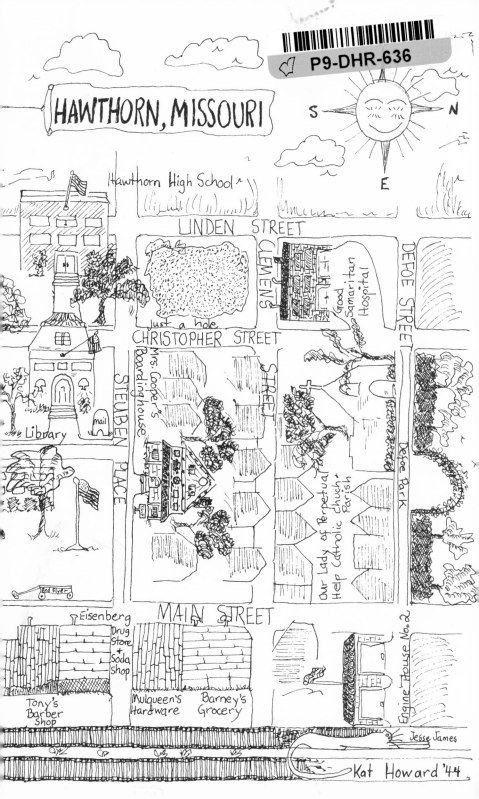

HAWTHORN, MISSOURI

Hawthorn High School

LINDEN STREET

just a hole

CHRISTOPHER STREET

CLEMENS STREET

DEFOE STREET

Good Samaritan Hospital

Library

mail

Mrs. Cooper's Boardinghouse

STEUBEN PLACE

Our Lady of Perpetual Help Catholic Church, Parish

Defoe Park

Red Flyer

MAIN STREET

Eisenberg Drug Store + Soda Shop

Tony's Barber Shop

Mulqueen's Hardware

Barney's Grocery

Engine House No. 2

Jesse James

Kat Howard '44

MRS. COOPER'S BOARDINGHOUSE

Mrs. Cooper's Boardinghouse

JOAN LINDAU

McGRAW-HILL BOOK COMPANY

New York   St. Louis   San Francisco   Düsseldorf   Mexico   Toronto

Book design by Anita Walker Scott.

Copyright © 1980 by Joan Lindau.

2 3 4 5 6 7 8 9 DODO 8 7 6 5 4 3 2 1 0

Library of Congress Cataloging in Publication Data

Lindau, Joan.
Mrs. Cooper's boardinghouse.

I. Title.
PZ4.L74235Mi [PS3562.I496] 813'.5'4 79-25189
ISBN 0-07-037882-7

The author is grateful to the following publishers for permission to reprint copyrighted material:

page 125: "Toot, Toot, Tootsie Goodbye," by G. Kahn, E. Erdman, T. Fiorito. © 1922, renewal 1950, Leo Feist, Inc. Used by permission. All rights reserved.

pages 153–154, 158, 184, 189, 208: The Complete Poetical Works of Amy Lowell, © 1955 by Houghton Mifflin Company. Reprinted by permission of the publisher.

pages 184–185: "When I Grow Too Old to Dream," by Sigmund Romberg and Oscar Hammerstein II. © 1934, 1935, renewal 1962, 1963, Metro-Goldwyn-Mayer, Inc. Rights throughout the world controlled by Robbins Music Corporation. Used by permission. All rights reserved.

Published in association with SAN FRANCISCO BOOK COMPANY

For Allyson Lowell Layne

MRS. COOPER'S BOARDINGHOUSE

Kathleen Howard stood before her bathroom mirror and stared into her fawn-colored eyes, wondering what the interviewer sent by the *New York Times Magazine* had seen. Had the woman noticed those fine hairs in her nose? The lines around her mouth? Smiling, Kat saw the lines deepen. Then opening her mouth, she examined the fillings in her teeth. She had a silver one in each of her back teeth and a gold one in a lower molar. She remembered the gold inlay because it had been so expensive.

"Did you always want to be an artist, Kathleen?" the woman had asked. "No," she'd answered. "When I was ten I wanted to be a major-league baseball player." Alone now, facing herself in the mirror, she wondered, "Why *do* you paint?" Twenty years barely eking out a living, going without meals and sleep and the friends who gave up on you because you didn't spend enough time with them. "For the same reason the birds sing," she said aloud, touching the gray hair swept back from her face. Only the hair at the nape of her neck was still fawn-colored like her eyes. "I wonder why my eyes don't turn gray?" She laughed softly, amused by her silliness.

When the interviewer left, she had called her brother long distance. She wanted to talk to someone who knew her and loved her. How good it made her feel to hear the surprise in her brother's voice when she said, "Hi, Raggedy Andy—it's me, Kat!" They didn't talk about the *Times* story. They talked about the good old days—about Mama, Papa, and Jesse.

A whistle interrupted Kat's reverie and she ran barefooted from the bathroom to the kitchen of her Greenwich Village studio. With a mug of hot tea in her hand and a cookie in her mouth, she left the kitchen and went over to her couch and sat down, stretching her long legs out over the oak coffee table and resting them on a stack of magazines. She had a faraway look in her light eyes and a child's sweet smile on her lips. Kat had been eight years old when Andy brought Jesse home to her. Andy had just enlisted in the army and had bought her the skinny white cat as a going-away present. Jesse's whiskers were broken off, and he had bald spots on his hind legs from trying to free himself from his cage. Kat named the scrawny creature after Jesse James and trained him to walk at the end of a leash.

Remembering those times, Kat got up, walked over to her window to peer down at the people and cars below, and imagined herself perched high above Hawthorn, Missouri, in the tree fort nestled in the giant oak behind her family home. She opened the window, and the evening breeze ruffled her pale blue cotton shirt and made her nipples harden. She slipped her hand underneath the open neck of her blouse and felt her breasts, then the soft hair under her arms. The September sun was setting, its orange light reflecting off the windows across the alleyway. Kat rubbed her fingers together in an unconscious gesture. She hadn't painted all day, and now the light was fading.

Leaving the window open, Kat walked back to the coffee table and straightened the magazines on it, then fluffed the pillows on the couch. As she started away from the couch, something caught her eye. She moved the marble ashtray on the oak table not more than an inch to the left, then walked over to her work area beneath the skylight. She took a clean paintbrush from a Maxwell House coffee can, thumbed the bristles, and put the brush to her mouth, enjoying the feel of the soft camel hair against her lips. Hanging on the wall before her was a painting of a baseball diamond with nine players dressed in white flannel uniforms and brown socks. Under each baseball cap was her ten-year-old face and the braids of hair she wore as a child. In the lower left corner of the painting was the date 1944 and the letters *AD*. Kat stood a long while gazing at the painting. Her serious expression relaxed. Her eyes glowed as she was reminded: "The real business of life is to enjoy it." She reached down and lifted the lid of her cherry-wood paintbox.

At three o'clock on that hot, muggy Friday, June 9, 1944, the school bell rang and shouts of joy went up in each classroom. The school year had come to an end, and the young students were free as the bluebirds in their Missouri sky. The mothers of youngsters in the lower grades stood on the lawn in front of Jefferson Elementary School, some with a younger brother or sister in their arms and a pet dog or cat at their side, waiting for their children to pour out of the red brick building, loaded down with lunch buckets, tennis shoes, and bookbags bulging with papers accumulated during the school year.

Inside, Kat Howard stood in the hallway outside her classroom, her head bent down shyly, waiting for her teacher, Marjorie Holmes. Kat hoped everyone would be gone by the time Miss Holmes was leaving, so she could talk to her privately and give her the hand-painted card she held against her chest.

"Aren't you coming, Kat?" called Annie Kramer as she passed Kat on her way out.

"Yeah, I'm coming in a minute, but first I've got something to do."

"What's Kat doing?" Betty Lou Ferrand asked Annie as she caught up with her.

"She's gonna talk to Miss Holmes, I think. Let's go get a seat at Eisie's."

"We'll save you a place," Betty Lou hollered back to Kat as she ran on with Annie.

Kat nodded and was glad her girlfriends hadn't decided to wait for her. That would have spoiled her plan. She looked critically at the card in her hand. The blue forget-me-nots were pretty, she thought, but the basket wasn't so good. It was hard to paint a basket. She wished she could have thought of something better to give Miss Holmes. Something really special. If she hit a home run for her, that would be special. But she hadn't been able to figure out how she'd get her teacher to go to the baseball field. And she didn't even know if Miss Holmes knew about baseball and how hard it was to hit a home run. Kat took in a deep breath, and for an instant the butterflies in her stomach settled. Would Miss Holmes take the card and rush off, or would she stop to talk and maybe even ask Kat to walk home with her? She'd probably have lots of books and things to carry, it being the last day of school. Kat decided she would offer to help carry some of her teacher's things—that way she could be with her a little bit longer.

Marjorie Holmes erased the blackboard, then walked over to the center desk in the front row of the classroom and took a seat. For three years she had taught the fifth and sixth grades at Jefferson. A class of thirty-five students was a handful, and she sighed with relief. The last anxious soul had scurried out moments earlier, leaving her alone with her thoughts.

As a ten-year-old, Marjorie had had one dream—to be beautiful like her mother and marry a wonderful man like her father. As a child she hadn't imagined how she would feel when that time came. She hadn't envisioned it well at all. She couldn't have known in her ten-year-old heart how attached she would become to thirty-five other hearts and minds. Looking down at her hands in the lap of her floral jumper, she noticed the spark of light in the small diamond ring on her finger. It reminded her of the sparkle she saw in David's eyes when she met him. He had been sent to greet her at the railroad station the day she arrived in Hawthorn. By whom? She'd never asked. He was the perfect candidate—strong enough to lift her heavy bags, with a courteous manner suitable for welcoming a schoolteacher, and willing to go out of his way to help a stranger, particularly a female stranger who was reported to be young and very attractive. In August she and David would marry.

The whistle of the afternoon train from St. Louis interrupted Marjorie's daydreaming, and she stood up and walked to the windows, smoothing down her jumper at her small waist. She was Hawthorn's loveliest creature, her silken brown hair and dark eyes contrasting dramatically with her fair complexion. She looked out the window at the children on the lawn below, then closed the windows and pulled down the shades. She gathered up her bookbag and purse and started out the classroom, looking over her shoulder one last time before she left the room and closed the door.

"Why, Kathleen, you're still here. I thought I'd be the last one out today."

"I was just getting ready to leave, but I have something to give you," said Kat, handing the card to her teacher but not daring to look up.

"How lovely, Kathleen. Did you make this?"

Kat blushed with pride and stole a look at Miss Holmes. She was so beautiful. She was the most beautiful person Kat had ever known. She had a little beauty mark on her right cheek which Kat sometimes stared at in class. "The basket's not very good," Kat apologized.

"It's very handsome. May I open it?"

"Sure." Kat watched closely as Marjorie read the words printed in her neat hand: "I hope you will forget me not, for I shall not forget you—Kathleen Howard."

Marjorie looked up from the card. "Kathleen Howard," she said, "the world will never be able to forget you."

Kat wanted to throw her arms around her teacher and tell her she loved her, but her arms were frozen at her sides and her throat was all caught up.

"Would you like to walk me home?" Marjorie asked.

Kat cleared her throat and managed a "Yes," and Marjorie touched her shoulder lightly.

Kat was too nervous to talk as they walked down Waller

Street to the corner of Main. She looked down at her feet and Marjorie's and matched her footsteps to her teacher's. When they reached Hannibal House they stopped, and Marjorie turned to Kat, smiling. Hannibal House, named after Hannibal, Missouri, where Mark Twain grew up, was the only hotel in Hawthorn. It was a residence hotel, with a few rooms rented to transients, and faced the town square. Marjorie Holmes lived in one of the resident apartments. Beside the hotel, also facing the square, was the St. Pierre Inn, the finest restaurant in town. Betty Lou Ferrand's mother ran the inn, and she and her daughter lived in an apartment above it.

"Kathleen, we don't need to say good-bye, do we?"

"Oh, no. I wasn't gonna say that."

"Mr. Webb and I are going to be married this August, and we'd like you and your parents to come to our wedding."

Kat was happy to be invited but stung by the reminder that Miss Holmes was going to marry David Webb and wouldn't be her teacher next year. "What are you going to do until then?" Kat asked. "Are you gonna be here?"

Marjorie grinned, amused by Kat's seriousness. "Yes," she said, "I've plenty to do to get ready. You get busy and read *The Last of the Mohicans,* and we can talk about it when you finish."

"I will. I'm going to get it from the library tomorrow. I've got lots of plans for this summer. I'm going to do some things too."

"I'm certain you are. Well, I've got to go now. We'll talk again soon. Thank you for your lovely card."

Miss Holmes started up the walk. Kat watched her until she was out of sight beyond the green canopied door, then turned and ran across and down Main Street to join her friends in Eisie's.

As Kat entered Eisenberg's Drug Store and Soda Shop she ran smack into a group of boys standing inside the door and overheard Daniel Brooks say, "Here comes Francis the fairy."

"He is not, Daniel Brooks! He's the Flowerman."

"What do you know, Kat," Daniel shot back.

"I know you're still mad 'cause I beat you at baseball today."
Francis Spenger was standing in the doorway. The boys had
been watching as he approached from the courthouse lawn
across the street. Francis was employed by the town of Hawthorn as its groundskeeper. Because he spent most of his time
outdoors he had a rosy tan. That and his trim form and blond
hair made him appear much younger than his forty-six years.
Francis had moved to Hawthorn from St. Louis more than
twenty years earlier and had been responsible for turning what
once was an open field of orchard grass into a well-manicured
park with gardens. Though the townfolk were openly proud of
Francis's work, most poked fun at the man.

Daniel Brooks had instigated a burlesque of Francis's lilting
walk and was now dumbfounded by Kat's upbraiding and the
presence of Francis. Daniel only flexed his muscles when he was
certain he'd not be challenged.

Kat turned and went to the table where her girlfriends were
sitting and didn't see Francis take a seat at the nearby counter.
Sliding into the booth beside Annie and across from Betty Lou,
Kat said, "Gee whiz, I wish you guys liked to play baseball
'cause you wouldn't get so mad if I beat you."

"Brooks's been bragging that he beat you today at recess," said
Annie.

"He's fibbing. He could never beat me."

"I think he likes you, Kat," said Betty Lou. "That's why he's
gotta beat you."

"Damnation!"

"Jiminetty, Kat, you shouldn't say bad words. Someone could
tell on you."

"There's nothing wrong with 'damnation,' Betty Lou. Reverend Wiley says it all the time, and any word that's okay in
church is okay in Eisie's."

Mr. Eisenberg came over to Kat and asked her if she wanted a
cherry soda like her friends.

"No, I feel like celebrating. I'll have a black-and-white." Kat
looked up at Mr. Eisenberg, wondering how he could see her
through his glasses, which were always speckled with dust and

dirt. Turning back to her friends, she whispered, "Guess what?"

"Kat, you always say that, and Annie and I can never guess you."

"I'm going to the World Series this year." Mr. Eisenberg set her drink down on the table.

"How are you gonna do that?" asked Annie.

"I'm saving all my money from my paper route this summer."

"That won't be enough to go all the way to St. Louis." Betty Lou knew better.

"I know that, silly. I'm getting another job too."

"How are you gonna do that? You're not old enough." Betty Lou twisted a blond sausage curl around her finger. She did this whenever she was questioning Kat. Kat wore braids, and Betty Lou was certain Kat was jealous of her curls, so she taunted her by drawing attention to her curls.

"I haven't decided that part yet, but I'll figure it out. I just know the Cardinals and Browns are gonna play against each other. I can feel it in my bones."

"Here comes Brooks," warned Annie. "Are you gonna say anything to him?"

"I've got nothing else to say. And besides, I've gotta go do my paper route." Kat slurped down the last of her ice cream soda and scooted out of the booth.

"Whatcha doing tomorrow, Kat?"

"Playing catch and looking into my plans," Kat yelled back to Annie. "Oh!" She remembered something and went back to whisper, "Betty Lou, don't you go broadcasting to anyone what I'm gonna do. I told you what I was planning in secret."

"Girl Scout's honor."

"You're no Girl Scout," Kat giggled.

"I've got honor just the same."

Kat looked to Annie.

"She won't blab," promised Annie.

Francis Spenger saw Kat get up, left a dime on the counter, and followed her out of Eisie's. As Kat ran across the square toward home, Annie's father, Frank Kramer, was coming out of the courthouse.

"Hi, Sheriff!" Kat boomed.

"Afternoon, Kat. Hello, Francis."

Kat turned around when she heard Francis's name and saw he was at her heels. "I didn't know you were there."

"I heard what you called me," Francis said.

Kat looked up at him, puzzled.

"Flowerman."

"Oh, that."

"Thank you."

"Daniel's got a big mouth, but he's not mean on purpose. He does it by accident sometimes."

"That's all right . . . Are you serious about wanting a job?"

Brother, thought Kat, it sure didn't take Betty Lou long to lose her honor. "What makes you think I am?"

"I overheard you talking about it in Eisie's. I've got an idea for you."

"A job idea?"

Francis nodded yes.

"I'm real smart. I can do fractions and name all the states, and I'm gonna read *The Last of the Mohicans* this summer."

"How are you at cleaning house and grocery shopping?"

"Golly, that's easy stuff. What's the job?"

"I've got a lot of work to do in the park this summer. I was thinking maybe you'd like to help me at the boardinghouse. I'd continue to do the heavy work, and Miss Parsons and Miss Renee do the cooking and dishes, but if you wanted to, you could straighten things up and pick up the groceries a couple times a week."

"Oh, I'd like that. I'm real good around the house."

Francis laughed and said, "I'll have to talk to Mrs. Cooper first. If she says it's okay, then—"

"Hot diggity!"

"I'll talk to her and tell you what she says when you deliver the paper tomorrow."

"That'd be great! Uh-oh, I'm late. I've gotta go and do my route. Thanks, Flowerman!"

"You're welcome, Kat. Tell me, did you think that up yourself?"

"You mean 'Flowerman'?"

Francis nodded.

"I guess so. I never heard it before I said it." And with that, Kat turned and was gone in a flash, her heels kicking and her braids flying behind her. She was bursting with good news to tell her mama and papa, but knew she best hold onto it until just the right moment.

＄2＄ Sol Eisenberg sat in the Morris chair in the corner of the boardinghouse sitting room. He was reading the evening paper by the light of the floor lamp, his pipe resting in the chrome smoking stand on his right side. Sol's wife, Sarah, sat across from him in a large chair fitted with a pink-and-green-flowered slipcover, her head against a white lace antimacassar that appeared tinged with age in the greenish yellow light of the room. Above her head was a painting of an Indian portaging a canoe in the wilderness.

Sol and Sarah were both balding, had thin lips, and wore flesh-colored bifocals. Married forty-five years, they seemed more like brother and sister than husband and wife. There was less affection between them than familiarity. They lived in a modestly furnished front apartment with private bath on the first floor of the boardinghouse. In the sleeping area were a teak bureau and twin beds, and in the lounge area an upholstered chair and ottoman, Sarah's swan's neck rocker and treadle sewing machine, and a walnut reading table. The hardwood floors and beige walls were bare. The other boarders lived in rooms on the second floor of the house—women to the right of the stairwell and men to the left—and shared a common bath.

When Sol Eisenberg was away at the drug store Sarah sat in her rocker. She didn't join the other boarders in the common rooms nor on the porch except when Sol was with her. When he was, as now, she would sit and watch him read. Sarah was unhappy living in the boardinghouse. In 1931, when the bank foreclosed on the Eisenbergs, Sol picked up the swan's neck rocker and moved it to Mrs. Cooper's. That and Sarah's sewing machine were the only pieces of furniture the Eisenbergs had been able to keep. Everything else had been repossessed or sold to keep the drug store and soda shop, which was their livelihood. Sarah had been sullen for thirteen years, but bitterness had taken hold of her years before that.

A familiar squeal came from the direction of the kitchen, and David Webb exited from the vicinity, a carrot stick in his mouth, and passed through the dining room to the magazine rack next to the sitting room sofa. The pair in the room did not look up. *Liberty* and *Colliers* magazines filled the rack, as well as a *Saturday Evening Post* with its Norman Rockwell cover missing. David glanced at the lady in the Woodbury Soap ad on the first page of the *Post,* then squatted in front of Sol's paper to glimpse the *Post-Dispatch* headlines. That was enough to satisfy his curiosity, and he went over to the Zenith console on the far side of Sol, then changed his mind and sat down at the player piano and put on the "Tiger Rag" roll.

When Miss Renee heard the piano she stuck her head around the standing fern in the archway dividing the sitting room from the dining room and cried out over the noise, "For pity's sake, David, turn that down!"

David winked as he smiled at her, then turned the piano off and went into the dining room. When he took the silverware from Miss Renee she blushed and skipped off to the kitchen. David delighted in the effect of his smile and touch. He was a dark, virile young man, well aware of his attributes. A plumber by trade, he also ran the projector at the Strand Movie House. Though he was engaged to be married, he received the blushing

12

attention of nearly every female in Hawthorn. Miss Renee was no exception.

Though she was without a real beau, Miss Renee had her dreams, her movie magazines, and her beauty parlor. Clark Gable and David Webb were her heart's desires; she dreamed about both as often as she dreamed about the sailor she corresponded with. Miss Renee passed for twenty-eight, but on close scrutiny looked her thirty-five years. She took great pains setting the French twist in her fashionably hennaed hair and painting the nails of her fingers and toes with bright red polish, leaving little white moons at the cuticles. There was a hint of despair beneath her girlish giggles and squeals. Pregnant at fifteen, she had left school and become a hairdresser. When the child was born, Gladys Pooley gave him up for adoption and moved from Independence, Missouri, to Hawthorn, where she took a new name.

Just as David finished setting the table, the cuckoo clock above the player piano announced the hour was six, and Miss Eva Parsons carried in a steaming casserole dish and placed it on the table. Eva was a tall, matronly woman in her late forties whose quick movements kept her from seeming years older than she was.

Eva returned to the kitchen for a dish of vegetables as Miss Renee carried in the water pitcher and Francis followed behind her with a white wicker tray. As Francis passed through the sitting room on his way upstairs with Mrs. Cooper's dinner, Sol and Sarah rose without looking at one another and went into the dining room.

"We won't wait for Francis this evening," Eva announced. "He's going to be a while."

Sarah Eisenberg mumbled something no one heard, and she and her husband took seats at the table with the others.

When Eva lifted her fork to begin, the others followed, and they all ate in silence for several minutes.

"The shepherd's pie is delicious," remarked Sol.

Eva wiped her mouth carefully with her linen napkin and smiled, her upper denture slipping slightly as her lips parted, then thanked Sol for the compliment.

"I suppose Her Highness is having something other than left-overs," Sarah said loud enough for everyone to hear.

"Eat your dinner and be grateful," Sol reprimanded her gently.

Sarah put her fork down. "Why does she get wine and I don't?"

"You don't drink."

"She doesn't know that."

"Why do you want something you don't like?"

Eva and David looked up from their plates at the couple. Miss Renee took one bite, then another, trying to ignore this customary bickering between husband and wife.

"She fancies she's the queen bee," Sarah spouted, picking up steam.

"If she's a queen, she's without domain," Sol answered.

"She has a *house*," Sarah said pointedly, getting in the lick she'd been waiting for.

Sol's shoulders slumped slightly and he put down his fork. David and Eva joined Miss Renee in uneasiness. Then, in a quieter voice, Sol said, "And she's locked in the tower, it would seem."

"That's her choice!"

"Is it?" Eva asked.

Everyone looked up, surprised at Eva's participation.

Regretting having called attention to herself, Eva changed the subject. "What's in the news, Sol?"

"The Yanks are moving toward Cherbourg. There's talk of surrender."

"The Germans won't stop fighting until the last American soldier is killed," said Sarah.

Sol bowed his head.

"Is there anything in the *Post-Dispatch* besides the war?" David asked.

"Yes," Sol answered, raising his head to look at David. "The Browns and the Cards are leading the leagues."

"I'll give you ten to one the Browns end up in the cellar."

"I don't understand how a young man fit to play ball can say

14

he isn't fit for service," Sarah pronounced.

"Sarah, a moment ago you were griping that all our men would die before the war's over. Now you want to recruit. What the hell, aren't you happy with anyone or anything?" She'd finally gotten to David.

"Favoritism," Sarah snapped, glaring at David across the table.

David threw his napkin on the table, but before he could stand up, Miss Renee touched his sleeve and stopped him. "What's playing at the Strand tonight, David?"

"*Stage Door Canteen* for the ninth week."

"Would I like it?"

"Yes, you like them all."

"Is Clark Gable in it?"

"No."

"Then maybe I wouldn't."

"What the hell is Francis doing up there?" David asked irritably.

"He said he had to speak with Mrs. Cooper," explained Eva.

"About what?"

"I don't ask, David. Would you like a second helping?"

"No thanks, Eva . . . How long have those two known one another?"

"He came here after us," Sarah said.

"Nineteen thirty-two," Sol answered. "Two years after she started taking in boarders."

"Nineteen thirty-three," corrected Sarah.

"This hasn't always been a boardinghouse?" David asked, surprised.

"Where have you been, David?" Sarah remarked.

"Mrs. Cooper lived here alone for a number of years," explained Sol. "When times got hard she took us in. Two years later Francis came. Since then all the rooms have been occupied. It was then that she stopped seeing people, coming down, going out."

"I need to see her," David said, turning to Eva. "To tell her I'm leaving."

15

"If you speak with Francis he'll tell her for you."

"She sees me!" Sarah interjected, then added, "Why are you leaving, David?"

"I'm getting married, remember? Where have you been, Sarah?" David stood up and took his dishes to the kitchen.

Eva excused herself to go powder for work—she ran the box office at the Strand Movie House—and the Eisenbergs retired to the sitting room to listen to "Fibber McGee and Molly" on the radio. Miss Renee was the last to rise from the table. She was lost in thought about David leaving.

Going up the stairs to the second floor, David met Francis on his way down.

"You missed a helluva dinner conversation," grumbled David.

"Sarah?" Francis asked.

"Jesus Christ, I wish someone would stick an old sock in her mouth!"

"Just ignore her, David. The rest do."

"Can I talk to you later?"

"Knock on my door when you get back."

"See ya later." David patted Francis playfully on the butt.

"I'll ignore that."

"You can't, any more than I can ignore that old prune."

George Howard crept up behind his wife in the kitchen and kissed the back of her head.

"Hi, darling," Janet Howard said, recognizing her husband's touch. "Dinner's about ready. Will you scare up that child of yours and see she washes the newsprint off her hands before she comes to the table."

George Howard and Janet Embers had been married twenty-two years. Both had been only children from St. Louis families. When they married they agreed they would have many children, but it had been a struggle for Janet. Eleven years and several miscarriages had come between Andy and Kat. Janet was thirty-three years old when Kat was born; she was now forty-three. Kat had been born the same year as the Dionne sisters. Her breech birth at eight months seemed as miraculous to the Howards as the quintuplets had seemed to Canada and the rest of the world. Nineteen thirty-three also was the year President von Hindenburg of Germany died and Adolf Hitler consolidated the offices of president and chancellor to become the Fuehrer.

George left the kitchen by the back door, careful to catch the screen before it slammed.

"Kat, dinner's ready!"

George Howard was five feet ten inches tall, with thick, dark eyebrows and mustache, a prominent nose, full lips, and large hands. His physical being was coarser than his intellect and disposition. He'd built the tree house in the giant oak behind the Howards' house for his son, Andy, but it had been a great effort for him. He was not especially handy with tools, though he looked like the type who would be. His rough features were those of an outdoorsman, not those of the scholarly student of language and history and the medical practitioner that he was. Although his rugged appearance often frightened new patients, his soft voice and gentle touch soon won him their confidence.

"Sweetheart, are you up there?"

Kat poked her head out of her tree fort. "Yeah, Papa, I'm coming!" The rope ladder unfurled, and George Howard held it taut while Kat climbed down. He watched his daughter's legs flex on each step and marveled at her agility. Kat leaped from the third rung to the ground and gave her father a terrific bear hug. Next to Andy he was her favorite human being in the world.

"Scat, Kat," said George as he patted her bottom, "and don't forget to wash those hands."

Jesse James poked his head out of the doorway above and meowed.

"Not you," George said, looking up. "You stay put."

Jesse flopped over on his side and rolled his head upside-down, begging for more attention than that. When George started off, Jesse got up and turned his back on the affront, his long white tail hanging out against the tree trunk.

At the Howards' victory garden George plucked a ripe tomato and carried it into the house.

17

"I see the roses are out," he said, joining his wife in the kitchen.

"Aren't they lovely? I cut some for the table."

George bent over the centerpiece on the dining room table. "Mmm, they smell wonderful—almost as good as you."

When Janet joined him in the dining room George took her into his arms. Standing eye to eye, they smiled and kissed. Kat joined her parents, hardly taking notice of the familiar embrace she found them in.

As George said grace, Kat peeked out from under her hooded eyes at her mother. She'd gotten into a habit of doing this and said that it "filled her up" to look at her mother this way. It also was Kat's expression that her mother "radiated like the sun" when she smiled. Janet Howard looked her age. Her blond hair was streaked with white, and her chin and bosoms were soft, but the extraordinary beauty that she had been as a young woman was present still in her fine features, sky-blue eyes, and graceful carriage.

Kat was an interesting combination of her parents. She had long limbs and broad shoulders like her mother, strong features like her father, as well as his hooded eyes, and a blend of her parents' coloring. From a distance the most arresting thing about Kat was her lithe body, but on close encounter it was her eyes, which were the same fawn color as her hair.

"How was school today?" Kat's father asked.

"Swell, Papa. I got a war stamp for having the prettiest workbook, and I got a double at recess and struck Brooks out."

"Who do the Browns play tonight?"

"Cleveland again."

"Kat, please swallow first."

"Yes, Mama. Did you ever go to a regular baseball game?"

"Your papa and I saw the Cardinals play in St. Louis before you were born."

"Did you like it?"

"I like doing just about anything with your papa."

"Is that why you got married?"

"That's why."

18

"I don't think I'll ever get married. I like doing things alone best."

"Someday someone will come along to change your mind."

"Could I go to a regular game by myself until then?"

"No."

"Why?"

"Ladies need escorts," answered her father.

"Why?"

"Because that's the way it is."

"Why?"

"Tradition."

"Like saying grace?"

"Like that."

"I think the Browns are gonna play the Cardinals in the Series this year and I'd sure like to go."

Janet took a serious look at her daughter when she realized Kat was not making idle conversation. "What's behind that, Kat?"

"Wouldn't it be swell?"

"Sure would," said her father.

"Hold on just one minute, young lady."

"I'd pay my own way, Mama."

"What about your escort?" asked her father.

"I'd pay his way too."

"How would you manage that?" he asked.

"My paper route and something else."

"What 'something else'?" Kat's mother asked, her voice raised a bit higher.

Kat hesitated, worried she'd jumped into this discussion too soon and hadn't laid the groundwork necessary for convincing her mother. "Flowerman has an idea for me." It was too late to retreat.

"Flowerman?" asked Janet.

"Francis Spenger."

"When did he become Flowerman?"

"Today. He has this idea that I could help out at the board-inghouse."

19

"Now I wonder who put that idea in his head?"

"He thought it up himself, Mama."

"And I suppose he thought it up that you'd be wanting a job?"

"Not exactly. He overheard me talking to Annie and Betty Lou in Eisie's."

"Goodness gracious, Kat," Janet said, shaking her head, "you haven't been on vacation a day and you're looking for a job. You're lucky you don't have to—why on earth would you want to spoil your summer working?"

"So I can go to the World Series." At times, Kat didn't understand her mother any better than her mother understood her. "Don't you see?"

"No, I'm afraid I don't."

"There's nothing wrong with Kat working," said George. "Most folks have to. What are the terms?"

"Terms?"

"What kind of work? How many hours a week? What are they gonna pay you?"

"I didn't ask all that. It's not set yet. Flowerman's gotta talk to Mrs. Cooper first and let me know tomorrow."

"I just don't know," said Janet.

George looked at his wife, waiting for her to say more. When she did not, he turned to Kat and said, "Finish your supper before it gets cold and we'll talk about this later."

While Kat took the dinner scraps out to Jesse, George and Janet talked in the kitchen.

"She's got her mind set on the World Series, and who knows if it will even be in St. Louis," said Janet.

"If anyone knew, it would be Kat. She can reel off the batting average of every player. She amazes me," George laughed. "The Series isn't until October and she'd have to be excused from school, but you're right, her mind's set on it."

"You won't be able to take her, George."

"I know. It would be one thing if it were just one day, but it's liable to be seven. Maybe Francis Spenger—he's a responsible man. Maybe he'd go with her."

"It's as certain as the spring rain that that man's no baseball fan."

"He's a Kathleen Howard fan. That's probably enough. How do you feel about Kat being at the boardinghouse and not at home helping you out?"

"I didn't expect her to be at home with me, but . . . I don't know about Mrs. Cooper. I've never met the woman, but Charlotte says—"

"Now, I know you don't believe everything Charlotte says."

"No, but it's strange that the woman never sees or speaks to anyone in town."

"Janet, I've seen and spoken to the old woman, and she doesn't seem strange to me. Would you feel better if I talked to her about this?"

"I'll leave that up to you, honey."

George picked up a towel and helped Janet dry the dishes. "I think it might be a good experience for Kat."

"Darling, I'm not trying to take anything away from her. I just want to protect her."

"You're the one who's always said God protects little children. Have we ever been sorry for putting our trust in Him?"

"No."

"And didn't we promise, those years we tried so hard to have a second child, that we'd accept His will? We can't pull back on that now."

"I know, but I've always had trouble with that promise. I'm never certain when it's God's will and when it's Kat's."

George laughed, then looked into his wife's eyes and said, "She's more self-sufficient than Andy was at her age. She can charm a snake and look a bully straight in the eye."

"Yes, but—"

"I hated hearing myself say she had to have an escort because that's the way it is."

"We wouldn't have let Andy go to St. Louis alone."

"I know. It's just that there's something to be said for breaking with tradition."

"Don't I know where she gets her ideas! Leave the dishes and

21

go talk to her. As sure as I'm standing here with suds up to my elbows she's out there fretting."

"I was watching her today and thinking someday soon she'll be lovely like her mother. Made me sad thinking of her all grown up."

"I used to look at Andy just that way, and now he's grown up and gone from me." Janet turned her face to the side.

"We're going to see Andy again soon," George reassured her, wiping a tear from her cheek. "Kat may get her ideas from me," he added, "but she sure gets her loveliness from you." Then he took his sweater off the kitchen chair and went out to the backyard.

Kat was sitting under the oak tree, petting Jesse. "Papa, I've been thinking, if Andy were here he'd be my escort."

"He sure would, honey."

"When's he coming home?"

"When the war's over, Kitty Kat."

"I miss him."

"I know you do."

"Why does a war take so long?"

"Want to walk down to the square with me?"

"That'd be swell."

"We'll get a soda at Eisie's when the show lets out."

"You always have the best ideas, Papa. Can Jesse come with us?"

"Sure enough."

Kat put the leash on Jesse and the three walked down Elm Street toward town. The red brick and white clapboard houses set back from the sidewalk were nearly obscured in the spring and summer months by the tall elms lining the street. Up ahead the public library stood on a slight elevation, its flag visible through the maple, chestnut, and hickory trees that filled the green. Kat, her father, and Jesse turned east down Waller, passing the St. Pierre Inn. Kat glanced up at the light in Betty Lou's window. Cutting across the courthouse lawn, which was well lit by the lampposts on the walkway, Kat noticed the mosquitoes and moths flying around each lamp light. George put his sweater down on the grass and a lightning bug flew over his shoulder.

Father and daughter sat close together on the sweater. Across Main Street facing the courthouse was Eisenberg's Drug Store and Soda Shop. Kat could see Mr. Eisenberg walking around inside getting ready to open up for customers. Next to the soda shop was Tony's Barber Shop, with its barber pole on the sidewalk out front. Kat couldn't figure where the stripes went when they spiraled to the top of the pole. They just kept spiraling. Next to Tony's was the First National Bank and Trust, then the post office with its flagpole. There were six flags in Hawthorn on regular days. One each at the elementary school and high school, and one at the library, courthouse, post office, and engine house No. 2, making six altogether. Of course, on Memorial Day and the Fourth of July there were more flags than a body could count. Next to the post office was the army–navy recruitment headquarters, and there was another flag there. That made seven flags in Hawthorn, Kat realized.

In this quiet moment Hawthorn seemed magical to Kat, as it did Sunday mornings when she did her paper route and at dusk on the occasional autumn day she walked home late from school, crunching fallen leaves beneath her feet and watching wisps of smoke curl upward from chimneys and drift together in the crisp air like hands clasping in the darkening sky.

"Is that where Andy went to sign up for the war?" Kat asked, pointing across the street.

"No, honey. He went to St. Louis. They didn't have a headquarters here then."

That was why she'd gotten mixed up on the flag count, Kat realized. There never used to be one there, and she hadn't done a check on the flags lately.

"You remember—he brought Jesse back from St. Louis that day."

"Sure, I remember that. I didn't forget you, Jesse," Kat said, scratching Jesse's back. "Papa, do you think Andy misses us as much as we miss him?"

"Maybe more. We've got each other."

"I think I'd rather be the one who goes away. I don't like being left."

"That's what happens when you grow up."

"What happens?"

"People come and go."

"I like the coming just fine. It's the going I don't like."

"That's for sure!"

"That's for damn sure."

George considered his daughter carefully, surprised by her language.

Kat turned away and looked at the boardinghouse on Steuben Place. It had a friendly look about it, pillars and a swing on the porch, and a sign out front that read: "Mrs. Cooper's Boardinghouse for Refined Ladies and Gentlemen."

"Did you ever meet Mrs. Cooper?" Kat asked her father.

"Yes."

"What's she like?"

"Like a grandmother."

"I don't know what a grandmother's like."

Didn't everyone know what a grandmother was like? George asked himself. But of course Kat didn't. His mother and Janet's had died before Kat was born.

"Papa, what are you doing?"

"Thinking about your grandmothers. I wish they'd lived long enough to experience you, and—"

"Vice versa?"

"Uh huh."

"I'll tell you something. I'm a little scared of her."

"No need to be, angel. She's not sociable, that's all. Being different is no crime."

"I know that, 'cause I'm different in a way."

"Yeah, your mama would agree with that, wouldn't she?"

"Yep, she says I'm like you more than her."

"You're like no one else, Kitty Kat."

"Did Mrs. Cooper ever come out?"

"A long time ago. But she always kept pretty much to herself, even then."

Kat lay back, feeling the prickly summer grass on the back of her neck and smelling its special fragrance as she watched the fireflies. "What's a fairy?"

"He takes the tooth from under your pillow while you're sleeping and puts the dime there."

"Why would someone call Francis a fairy?"

"Who called him that?"

"Daniel Brooks, but I told Brooks he wasn't a fairy, he was a flowerman."

"You like Francis Spenger, don't you?"

"Yeah, Papa. He's real nice and he makes things grow."

"Maybe he would be your escort."

"You mean you're gonna let me go?" Kat sat up.

"You'll have to see about the job first."

"Hot diggity!"

"And I think you ought to speak with Mrs. Cooper before you accept the job, if it's offered to you."

"Do you think Francis would go with me? He's as old as you."

"I'd go with you if I could."

"Yeah, I know you can't 'cause someone could get sick."

"First things first. See about the job."

"What should I say to Mrs. Cooper?"

"Tell her about yourself."

"Like what?"

"Oh, Kat, you know. You talk about yourself all the time."

"Not to strangers."

"Then ask her what your duties will be. If she asks you to do something you don't think you can do, you should tell her. It wouldn't be fair if you didn't. And ask her how much she's willing to pay you for your services."

"How much should she?"

"That depends on the job. A quarter for an hour's work is pretty good, but you'll have to decide that. Figure out how much money you need and divide it by the total number of hours you'll work. That'll tell you how much you need to make each hour of work."

"Will you help me figure it if I need you to?"

"Sure will. You might suggest that you work two weeks on trial. Then, after the two weeks, you and Mrs. Cooper can have a talk to see if you're both satisfied with the arrangement."

"That's a good idea, Papa."

"Let's get a soda. It looks like Eisie's has opened up for business."

Later, on their way home from Eisie's, George put his sweater and his arm around his daughter. Kat could smell the faint pipe tobacco scent in the brown cardigan. She could tell her papa by his smell as easily as by his touch and the sound of his footsteps.

"It's such a pretty night I'm gonna sleep in my fort."

"No, you aren't, Kat. You put Jesse up there and then come in. Don't go up and read. Do you hear me?"

"Yes, Papa, only—"

"Don't press your luck."

"Yes, Papa."

❧3❧ Francis was sitting in a chair in his boxer shorts with his feet up on his bed reading Lillian Smith's *Strange Fruit* when David knocked on his door.

"Is that you—"

Before he could say "David," David stepped in. "What the hell are you sitting around like that for?"

"It's hotter than blazes."

"Damn it, Francis, you could have put something on. You knew I was stopping in."

"And who are you that I should get dressed up for?"

David stood uncomfortably inside the door. There was no place for him to sit except on the bed, and he sure as hell wasn't going to sit on Francis's bed. He knew the older man found him attractive, and he teased him when it was impossible for Francis to do anything about it. Alone with him, David was careful not to provoke any response from Francis which he didn't want to deal with.

"How was the movie?" Francis asked, putting down his book and getting up to give David his chair.

"No, thanks, I'll stand," said David, putting his hands in his pockets. "I run the projector; I don't look at the movies."

Francis put on his robe and sat on his bed. David decided to sit after all, and he took the chair.

Looking down at Francis's bare feet on the hardwood floor, David was reminded of two jokes that were told around town: one that Francis's lilting walk was a result of being shot in the rear end in World War One; and the other that Francis had been rejected by the army because he was such a fruitcake, and the "wound" something he'd gotten in bed, not on the battlefield. David laughed at both jokes but believed neither.

"Well, what did you want to talk about?" Francis asked.

David lifted one of his legs and rested it squarely on his other. "Do you think I'm a coward because I'm not in the army?"

"Good god, a Machiavellian like you?"

"What kind of bullshit word is that? Answer my question."

"No."

"No, you won't answer—or no, I'm not a coward?"

Francis looked at him closely and said, "Why the hell do you have to ask?" But Francis knew why, knew that David struggled with doubts about his manhood and sought him out for reassurance rather than Johnny McGee or Tony Rossetti. In front of the "regular guys" David didn't dare display any self-doubt. "David, I don't give a damn that you're not in the army."

"You were."

"I was a scared kid—that's why I joined. Too scared not to, and scared out of my wits in it. How do you suppose I got a bullet in my ass? I was running—running for my life. They gave me a medal for bravery when all I was doing was saving my skin."

David put his leg down and waited a long moment, then said, "It's not that I'm scared. I tried to enlist but—"

"Hey, if you aren't scared, you're a damn fool."

"Do you want to know why they wouldn't take me?"

"Is that what you came here to tell me?"

"No, damn it, I came here to tell you when I was leaving so the old lady could rent my room."

There was another long silence before Francis asked, "Well, are you going to tell me?"

"I had TB when I was a kid."

Francis looked at David's handsome face. Above the shadow of his beard were the two dark eyes and a vulnerability deep within David evidenced in them. "I'm sorry, that wasn't what I was asking. When are you leaving?"

"August nineteenth ... I had it when I was fourteen. Overheard my old man say to my mom that she'd only given him one son because I was a weakling. My older brother was his favorite. I ran away from home once, and when I came back my dad said, 'Have you been gone?' like he hadn't even noticed."

"Looks to me as though you've recovered."

"Hell, yes, soon as I left home for good."

"David, it's not what you look like or what you do, but how you think that makes you a man. It took me a helluva long time to figure that one out. Maybe it won't take you so long."

David lowered his head, then stood up and put his hands in his pockets again. "Shit, I don't know why I told you all that crap. You'll tell her when I'm planning to leave, huh?"

"Yes, David."

"See ya later," David said glumly. He turned and left the room.

Francis reached for his book and sat down in his chair again, but he didn't read. Instead, he thought about David and wondered if perhaps David teased because he was looking for some response his father never gave him. David's bravado had never fooled Francis. And it was that as much as the muscular young body and handsome features which Francis found arresting.

❦4❦ Kat arrived at the railroad station Saturday afternoon before the train from St. Louis. Mr. Quinn, the railroad clerk, was waiting on the platform. He was a gruff man with a red knob of a nose. Kat nodded to him and then looked down the tracks. The train was not yet in sight. To kill time Kat tossed her baseball over her head, squinted, then caught it in her mitt. She repeated this game of catch with herself half a dozen times, looking over at Mr. Quinn and then down the tracks between tosses.

"It's three P.M.," announced Mr. Quinn as he snapped his pocket watch closed.

Two long whistles sounded down the tracks, and Kat saw the black engine car of the Union Pacific heading toward the station. Soon a bundle of the *St. Louis Post-Dispatch* was tossed onto the platform.

After counting them, forty-five in all, Kat stacked them in her Red Flyer and called to Jesse. The lanky white cat leaped onto the wagon and sniffed the newspapers. When he lifted his hind leg Kat hollered, "No!" Jesse meowed in protest, scratched the papers with his front claws, and raised his leg again. "No, Jesse, don't spray. I won't let you ride in the wagon if you're naughty." Jesse eased down and tucked in his front paws. "I don't need any trouble from you today," Kat said firmly.

"So long, Kat. See you tomorrow morning."

"Bye, Mr. Quinn." Tomorrow morning? Oh, that's right,

thought Kat. Tomorrow's Sunday. On Sunday the *Post-Dispatch* had an early edition. It was hard telling the days of the week once school was out.

As Kat passed the Strand Movie House on Main Street she saw Eva Parsons in the ticket booth and stopped.

"Hi, Miss Parsons."

"You missed the matinee, Kat."

"Oh no, I've got business today. Did you see Annie and Betty Lou?"

"Yes, they were here, but the matinee let out an hour ago."

"Thanks. Did you see which way they went?"

"No, child."

Kat waved good-bye and started down the street. She delivered the ten papers on Bryant Street, turned right onto Christopher to Clemens Street, then turned right again. Annie Kramer's house was on Clemens Street, across from the rectory. Rather than leaving the paper under the Kramers' doormat Kat tapped on the screen door.

"Here's your paper, Mrs. Kramer. Is Annie home?"

"No, she's over at Betty Lou's. No, Jesse," scolded Mrs. Kramer. Jesse was stalking something in the Kramers' flowerbed.

"Stop that, Jesse!" hollered Kat. "I'm sorry, Mrs. Kramer, he's been a bad egg today. And me with so much on my mind."

"Are you going to stop off at Betty Lou's?"

"After I finish my route."

"When you see Betty Lou's mother will you ask her to please give Annie a sugar coupon?"

"Are you gonna make some of your sugar cookies?"

"No. Mrs. Ferrand asked me to bake a cake for her daughter."

"Oh, gosh, I clean forgot! Tomorrow's Betty Lou's birthday."

"Don't spill the beans to Betty Lou."

"Oh, I won't. I'll say you're gonna make some of your delicious cookies."

"You don't need to say anything."

"Just if Betty Lou gets suspicious, then I will."

Kat set Jesse on top of the newspapers in the wagon and

pulled the Red Flyer down the walk, wondering if Francis had talked to Mrs. Cooper yet. Maybe he won't let me see her, she thought, and Papa won't let me work there if I don't talk to her.

On Main Street Kat dropped off a paper at each store, stopping at the barber shop to say hello to Tony Rossetti. Tony was a World War One veteran; one Saturday nearly a year earlier he had told Kat about getting shot in battle and how a doctor cut off his leg, giving him no anesthetic, because gangrene had set in. The story was gory and Kat hadn't liked hearing all the details; but Tony had liked telling them, so she listened and pretended it didn't bother her. When Tony was through telling the story he looked like he was going to cry. Ever since then, Kat had stopped to talk to him when she delivered his Saturday paper. Tony had a customer in his chair this particular Saturday, so he just waved. Kat was glad because her mind was on her appointment.

The Red Flyer squeaked up Steuben Place. Kat counted two more houses. Her heart began to pound and she could feel her pulse in her ears as she pulled her wagon in front of Mrs. Cooper's Boardinghouse.

"Stay in the wagon, Jesse, and be a good kitty." Jesse rolled over and stared up at Kat with his large yellow eyes. Kat put her face in his belly and kissed him, then whispered, "Wish me luck."

David Webb was sitting on the porch swing with his arm around Marjorie Holmes.

"Hello, Kathleen," Marjorie said gaily. "How's it feel being on vacation?"

"Just swell, Miss Holmes." Kat tapped on the porch door.

"What are you up to, Kat?" asked David.

"Nothing."

"Like hell, you've got on your serious face." Marjorie frowned at David for swearing.

"Flowerman and I've got some business to discuss," she answered without looking around.

David raised an eyebrow.

"Don't give her a hard time," whispered Marjorie.

31

"Come on, Kat," said David, getting up. "I'll see if I can find you a flowerman."

The two walked inside. Kat sat in the Morris chair in the sitting room and waited while David called up the stairs, "Is there a flowerman in the house?" Kat looked around the sitting room from where she sat. It was a strange room. None of the furniture matched, and all of the big pieces were at one end, making the room lopsided. The pictures on the walls were small and hung high, leaving large blank spaces.

Francis entered quietly from the hall and surprised Kat. She flinched, then blushed. Francis stood smiling, his hands at the waist of his khaki trousers, and said, "It's all set, Kat."

"It is? You mean—"

"You can start work next week."

"Yippee! Can I talk to Mrs. Cooper?"

"She said it's okay."

"But I need to talk to her."

"I can tell you everything you need to know."

"My papa says I've got to talk to her."

"She doesn't—"

"But I can't take the job unless—" Kat stopped because she felt herself almost starting to cry from her nervousness.

"I'll go see. You wait here."

Kat pulled her long legs up into the chair and hugged herself for security. Soon Francis was back.

"She'll see you, but not today. Can you come by tomorrow?"

"Tomorrow? Sure, I can come then. After church?"

"See you then."

Kat loved getting up before anyone on Sunday. Tiptoeing out the back door in her bare feet, her shoes in her hand, she opened and closed the screen door carefully so as not to disturb her parents on their one morning to sleep in.

The wet grass felt good on Kat's bare feet as she walked across the lawn to the foot of the old oak. Whispering, she called to Jesse. "Come on, lazy bones."

Jesse peeked his head out of the doorway of the fort and yawned wide before stretching his legs and meowing for Kat to come get him.

"You should learn to come down a tree by yourself," Kat said as she climbed up for him. "If you can walk on a leash, you can do that. You're spoiled."

Jesse held onto Kat's cotton tee shirt with his front and back claws as the two descended the rope ladder, then leaped from her once they were safely on the ground.

Reaching deep into her shorts pocket, Kat pulled out some food scraps. While Jesse ate his breakfast Kat walked to the side of her house to smell the roses. The sun glistened on the yellow and salmon. She reached out and touched a teardrop on the palest salmon petal, then put her finger to her lips. She smoothed down the front of her blue tee shirt, liking the soft feel of the cotton, and tucked the tails into her shorts. Betty Lou has breasts, Kat thought as she looked at her narrow chest, wondering if she'd have them when she turned eleven. Then Kat remembered Betty Lou had the beginnings of breasts when she was ten. But Annie didn't, and neither did the other girls in her class, so Kat decided Betty Lou was just advanced in this way and it was okay that she didn't have any yet. Once Betty Lou had showed Kat her breasts when they were alone in Betty Lou's bedroom. She'd asked Kat to touch them, and when Kat touched Betty Lou's nipple with her finger, her girlfriend had giggled. Then Betty Lou touched Kat's. It didn't tickle Kat like it did Betty Lou, but it felt real nice.

On Sundays Kat delivered the papers in her bare feet, taking along her shoes to put on at the very last minute, when she neared home, so her mother wouldn't catch her barefooted. The cut grass tickled the bottoms of her feet as Kat walked across the front lawns on Elm Street. When Kat passed the St. Pierre Inn on the corner of Elm and Waller, she glanced up at Betty Lou's window, then found a small pebble and tossed it at the window. It pinged against the glass, and a sleepy head poked out. "Happy Birthday, Betty Lou!" called Kat.

"Hi, Kat, whatcha doing?"

"I'm gonna do my paper route. Am I the first to wish you a happy birthday?"

"Uh huh."

"Good, I like being first. See ya later." Kat waved, then made her way down Waller Street to the railroad station.

The seven o'clock train from St. Louis brought the final sections of the Sunday paper: the hard news and sports. The other sections arrived a day earlier, and Mr. Quinn kept them in the railroad office. As Kat put the sections together on the platform she could smell the wild honeysuckle that grew on the other side of the tracks. The rising sun felt warm on the back of her neck as she bent over the papers reading the sports page. The Browns had beaten Cleveland Friday night and were holding onto first place. "Hot dog!" she said out loud. Everything was working out just right—the Browns were winning, and she was going to be able to go to the World Series.

As Kat and Jesse and the Red Flyer headed down Main Street, a butterfly caught Jesse's attention, and he ran across the courthouse lawn, leaped into the air, and did a pirouette. Kat followed Jesse across the lawn and tried jumping and turning in mid-air as he had done. It must be easier, she decided, when you had four legs to jump with.

Just then Sheriff Kramer and Johnny McGee came out of the courthouse. "You stay away from those whiskeys at Joe's," Annie's father was saying. "I'm getting tired of locking you up every Saturday night and listening to you grumble on Sunday morning."

Johnny walked off grunting something with his arm raised, not waving good-bye so much as waving off the reprimand.

"Hi, Sheriff," called Kat.

"Morning, Kat. What's new?"

"The Browns and the Cards are still on top."

"First in shoes and first in booze and last in the American League."

"Not this year. This year St. Louis is gonna be first in all three." Kat took five papers into Hannibal House, deciding that was what she would talk to Mrs. Cooper about. She would tell Mrs. Cooper about the Browns and then about her tree fort and Andy and Jesse. That would be enough. She came out of the hotel and continued up the street.

When Kat finished her paper route she sat down in her empty wagon and picked out the grass from between her toes, then wiped the bottoms of her feet with her hands before putting on her shoes and starting down Elm Street toward home. When she got home she found that her mother had hung her Sunday dress on the knob of her dresser and set her mary-janes below it. This Sunday in church Kat would say a little prayer, asking to do well at her meeting with Mrs. Cooper. Kat's mother had told her it wasn't right to ask God for things, but asking him to help you do your best at something was okay.

Reverend Wiley nodded to the choir, then stretched his arms out wide as though embracing the world, and said, "Let us sing."

The congregation rose to its feet and sang:

> This is my father's world,
> And to my listening ears
> All nature sings and round me rings
> The music of the spheres . . .

When the hymn was over, Kat reached for a tithing envelope and pencil from the rack on back of the pew in front of her and doodled while Reverend Wiley gave his sermon, entitled "On the Side of Righteousness," telling the congregation that God was on the side of the Allies and therefore the Allies were certain to win the war in Europe. George Howard put his arm around Kat to his wife on her other side, and Janet took her daughter's hand in her own as Reverend Wiley finished up, saying, "Let us pray."

Janet Howard gave thanks for the blessing of her dear child beside her. Then she asked God to watch after her boy and wondered if it were His will that young men fight one another to the death. How, then, did one reckon with the sixth commandment? Janet knew mothers who had lost their sons and were proud of the sacrifice. In her heart she wanted her boy at home and was angry with herself for having this secret, selfish wish.

After church the Howards walked home, three abreast, and Kat asked her father if the royal blue robes the choir wore were the same robes the graduating class from Hawthorn High had worn the week before. Her father explained that though they were the same kind of robes, they were not the exact ones.

At home, Kat hung her Sunday dress in her closet, then took a pair of tan shorts off her clothes tree and stepped into them. She knew Betty Lou would be all dressed up for her birthday party, but Kat had to go for her appointment with Mrs. Cooper first, so she was going to wear her regular clothes. Kat thought she'd feel more comfortable that way, and besides, she didn't want Mrs. Cooper to get the impression that she was a fussy girl and not a good worker.

After Kat slipped her tee shirt over her head and her feet into her brown sandals, she sat on her bed to think about her appointment and prepare herself for meeting Mrs. Cooper. The old woman knew her father, so they wouldn't be absolute strangers. Kat reminded herself what her papa had told her to find out: what her duties would be, how much she would be paid for doing them, and setting up a trial period. Her father felt that Mrs. Cooper would approve of the trial run, and Mrs. Cooper already had agreed to her working there. Kat wouldn't have to talk the woman into anything—she just had to meet her and hope she didn't change her mind about the job. It would be fun to find out what a grandma was like anyway, thought Kat, and then she'd have lots to tell Annie and Betty Lou at the party.

Kat got up from the bed, ready for her adventure. She took Betty Lou's birthday present off her dresser, picked up Jesse's leash, and ran down the stairs.

6 The stairway up to the second story of the boardinghouse was real nice, thought Kat. The light coming in through the stained glass window made pretty colored patterns on the walls. By contrast, the stairway got kind of scary going up to the third story. It was dark, and Kat could barely see Francis's long legs climbing in front of her. Francis put his hand on Kat's shoulder as he knocked on the door to Mrs. Cooper's sitting room.

A voice came from inside the room: "Yes, Francis?" Kat felt her stomach leap to her throat.

"Miss Howard," announced Francis.

"Show her in."

Francis opened the door, and the bright light in the room blinded Kat for a long moment.

"Come forward, child."

Kat blinked her eyes and took a step forward.

"Francis, are you still there?"

"Yes, ma'am."

"Please bring up some cookies and milk."

"Will do," Francis said, leaving them.

When Kat's eyes adjusted to the light, she saw an old woman with snow-white hair sitting in a chair by the window. The woman had on a long black skirt, a gray collarless man's shirt with long sleeves, and a gray shawl across her shoulders. She put out her hand and motioned for Kat to come near. As Kat approached the woman, she heard the floorboards squeak.

"I'm Kathleen."

"You look like your father."

"Yes, ma'am. That's what everyone says, including me."

"He's a fine young man, your father."

Kat stared into the woman's filmy gray eyes. "Yes, ma'am," she answered, though she thought it odd that the woman had called her papa a young man.

"Sit, please." Mrs. Cooper motioned to the dark blue needlepoint footstool in front of her chair. Kat was glad to sit on the stool, where her feet could touch the floor. The woman's hands were in her lap. Kat looked at them. They were large and pink and very smooth. The old woman sat back, studied Kat, and said nothing.

"Do you want me to tell you about me?" asked Kat.

A faint smile waved across the old woman's face and then was gone. She made a sound that sounded like a yes to Kat, so Kat began, "I'm ten, and I'm going into the sixth grade next year." The old woman turned her face from Kat's gaze. "My real name is Kathleen, but I could never say Kathleen when I was little, so my brother—his name is Andy, actually Andrew, but we call him Andy and I call him Raggedy Andy—he shortened it for me. My papa sometimes calls me Kitty Kat, but everyone else calls me just Kat." The old woman turned back and faced Kat. "Should I tell you more?"

"If you have the energy."

"My brother's in the army. He gave me Jesse James when he left."

Mrs. Cooper laughed hard and startled Kat so she nearly fell off her stool.

"Did I say something funny?"

"Jesse James," said the old woman, and she smiled again, this time a big smile which made a pattern of wrinkles appear on her face.

"Oh, not the real Jesse James. He's in jail, I think. The Jesse

James I'm talking about is my cat. He walks on a leash and goes almost everywhere with me. He's outside right now waiting for me."

The old woman put her hands on her knees and asked, "Is Jesse James your sidekick?"

"We belong to each other," said Kat.

"Well, then, we'll try not to keep him waiting long."

Francis knocked before entering with a plate of cookies and two glasses of milk on a white wicker tray. As Francis passed Kat on his way out, he touched the top of her head with his hand. That helped Kat relax, and she took a bite of cookie.

"Did you make these?" Kat asked Mrs. Cooper.

"No. Why do you want to work here, Kathleen?"

"So I can go to the World Series. I'm sure the Browns are gonna play the Cardinals in the Series this year, and I want to see it."

"Who are you rooting for?"

"The Browns 'cause they've never won before."

"Do you always root for the underdog?"

"Yes, except when I'm playing. Then I root for me."

"And you're never the underdog?"

"Not in baseball. Nobody but Andy knows this, but I'm going to be a baseball player in the major leagues when I'm finished with school."

"What position do you play?"

"I haven't picked one yet. Do you like baseball, Mrs. Cooper?"

The old woman turned and looked out the window again, saying, "If you will try out all the positions, you'll discover the one which matters most."

Kat looked at the woman's profile. She had a double chin and wrinkles around her neck, and her white hair was held back in a bun. When the woman turned back she took the shawl off her shoulders. Kat thought she smelled lavender in the room and noticed that Mrs. Cooper did not wear a brassiere. Kat put her empty glass on the tray beside the woman's full glass.

"So you think the Browns are going to play in the Series this year?"

"Yes, ma'am. I can feel it in my bones."

The patterns appeared on the woman's face once again, fascinating Kat. "Well, Kathleen, you may be right then. And so you're going to go to St. Louis to see them?"

"Yes, ma'am. That's why I need two jobs."

"Two?"

"I have my brother's paper route too."

Mrs. Cooper got up slowly. She walked deliberately—as if she were not quite sure her stiff knees would be able to support her—to a rolltop desk in the corner of the room and returned with a piece of paper.

"I wrote down these instructions for Francis, but I'll give them to you instead." Next to the days of the week Monday through Saturday were listed the duties to be performed that day: Monday, water the plants, one hour; Tuesday, dust, one hour; Wednesday, grocery shop, two hours; Thursday, dust, one hour; Friday, change bed sheets, one hour; Saturday, grocery shop, two hours. "There are eight hours listed. You'll be paid two dollars on Saturday of each week. I'd like you to do your work before noon each day. Francis says you have a wagon you can use to carry the grocery bags."

"Yes, ma'am, my Red Flyer. I use it for my paper route."

"Well, what do you think, Kathleen? Can you do what's listed there?"

"Yes, ma'am, I'm certain I can, but ... "

"Yes, child, is something wrong?"

"Oh, no, this is just swell! It's just ... well, you see, my papa told me I should ask if I can work two weeks on trial, and then after the two weeks you and I would talk about me and decide if everything is going okay."

"That would be fine. July second we will visit again. Can you begin work a week from Monday?"

"Yes, ma'am. I could have started today except it's Sunday."

"Very well. You take that piece of paper home with you and show it to your papa. Francis will show you where things are, give you the grocery list and coupon book on Wednesdays and

Saturdays, and pay you each week. If you have any questions, please ask him. Any problems, tell him."

"Yes, thank you."

"He says you're a very special friend, and I trust his word."

"Yes, ma'am."

Mrs. Cooper pushed a buzzer near her chair. "Now you better get out to Jesse James."

"Yes, ma'am. Thank you for the cookies. I had a real nice time."

Francis knocked on the door.

"Francis, show Kathleen out, please, and you may take the tray."

Kat looked around the room quickly before she left. She'd been paying such strict attention to Mrs. Cooper she hadn't seen the bookcase that went from the floor to the ceiling behind the desk.

"I'm going to read *The Last of the Mohicans* this summer," Kat said proudly.

The old woman didn't hear her. She had turned around and was looking out her window toward the square.

◄§ 7 ◊► **B**etty Lou was dressed in a pink pinafore with four pink ribbons in her hair. Kat was glad she had worn shorts because even Betty Lou looked uncomfortable in her dress. She kept tugging at the skirt because, Kat noticed, Betty Lou was longer-waisted than the dress. Kat thought her friend did a wonderful job oohing and ahing over her gifts, acting surprised at each one; but she knew it was a performance because Betty Lou had told everyone what she wanted and had gotten exactly that.

Betty Lou saved Kat's present till last, recognizing which one it was by the white wrapping paper with the hand-painted bird. Since the second grade Kat had wrapped all her gifts in white butcher paper; rather than tie a bow around the package, she would paint a picture on the top and sometimes the sides and bottom of the package as well. Betty Lou was truly surprised when she saw the paper doll and clothes cut-outs inside—she hadn't gotten the toilet water she'd hinted for. She put down the opened gift and went over to Kat to kiss her on the cheek. It wasn't the gift so much as the giver Betty Lou was happy with, but the gift was the perfect foil to use to get close to the one she secretly adored. If the others were wise to Betty Lou, Kat certainly wasn't on this score. She was as unaware of Betty Lou's affections as she was of Daniel Brooks's.

After the gifts were set aside, Betty Lou's mother ushered the dozen young guests out to the front steps of the St. Pierre Inn for the picture-taking. Betty Lou sat down front center. Annie and Kat were off to one side, and Daniel Brooks was in the back row. Mrs. Ferrand made all the girls and boys squeeze close together so she could frame them within the perimeters of the black box she held against her chest.

"Now, don't anyone move a muscle when I say smile."

"How can we smile if we can't move a muscle?" asked Daniel.

"Smile and then hold your breath," Mrs. Ferrand answered.

Daniel didn't want to smile because his dead tooth would show.

"Is everyone ready?" Mrs. Ferrand asked in her serious tone.

Betty Lou stood up, whispered something in her mother's ear, and ran inside.

"Everyone relax," said Mrs. Ferrand, "but don't get up, please."

Kat turned to Annie and whispered, "Betty Lou's got to go to the bathroom, I'll bet." Annie giggled. "It never fails. She's always gotta pee when she's 'sposed to hold still." Annie giggled again.

"Annie, you're out of my picture."

When Annie moved in closer to Kat, she whispered, "Mrs. Ferrand is stricter than the teachers at school."

Kat didn't answer Annie. Instead, she studied Mrs. Ferrand. Betty Lou's mother looked older than Kat's mother, though she wasn't. That was because she had dark circles under her eyes and looked tired all the time, Kat figured. Mr. Ferrand was away in the war and Mrs. Ferrand worked long hours at the inn. What free time Charlotte Ferrand had she volunteered at the Red Cross. The dark dresses and closed collars she wore made the circles stand out, and the seriousness, too, thought Kat. While Mrs. Ferrand took great pains to make her daughter look like a princess, she did nothing to enhance her own appearance.

Betty Lou returned, and everyone sat up straight for Mrs. Ferrand.

"Smile," said Betty Lou's mother, and Daniel Brooks held up a fan of playing cards in front of his smile as the camera clicked.

"Brother," Kat sighed. "I'm sure glad that's over with."

"Everyone back in for cake," directed Mrs. Ferrand.

There was a frantic dash for the door, and Kat grabbed Annie's arm. "Wait a sec'. I've got something to tell you."

After the others were inside Kat said, "I got a job."

"You did? That was quick."

"I'm gonna work at the boardinghouse."

"That's great, Kat. Now you can go to the World Series."

"I had my interview with Mrs. Cooper today."

Annie asked how the meeting went, and just as Kat was about to tell her Betty Lou appeared.

"Aren't you coming in?" asked Betty Lou with a forlorn expression on her face.

"Kat got a job," sang Annie.

"You did? How come you didn't tell me first on my birthday?"

"I was gonna tell you, Betty Lou, but you've been too busy opening gifts and stuff."

"Are you gonna tell me now?"

"I'm gonna work at the boardinghouse."

"Doing what?"

"Watering plants and stuff. It's all here. Mrs. Cooper wrote it down for me."

The three girls bent over the piece of paper Kat had pulled from her pocket.

"Betty Lou!" Mrs. Ferrand shouted from the window above them. "Everyone's waiting on you!"

"I've gotta go make my wish and blow out the candles. You're coming, aren't you?"

After the cake had been devoured the party broke up. Kat and Annie stayed to help Betty Lou and her mother wash dishes.

The Ferrands had a small kitchen on the second floor, above the restaurant. Betty Lou and Kat sat on the chrome chairs at the kitchen table while Mrs. Ferrand rinsed off the Kramers' cake platter and handed it to Annie to dry.

"Put it on the table so you won't forget to take it home with you," Mrs. Ferrand said to Annie, who placed the platter on the yellow-flowered oilcloth in front of Betty Lou and Kat.

"Now you can tell us about your job," cooed Betty Lou, gazing at Kat.

"I had my interview with Mrs. Cooper before I came here. I'm gonna work two weeks on trial first."

"What's Mrs. Cooper like?" asked Betty Lou.

"My papa says she's like a grandmother, but since I never had one I don't know. She's old like a grandmother, and she walks kind of bent over and slow. But she's got a real loud laugh and smells like lavender."

"That's the kind of toilet water you were supposed to get me," said Betty Lou.

"Betty Lou, birthday presents are supposed to be surprises. There'd be no point in wrapping them if you knew what they were."

Betty Lou caught her mother's critical glance and said, "I like the paper doll. I didn't mean that. I was just thinking it was a coincidence."

"Practically no one has ever seen Mrs. Cooper," said Annie. "I bet you're the first in our class who has."

"Were you nervous?" asked Betty Lou.

"Kind of, but not really. I mean at first I was, but not after I talked and we had milk and cookies."

"What did you talk about?" asked Betty Lou.

Mrs. Ferrand put the last dish in the sink rack to drain, wiped her hands on her apron, and turned around to look at Kat.

"She asked me why I wanted to work there, and I told her because I wanted to go to the World Series. I think that interested her."

Mrs. Ferrand stepped to the table. "Does your mother know about this?" she asked Kat.

"Sure," Kat replied.

"And she's letting you work at that house?" Mrs. Ferrand's sharpness caught everyone's attention.

"Yes, ma'am," answered Kat.

"Doesn't she know about that old woman?"

Mrs. Ferrand seemed disturbed, but Kat couldn't imagine why. Betty Lou evidently couldn't either and asked, "What about her, Mummy?"

"She sits up in her room in that house and never comes out or sees anyone."

Kat pulled herself up straight and said, "My papa says she's just not sociable."

"Your papa doesn't know what others know."

Kat wasn't prepared to defend the old woman, but she would defend her papa to her death. "My papa knows as much as anyone about anything."

"I wonder," Mrs. Ferrand answered back.

Betty Lou and Annie leaned toward one another, away from the crossfire. Betty Lou knew her mother was referring to something important, like morals, by the look in her eyes and the way she was swallowing. She also knew Kat got enraged whenever

45

anyone doubted her or her family. And Betty Lou didn't want her mother, whom she loved above anyone else in the world, and her friend, whom she also loved, to be mad at each other and argue. She licked her lips nervously, wondering if she should say something. Annie, who was uncomfortable around the slightest conflict, stared down at her mother's platter on the table, wishing she could grab it and run off.

After a long pause Kat said, "I don't wonder, Mrs. Ferrand."

"You are a child."

"I'm a grown-up child."

"There's no such thing, and because your parents don't know enough to warn you, it is my duty to do so. Mrs. Cooper does not show her face because she did something which is too dissolute to describe. I would not permit Betty Lou to be in her house, but since you say your parents are permitting you to do just that, I advise you to avoid the woman."

"Will you spell 'destitute' for me, Mrs. Ferrand?" asked Kat.

"I said dissolute. D-i-s-s-o-l-u-t-e."

"I don't know what that means, Mrs. Ferrand, and I don't know Mrs. Cooper hardly at all, but I'm not scared of her and I'm glad I got the job there. And I'm going to the World Series." Kat stood up. "I think I'll leave now. Thank you for the invitation."

Betty Lou looked up, pained, and Annie grabbed up her mother's plate.

Soon the three friends were standing once again on the sidewalk in front of the inn. Annie started home without a word, while Kat patted Betty Lou's shoulder, saying, "I'm not mad, Betty Lou. Don't worry." Then Kat, too, started for home, forgetting Jesse, who had been lying in the shade under one of the small evergreens at the entrance to the inn. When Kat reached the Elm Street corner, she suddenly remembered her sidekick and called for him. Jesse ran out from under the tree, dragging his leash behind him.

When Kat arrived for her first day of work it was Eva Parsons who greeted her at the front door.

"Was I supposed to be here before ten?" Kat asked as she followed Eva to the kitchen.

"No, dear. Francis thought he'd be here all morning, but last night the peonies were torn up, by a dog perhaps, and he had to go to the park first thing this morning to see to those that could be saved. When I finish this jam I'll take you around the house."

"What kind of jam?" Kat asked, taking a seat on the step stool beside the pantry and noticing that the room smelled like sandwiches, the way her lunch pail did. Kat wouldn't let her mother wash out her lunch box. There was something about the smell of it that was comforting to her, like the smell of bed sheets right off the clothesline and the smell of oak in her tree fort. Kat lived close enough to school to go home for lunch, but she liked having lunch with her friends, so she had carried her lunch to school for the last two years.

"Peach," answered Eva. Kat had been taking in the room and had forgotten the question she'd asked a moment earlier. "Got out a jar of last year's canned peaches this morning to make jam," Eva explained.

"How do you do that?"

"Add two cups of sugar to each jar, then let it boil till it's nice and thick."

"It smells real good. I like this room," Kat said, looking up at the blue willow plates and cranberry glass on the cupboards just below the ceiling. "Am I supposed to dust them? 'cause I don't know how I'd reach up that high even on this little ladder."

"No, dear. Hold your horses now and I'll tell you what you're supposed to dust and what you're not."

Kat didn't mind Miss Parsons telling her to be patient because she didn't sound like she was scolding. "Were you the one who made the cookies I had with Mrs. Cooper?"

"Yes, dear."

"They were about the best cookies I've ever had."

"Thank you. When you finish watering the plants today you may have another."

"Thank you, that'd be swell." Kat watched Eva skim off froth from the mixture in the pan, then pour the jam into a Mason jar and set it on the window sill to cool. She knew she was going to like this job. There was lots of new stuff to see and learn.

After Eva had placed the sticky jam pan in the sink to soak, she fetched the green watering can from a narrow broom closet beside the stove and led Kat to the Eisenbergs' apartment on the first floor. Eva was wearing a long skirt like Mrs. Cooper, but she wasn't nearly as old, just old fashioned, observed Kat. As she walked, she picked up her skirt just a little, and Kat saw she was wearing slippers on her feet, not shoes. Kat also noticed that Eva walked with her back held straight; Kat's mother would describe Eva as "correct." For the longest time Kat thought when her mama said this about a person she meant the individual was real smart. Kat knew now that her mother meant correct manner-wise, not smart-wise, though Kat understood the two qualities could be present in the same person.

Eva tapped lightly on the Eisenbergs' closed door and announced herself. A woman's voice answered, told her to come in.

"Mrs. Eisenberg, this is Kat Howard, George and Janet Howard's child."

Sarah stopped rocking. "What's she doing here?"

"She's going to work here this summer."

"Work here?"

"Yes, Sarah."

"Why isn't she home helping her mother?"

Kat wondered if Mrs. Eisenberg knew she was standing there, because she didn't look at her and she was directing all her questions to Miss Parsons.

Eva didn't answer Sarah's question. Instead, she motioned for Kat to follow her to the window sill, then handed her the watering can she'd been holding. Kat tipped the spout and watered the crowded geraniums as Eva instructed her. Hearing the floorboards creaking behind her she turned around and saw that Mrs. Eisenberg was rocking again.

"You live in that big house on Elm Street, don't you?" Sarah asked Kat.

"Yes, ma'am," Kat answered, surprised that the woman had addressed her.

"That's where you should be."

Kat turned to Eva Parsons for help, but Eva showed no reaction to the woman or her remark. Instead, she nodded to Kat that it was time to go.

Back in the hall, Eva said, "We'll go up and see Miss Renee next. She's home today. She works Saturdays at the beauty parlor, so Sunday and Monday are her holidays."

Kat had heard Eva's teeth make a strange clicking sound, and was curious about that, but Eva turned away from Kat's stare and started up the stairs before Kat could question her.

Eva Parsons was a very different kind of lady than Kat had ever known. She wasn't like a schoolteacher or a mother or a grandmother. Kat knew she was Judge Lionel Parsons's daughter. She looked like the judge and was hard to figure like him. The kids at school sometimes made fun of Eva. They called her an old maid. But everyone in Hawthorn knew Eva Parsons could have married widower Mulqueen of Mulqueen's Hardware if she'd wanted to. Mr. Mulqueen had had seven years of bad luck courting Eva ever since Mrs. Mulqueen died of pneumonia in 1937. Eva didn't seem like the romantic type to Kat, and that, Kat assumed, was why she didn't want a husband.

Miss Renee, on the other hand, seemed very romantic to Kat. She was lounging in a bright green dressing gown with white angora around the neckline when Kat and Eva arrived to water her plants. The first thing Miss Renee said when they entered her room was, "Don't touch the bed or you'll mess my nails." She was lying across her bed, a movie magazine at her elbow, applying cherry-red polish to her fingernails.

After being introduced, Kat, watered Miss Renee's lipstick plant, careful not to drip any water on the maple dressing table.

"Now you've met all the ladies of the house," said Eva.

"Have you met Mrs. Cooper too?" Miss Renee asked Kat as she blew across her hands.

"Yes, last week."

"What did you think of the antique?" Miss Renee asked with a smile, then rose and went to the cheval mirror. She raised her hands to her white angora neckline and looked admiringly at her nails in the mirror.

"Is she really a hundred years old?" Kat asked in earnest.

Miss Renee squealed with delight and Kat giggled. Then Eva stepped out of the room into the hall and motioned for Kat to join her.

After the two had visited each room and Kat had listened carefully to Eva's watering and dusting instructions, they returned to the kitchen. While Kat ate her cookie Eva put soup on the stove for the lunch meal.

"Is cooking your hobby, Miss Parsons?"

"Baking is my hobby and cooking is my work."

"Is it cooking when you do it on the stove and baking if you do it in the oven?"

"That's close enough."

"I think I'm going to like it here."

"The best thing to do, dear, is to listen to everyone, do the best you can to do as they ask, and don't get entangled in their eccentricities. Mind your own business and keep your own counsel."

"That's how you do it, isn't it?"

"Yes, dear."

"You do it good."

Eva smiled for the first time since greeting Kat at the door. Then, lifting the spoon from the boiling pot to sip the broth, she said gently, "You may go now. I'll see you tomorrow."

"Yes, ma'am," said Kat, standing up and wiping her hands on the back of her shorts. "Thanks for helping me."

Eva nodded as she tasted the soup, and Kat headed toward the front door.

As Kat started down the walk she glanced back at the boardinghouse and looked up at the two windows on the third story. The old woman was sitting at the window on the right. Kat started to raise her hand to wave, then remembered what Betty Lou's mother had said a week earlier and what Eva Parsons had just said and put her hand in her pocket. She was going to be careful not to mess up on anything. Thinking she'd get her mitt and ball and find Daniel Brooks to play catch, she pulled a stick of gum out of her shorts pocket, popped it in her mouth, and skipped down the walk.

While Eva Parsons put Wednesday's groceries away in the cupboard and ice box, Kat sat on the step stool in the boardinghouse kitchen dunking a cookie in a glass of milk. She watched Eva put the last item away, then placed her empty milk glass on the counter, licked sugar off her fingers, and left for the day.

Moments after Kat was gone, Sarah Eisenberg rushed into the kitchen. She had been watching for Kat at her front window. When she saw the youngster run across the town square toward home she left her rocker in search of Francis.

Eva breathed a sigh of relief as Francis entered the kitchen behind Sarah, who was insisting upon seeing Mrs. Cooper right away. Francis carried this message to the old woman upstairs when he took up her lunch meal. Mrs. Cooper reluctantly agreed to speak with Sarah that afternoon.

When Sarah arrived upstairs she saw the chair standing, as usual, in the middle of the room and sat down on it, then waited until Mrs. Cooper, seated at the window, turned and acknowledged her. Just as Sarah opened her mouth to speak Mrs. Cooper raised a hand to stop her. The old woman would have the first word, as always. Sarah seethed inside. She hated having to sit in the center of the room, not permitted to speak until spoken to.

"Sarah Eisenberg, I understand you are unhappy today."

"I don't want that child coming into my room and moving my things."

"I assume you are speaking of Miss Howard," Mrs. Cooper said calmly.

"Yes, of course."

"Miss Howard is in my employ. It is my opinion that her services are needed here. If she has done something specific which has injured you, please speak up and I will see to the matter."

"She should be in her own home helping her mother."

Staring intently at Sarah, Mrs. Cooper said, "That would seem to be up to her and her mother, not you or me."

Sarah turned from Mrs. Cooper's gaze and looked about the room. Her eyes stopped on the victrola. "Everything I owned was taken from me," she grumbled. "And at no fault of my own! I am an old woman now, with nothing. Is it not my right to have my privacy? To have my personal things, my bureau articles, left alone and not disturbed by a child's careless hand?"

"Has anything been lost or damaged?" asked Mrs. Cooper.

"You don't understand, though God knows you should since no one is allowed to come near you!" Sarah had meant to say "near your things." Her displeasure over being kept at a distance in the center of the room was made obvious by this slip of the tongue.

"Have you spoken to Miss Howard and told her how you feel?"

Sarah didn't answer. She fidgeted in the chair.

"I can see you are quite upset and uncomfortable, Sarah. Relax and I will give this some thought." Mrs. Cooper leaned back and closed her eyes. After several moments she opened her eyes and said, "You are quite right to ask that your privacy be protected and your things untouched. I will speak to Miss Howard and excuse her from dusting your bureau. Do you wish for her to continue watering the plants in your room?"

Sarah felt victorious, smiled, and clasped her hands in her lap. "She may continue to water the plants. For now."

"Very well. If that is all . . ." Mrs. Cooper turned her head to the side, expecting Sarah to excuse herself and leave.

"It's not the same for the others. I don't expect them to understand. They didn't have a house once."

"Dear Sarah . . ." Mrs. Cooper said with a tenderness that surprised both women. Before she could go on with her thought, she was interrupted by Sarah's outcry.

"I had a family and friends once. Parties in my home. I am a God-fearing woman, not like you. Why am I punished? You're the one who—"

"I must stop you, Sarah. I don't wish to hear what you think of me."

But Sarah was not about to be stopped. "You have a house. Why? Why must I live in your house?"

"Sarah, if you wish to live somewhere else, where you would feel more comfortable, you're free to go."

"I have nowhere to go and no one."

"That is something for you to discuss with Mr. Eisenberg or your God, not with me." Mrs. Cooper was growing tired and impatient, and her voice was no longer soft.

"Do you think he listens? He's never listened to me. If he had, do you think we would have lost everything?"

"I think you enjoy being a victim."

"Of course. I shouldn't expect you to understand. What have you ever had to lose?"

It was, as always, impossible to communicate with Sarah. Mrs. Cooper's anger subsided in a kind of hopelessness. "I'm no comfort to you, Sarah. You shouldn't come to me. It does neither of us any good. In the future Francis will hear your complaints and see to your needs. That is all, Sarah. Please leave."

"You can't do this." Sarah stood up. "Cut me off. I'm an old woman like yourself, alone."

"Sarah, it was you who said I was not like you. And that I am unable to understand your dilemma." She reached an arm out and rang the buzzer for Francis.

Sarah was desperate. "You make me sit in the center of this room like a child. And I can't talk until you talk first. You think because this is your house you're better than me." There were no tears in Sarah's eyes, only rage. "I'm not ashamed of anything I've done in my life, but you . . ."

Mrs. Cooper turned around and looked out her window. She would listen to no more.

"You can't turn away from it," Sarah spouted. "You turn because you don't want to face the truth of who you are. You turn from me because I'm an old woman who isn't afraid to say what you are." But she was afraid to say it, and when Francis heard the ruckus he opened the door without knocking, and Sarah left without another word.

Sarah's visit had been a strain on Mrs. Cooper, and she was glad she would not have to go through it again. Though she didn't seek approval from others, cruel words sometimes hurt, even Sarah's feeble attacks.

Comforted by the sight of the trees outside her window, Mrs. Cooper rose from her chair and went to her closet to get down a puzzle. She wouldn't be able to read just yet—after the puzzle perhaps. She laid out the pieces on the table in front of her settee, located in an alcove to the right of the door as one entered the room, cater-corner from the window.

The old woman's hands felt cold and clumsy. How frustrating to grow old, she thought. One's body cannot keep up with one's mind. She could spot the appropriate piece, but it took so long to pick it up and put it in place. As she worked she remembered what Sarah had said: she didn't want the child's careless hands on her things. No, Mrs. Cooper thought, rubbing her hands together for warmth, not careless. Children care deeply. They cannot help that they are inexperienced.

Sometime later the old woman heard a soft rap on her door and looked up to see that the room had grown dark. She had dozed off, and Francis was there with her dinner tray.

"Come in, dear."

54

"Were you napping?" Francis asked.

"Yes, but I'm hungry now. Put the light on and bring the tray here."

"I'm sorry about this afternoon. I saw she was quite angry. I should have put her off a day."

"I shall not see her anymore, Francis."

"I understand."

"Please sit. I want to ask you a question."

Francis took the chair still standing in the center of the room, where he'd placed it hours earlier, and carried it to the settee.

"How do the others feel about the Howard child?"

"Eva's the only one who's spent any time with her. She says Kat's a good worker. Does her job well in half the time. Very businesslike, I think Eva said. You know, takes it very seriously."

"And how do you feel about her?"

"You know how I feel. She's a terrific kid. She's quite remarkable. I forget she's only ten. Sees everything and catches on quickly. She's got Sarah figured."

"How's that?"

"Doesn't make conversation with her. Answers her with a 'Yes, ma'am' or a 'No, ma'am.' I think it irks Sarah not being able to get her goat. Eva overheard Sarah telling Kat she was abnormal because she played baseball and Kat answer 'Yes, ma'am.' Tickled the heck out of Eva, though of course she covered up her pleasure. She had to tell me though."

Mrs. Cooper took a sip of wine. "No wonder Sarah wants her to continue watering her plants. She's hoping to get to the child eventually."

"Sarah won't be happy until everyone around her is as miserable as she is."

"She's a one-woman crusade in that cause, isn't she?" Mrs. Cooper chuckled.

"She gets to David terribly. The others ignore her as best they can. Which reminds me. David is leaving August nineteenth. Since Marjorie is going to be leaving Hawthorn, too, there'll be a new schoolteacher coming in. Maybe David's room?"

"You will see to that, won't you, dear heart?"

"Yes, of course." Francis smiled reassuringly as he stood to go.

"When Kathleen comes in tomorrow, you had better tell her to skip—no, I'll tell her myself. No, I won't be seeing her for another week. Tell her to skip Sarah's room on Tuesdays and Thursdays. I'll explain why to her later."

Francis nodded and started toward the door.

"Is she awfully sensitive?"

"Kat?" Francis asked, turning around. "Yes, I think she is."

"Make certain she doesn't feel she's done anything wrong."

❧ 10 ☙ Perched in the crook of the oldest oak in Hawthorn was a gray clapboard tree house built by George Howard for his son, but which now belonged to his daughter. Painted above the doorway in large black letters was the warning: "Beware of Kat." Kat called the tree house her fort; it was here she went to read and write, daydream, or just hide away. A hatchway in the roof of the fort made it possible for Kat to lie on her back on the oak floorboard and gaze up through the opening at the tree and sky above. There were windows at the back of the fort facing Christopher Street and two windows and a door at the front facing the back of the Howard house.

Inside, the walls of the fort were covered with Kat's drawings, picture cut-outs, newspaper clippings, a piece of manila paper on the door with large green-crayon letters spelling out "Private Property," and a photograph of Andy in his army uniform beside the calendar that hung on the wall between the two back windows. Marked in Kat's neat hand on the days of the week were her boardinghouse duties and the Browns' and Cardinals' home games in Sportsman's Park. Throughout the calendar were red stars marking the birthdays of friends and family.

Kat kept her most prized possessions in her fort. In one corner, alongside a stack of four Nancy Drew mysteries, a picture book of birds and flowers that had been soaked with rainwater and now swelled in its binding, a book on baseball with its front cover missing, and a dictionary with Kat's name embossed in gold letters on its cover, was a doll in a calico dress which Kat had named Peggy Sue. Kat no longer played with Peggy Sue, but she did talk to her doll once in a while when Jesse wasn't around. In another corner of the fort were two baseball mitts—Andy's old first baseman's and Kat's outfielder's, which held a gray hardball with worn-out red stitching. Hanging from a large wooden peg above the mitts were a flashlight and a whistle. The flashlight was Kat's night light, and the whistle was for signaling an SOS to her parents.

Kat leaned against a side wall of her fort with her knees propped up supporting her Mohawk writing tablet. On her right was a round tin containing a pair of scissors, a gum eraser, three sharpened pencils and a pencil sharpener, a Crayola crayon box, some string, a yellow golf tee, a black comb, her war stamp book, and a Boy Scout patch Andy had won for starting a fire with flint and stone. On top of the tin were a knife that once belonged to Andy and a stack of baseball cards with a brown rubber band around them; next to it stood a pink piggy bank with bright blue eyes and a red snout which Kat had named Piggy Blue, along with Jesse's water bowl, a fallen oak leaf floating at its top. On Kat's left was a cigar box containing letters; lying across the box, his head on an outstretched paw, was Jesse James.

The fort smelled of oak and the gardenia toilet water which Kat splashed on liberally from the green glass bottle resting on the shelf over her heard. Above, the lambent sun shimmered past the oak branches through the fort's hatchway onto the calendar inside. Kat looked at the calendar, wrote "June 26, 1944" at the upper-right hand corner of the tablet page, and continued:

Dear Raggedy Andy,

I just got home from dusting and straightening the rooms at Mrs. Cooper's. I started my job last week and I'm going to make two dollars a week, which will be just right. By the end of August I'll have twenty dollars. I'm going to use it to go to the World Series. The reason I need so much is because I have to have an escort and pay two ways.

The newspapers call the Browns a plucky team, and they are. They're still in first place. I have to admit the teams are pretty bad a lot of the time. On June 8 Cuccurullo, he's the rookie pitcher for the Pirates, threw a wild pitch into the stands with the bases loaded. The Cubs scored three runs. The Cards are doing like always. They beat Cleveland 18 to 0 last week. They haven't lost players like the other teams, so it's a real massacre, like when I play Brooks. I told Mrs. Cooper I was going to be a major-league player when I'm finished with school. I don't know why I told her my secret. I've only seen her once. I'm going to see her again on July 2 to decide if I can keep my job.

Betty Lou is eleven now. Annie's mother fixed her a chocolate cake and we got to lick the frosting from the bowl. I gave Betty Lou a paper doll and cut-outs. She used to cut them out of the newspaper comics. Annie gave her a paintbox. It's really swell. I almost said she could get one for me just like it when my birthday comes, but I remembered in time. I hope you'll be home for my birthday. I miss you a lot, Raggedy Andy.

I go to the grocery store two times a week and get to squeeze the oleo margarine to make it yellow. It comes with a red pill that bursts to make the color. Eva Parsons, I call her Miss Parsons to her face, is very nice and cooks swell, but she has bad teeth. They click when she talks and jump when she laughs. I think that's why she doesn't laugh as much as Miss Renee, whose name is really Gladys Pooley. She doesn't tell anyone that, but Flowerman knew and he told me. He's my favorite. He's Francis Spenger, but sometimes I call him Flowerman because he's a gardener and wears a flower by his ear in the thing around his head like Indians wear. He got me this job and pays me on Saturdays. We talk a lot but not like you and me. I wish you were here so we could talk like we used to. Jesse misses you too.

The cat next door at the Bennetts' is going to have kittens. Papa says Jesse is the papa. Jesse won't say. Ha, ha. He just falls over on his side and purrs. I would be real sad if it wasn't for Jesse. He makes me laugh all the time. He won't climb up the tree like a regular cat. He uses a ladder like me. Maybe he thinks I'm a cat because he hears everyone call me Kat.

Miss Holmes, my teacher, is getting married to David Webb in August. I don't like him too much but I don't tell anyone that. Miss Holmes is beautiful. I wish you were going to marry her. Then she would live with us. I like talking to her but I don't anymore because she's always with him.

I'm writing the longest letter ever because I miss you. I'm in the fort with Jesse. He's asleep. His head is on the box where I put your letters. He looks real cute because his paws are covering his eyes like he was praying. I hope the war will be over soon and you'll be home.

I love you.

Your Kat

P.S. Do you know anything about Mrs. Cooper? Betty Lou's mother doesn't like her and she made me worry, so if you know something you can tell me.

Kat put the letter in her pocket, threw the baseball mitts out of the fort, and unfurled the rope ladder. "Come on, lazy bones!" she called to Jesse. The lanky white cat balanced on Kat's shoulders as she climbed down to the ground. After she put Jesse's leash on him, she lifted the heavy rock beside the back door and anchored the leash to it, holding Jesse there while she went into the house. As she opened the screen door she saw her mother at the kitchen table and quickly caught the door before it slammed.

"I have a letter to send to Andy, Mama."

"Get me an envelope and my purse and I'll address it for you."

Kat ran from the kitchen and returned with an envelope and her mother's purse. "I'm gonna play at the square; then I'll come home after I do my route."

"Here's my last stamp and a quarter. Get me some stamps when you mail this," said Janet, addressing the envelope for her daughter and handing it back to her.

At the back door Kat hesitated, turned around, and asked, "Can you tell if a person is lacking in moral restraint?"

Janet looked up from the dress pattern she was cutting on the kitchen table. "That sounds like something out of the dictionary, not your head."

"It is. I looked up 'dissolute' and that's what it said."

"Where did you get that word?"

"Betty Lou's mother said it."

"You probably misunderstood her."

"Uh uh. She spelled it. She said I shouldn't be at the boardinghouse because Mrs. Cooper was that word."

"It's not a very nice word to call someone."

"How come Mrs. Ferrand did?"

Janet put the scissors down and leaned on the table with both hands. Kat watched her mother intently, waiting for her to explain things and set her mind at ease.

"I don't know why Mrs. Ferrand said it or what she meant by it," said Janet.

"I think she meant Mrs. Cooper was bad."

"Do you think Mrs. Cooper is bad?"

"No, I don't think so," Kat said, but her face showed she was still troubled.

"Come here, Kat, and sit down beside me." Janet sat down and pulled out a chair for her daughter. "When you had your talk with Mrs. Cooper, did she frighten you?"

"No, Mama," Kat answered, then added after a pause, "I was a little nervous in the beginning because she's new."

"Just between you and me, Mrs. Ferrand gets excited sometimes and says things stronger than she feels."

"You mean she exaggerates?"

Janet nodded.

"I do that sometimes."

"Everyone does from time to time to get attention, but it's better not to because it confuses people."

"I know," Kat said. Janet stroked her daughter's head, wondering if she'd said too much or not enough. "If a person was bad, I'd know it," Kat said confidently.

"Yes, I think you would. And you also know you can always come to me or your papa when you get confused."

"Yeah, I know."

Janet looked into her child's clear eyes and marveled at how open she was. In an instant Kat would be up and gone, though Janet wished she could keep her there a while longer.

Kat scooted her chair away from the table and hopped up. "I'm going now. Bye." In a moment she was out of the house, the screen door slamming shut behind her.

"Kat!"

"Yes, Mama?"

"Please don't slam the door."

"I'm sorry. I forgot."

"Don't forget the stamps."

"I won't. Bye."

Jesse sat up tall in the Red Flyer as Kat pulled it toward the town square whistling the theme song from "Jack Armstrong, The All-American Boy." Behind her, approaching fast on his bike, was Ralph Quinn, Mr. Quinn's fourteen-year-old son. He whizzed around the wagon and spit out a mouthful of water at Kat.

"I'm gonna clobber you, Ralph Quinn!"

"I'm not afraid of stupid girls!" Ralph hollered back over his shoulder.

Kat wiped the front of her shirt, heaved a fist in the air at Ralph as he rode off toward the railroad station, then went into the post office to mail her letter and get her mother some stamps. When she came out of the post office she saw Daniel Brooks sitting across the street on the courthouse steps and ran to greet him.

"Want to play catch, Brooks?" Kat asked, out of breath.

"I haven't got my mitt."

"That's all right 'cause I've got both of mine. How come you forgot yours?"

"My mom's mad at me, so I left home without it."

"How come?"

"How come she's mad?"

"Yeah."

" 'Cause I bought these shoes."

Kat looked down at Daniel's feet and saw two white bucks. "They're real nice, Brooks."

"Mom says they aren't practical and won't last and I can't have another pair because we don't have any more coupons."

"You can go barefoot then. That's even better."

"Yeah."

"You'll feel better once you play catch."

"Not if you beat me."

"Brooks, you can't get sore every time I beat you. Besides, we're only gonna play catch, not three swings."

"Oh, all right."

Mrs. Cooper had been sitting at her window reading. She put down her book and looked out at the square at the two youngsters playing ball. She watched as Kat mopped her brow with her hand, then wiped her hand on the back of her shorts. Daniel threw Kat a grounder, and she reached down, snatched it up, and tossed it back to him in one graceful movement.

An idea flashed across Mrs. Cooper's face, and she left the window and returned with a sketch pad and a charcoal pencil. This time she saw Daniel wind up and throw the ball high above the trees and Kat run under it and catch it. When the next ball sailed into the air, Mrs. Cooper heard herself urge Kat to catch it. Kat did, and the old woman turned to her pad and began sketching.

Several minutes passed as Mrs. Cooper sketched the scene in the square. When she had completed four drawings she laid her pad and pencil aside and continued to observe the activity from her window. Kat threw a fast ball to Daniel, and he missed it. Jesse chased the ball into the shrubs beside the courthouse. Just as Kat was retrieving the ball, Francis rounded the corner and waved to Daniel and Kat. When Kat ran to join Francis, Daniel ran off toward home. Francis greeted Kat, tapping the visor of her baseball cap, and the two friends sat down on the courthouse lawn. Mrs. Cooper smiled at the sight of them, remembering Francis as a youngster. Sighing, she said, "*Il y a longtemps, hier,*" then closed her eyes and pictured in her mind's eye those days long ago.

The squeak of the Red Flyer startled the old woman from her daydream. "*Qui est là?*" she asked aloud. Looking down, she saw a long, skinny, white cat stretched out on a stack of newspapers in a red wagon and the youngster with pipe-stem arms and legs skipping up the walk with the evening paper. "Yes, Francis," Mrs. Cooper said in a hushed voice, "*je vois ce que vous voulez dire, remarquable.*"

11 The first days of summer passed quickly for Kat and suddenly it was July. She had not seen Betty Lou or Annie since the birthday party, and it had been nearly a week since she had played catch with Brooks. Learning to get along at the boardinghouse was foremost in Kat's life. It hadn't been easy. It wasn't like working around her house nor straightening her own things. She had to be more cautious, knock on doors before entering, and be extra careful when touching things. At home accidents were tolerated. Kat was certain Mrs. Eisenberg didn't tolerate mistakes, and she wasn't certain Mrs. Cooper or Miss Parsons did either. By the end of her second week of work Kat knew what was expected of her and was familiar with where things were. Though she was becoming friendly with each of the boarders, she followed Eva Parsons's advice of that first day and concentrated on her duties, not the personalities of the boardinghouse. Thus an element of mystery surrounded the place and the people, particularly Mrs. Cooper, whom she'd seen just once and would see again in a day.

On Saturday, the first day of July, Annie and Betty Lou asked

Kat to go to the matinee with them. When Kat hesitated longer than usual before agreeing to join her friends, Janet Howard stepped in and encouraged her daughter to go.

After loading up at the movie theater's candy counter the three chums fumbled in the dark for seats. Annie sat in the middle. Kat was on her left, with shoes off and bare feet up on the red velvet seat, and Betty Lou on her right, inwardly disappointed that she wasn't sitting beside Kat.

During the newsreel Betty Lou whispered to Annie that she had something extremely important to tell Kat and had to trade seats with her in order to do so. Annie fussed, but Betty Lou insisted, "It's about my daddy and the war." A boy behind them shushed the two, and Annie gave in, trading seats with Betty Lou.

Leaning close to Kat, Betty Lou whispered in her ear, "Want to come home with me afterward and play in my room?"

"I've got to do my paper route first. Then maybe I'll come over and play with you and Annie. But I'm not promising 'cause I may decide I don't want to."

Betty Lou hadn't intended to invite Annie, and she might have worked on Kat some more if the boy behind her hadn't begun banging the back of her seat for quiet. She'd have to wait until the movie was over and invite Annie too.

The movie ended with Roy Rogers singing to Trigger and Kat working on the Jujubees stuck between her teeth.

"Come on, Kat, let's go," urged Betty Lou.

"Wait a sec'. I wanna see the credits."

"Why do you want to see them?"

"I just do." But the commotion in the theater broke the magic spell, which was what Kat wanted to hold onto longer, and she succumbed to Betty Lou's tugging on her sleeve.

Outside in the sunshine Annie glanced down at Kat's feet and said, "You forgot your sandals."

Kat ran back inside the pitch-black theater, fumbled around among the discarded popcorn and candy wrappers, retrieved her sandals, and then joined her friends outside.

"Let's go to my place," said Betty Lou, resigned to inviting

Annie as well. "We'll play movie, and I'll be Dale Evans and Kat can be Roy Rogers."

"Who am I gonna be, Trigger?" asked Annie.

"You can be the Sons of the Pioneers," replied Betty Lou.

"I don't want to be that."

"Then you don't have to come." Betty Lou saw this as her last chance to get rid of Annie and have Kat all to herself.

"I've gotta do my paper route," said Kat. "Then I may just go home."

A slight edge to her voice, Betty Lou asked, "You're gonna go over to the boardinghouse, aren't you?"

"No, I've already done the grocery shopping."

"You spend more time there than anywhere. We don't ever see you." Betty Lou had been expecting disappointment.

"It's my job, Betty Lou."

"You like them better than us." Betty Lou chose the collective pronoun to keep from exposing the real wound.

"You're crazy, Betty Lou. I do not."

"You're the crazy one for liking old people better than your friends—and especially Mrs. Cooper, who isn't even a nice person."

"You're saying something you don't even know, Betty Lou. I've just decided I'm not coming over to your house. I'd rather be alone."

Kat's reproach stung her, and Betty Lou looked away.

"I'll be Roy Rogers then," Annie offered.

"No, you aren't tall enough," said Betty Lou, not bothering to look at Annie.

"You just don't like me," said Annie, now the one hurt.

The three had reached the St. Pierre Inn, and Betty Lou sat down on the stoop. Afraid she was about to be abandoned by both friends, she cooed, "Yes, I do, Annie . . . We'll play beauty parlor instead of movie, okay?" Then she twisted a curl around her finger, adding, "If you come play, Kat, you can have curls too."

"I don't want curls. I like my hair the way it is."

"Don't you want pretty hair like Dale Evans?" asked Annie,

wrinkling her nose and drawing Kat's attention to the row of freckles that bridged it.

"No, it'd get in my way when I play catch."

Annie sat down on the stoop beside Betty Lou and asked, "Did you see Ralph Quinn and that boy fighting?"

"When?" asked Kat.

"When we came out of the Strand. He was twisting his arm and making him red in the face, and I think he was crying too."

"Ralph Quinn was crying?"

"No, Betty Lou, the boy he was hurting."

"I'll bet the boy was smaller than Ralph," said Kat.

"Yeah, he was. Remember when Ralph chased Brooks with a knife?" Annie asked Kat.

"I never saw Brooks run that fast ever!"

"Why was Ralph chasing him?" asked Betty Lou. "Did Brooks call him a bad name?"

Kat shook her head and sighed, "Ralph doesn't need a reason. He's just mean." Then she started away.

"You coming back?" Betty Lou tried again.

"I don't think so. It'll be too late, and tomorrow's church, and then I've got my second—" Kat stopped herself just as she was about to say she had her second meeting with Mrs. Cooper.

"Bye," called Annie. "See ya in church."

Kat waved, and Betty Lou turned to Annie and whispered, "Do you think she's telling the truth about not going over to the boardinghouse afterward?"

"You're jealous of a boardinghouse, Betty Lou."

"I am not. I'm just worried about her."

"Kat doesn't lie and she's not afraid of anyone, so you don't need to worry."

"But she could get hurt."

"You said she was like Roy Rogers, and he doesn't ever get hurt."

"That's only because she's the tallest that I said that. Mrs. Cooper could hurt her."

"Are we gonna play beauty parlor or not? 'cause if you're just gonna talk about Kat I'm going home."

"Yeah," Betty Lou said as she got up. "I've got some fingernail polish. We can give manicures, too, if you want." The two went inside.

An hour later Annie left Betty Lou's with tangerine fingernails and headed across the square toward home. Farther in thought than distance from her friend, Kat ambled up the boardinghouse walk to deliver the Saturday paper. She glanced to the third story and saw the old woman sitting in the window on the right. As always, Kat felt an urge to acknowledge her awareness of the woman and, as always, she held herself back from doing so. This time, though, when she returned to her wagon on the sidewalk, she turned around, looked up again, and waved. She thought she saw the old woman wave back, but it could have been the curtain that moved. It didn't matter to Kat. It had felt good to wave. I'm not going to let Betty Lou or Betty Lou's mother stop me from waving if I want to, she said to herself. That was all there was to it, and the Red Flyer rolled down Elm Street with the last ten papers to be delivered.

◄§12§► K

Kat hadn't been on the stairway to Mrs. Cooper's quarters on the third floor since her interview with the old woman. She stepped carefully, holding onto the railing in the dark. When she reached the third-story landing she noticed that the stairway turned to the left and continued upward, becoming darker and narrower still. There was a door to the left of the stairway off the hall as well as the one to the right which Francis had led her to three weeks earlier. Kat approached the one on the right, curious about the other, and rapped on its wood frame.

A voice inside responded. "Who is it, please?"

"It's me," Kat announced.

"Come in, dear."

Kat opened the door slowly and peered into the sunny room.

"For heaven's sake!" Mrs. Cooper exclaimed. "I hardly recognize you."

"It's me," Kat repeated.

"You look like an angel."

"I've just been to church, that's why."

Kat stood in the light that flooded the room. She was dressed in a white pinafore with starched ruffles at the shoulders and dickie, white knee socks, and black patent-leather shoes. Her hair wasn't braided but was tied back with a white ribbon, the fawn waves reaching down her back to the dress sash tied at her waist.

Mrs. Cooper studied the angelic creature before her and was struck by the ardor in the child's eyes. She was catlike, thought the old woman. Some wildness smoldered beneath those slightly hooded eyelids. Like a lioness crouched behind Kenya grass, she would have to be reckoned with.

"Have a seat, Kathleen." Mrs. Cooper gestured to the stool beside her.

Kat sat down, smoothing the skirt of her dress as she did so, then looked up at the old woman. She was wearing an amber-colored dress with a high collar and an amethyst lavaliere dangling from a gold chain around her neck. "You look real pretty in your dress-up too, Mrs. Cooper," Kat said as she clasped her hands around her knees.

The old woman gave Kat a generous smile, and the pattern of wrinkles appeared on her face. Kat was fascinated by these patterns that came and went so quickly.

Beyond the woman, Kat saw the rolltop desk and the bookcase she'd noticed on her first visit. There was a stillness about the room which reminded Kat of a library. She took in a deep breath, recognized the lavender scent, then lowered her eyes to Mrs. Cooper's lap, where the woman's two hands hugged one another. Something in the way they moved made Kat ask, "Are they all right?"

"They're old and not as limber as they used to be," answered the woman.

"I've never seen big knuckles like that."

"Arthritis," said Mrs. Cooper. "I've got it in my knees too," and she raised her skirt to show Kat.

Kat looked at the woman's knees and saw that they were swollen also. "Does arthritis hurt?" she asked.

"Would you like a candy, Kathleen?"

"Yes, thank you."

Mrs. Cooper reached for the glass candy jar on the table beside her and offered Kat a spearmint wrapped in cellophane. On the table beside the jar were two books. The larger was *The Last of the Mohicans*. The other book remained a mystery to Kat, for she was unable to see the title on its cover.

"Do you like your job, Kathleen?"

"Yes, ma'am."

"Are you having any difficulties?"

"No, ma'am."

"Francis tells me the house has never been as tidy."

"I'm good at that."

"Yes, it appears that you are. Mrs. Eisenberg would prefer that you not straighten her things."

"I know. Flowerman told me. But she needs me more than anybody. Her room gets real dusty and her things aren't balanced."

"Do as she wishes."

"Oh, yes, ma'am, I am. I mean I'm not. I mean I'm not doing her room because I'm doing as she wishes."

"Very good."

"I don't mind skipping her. I don't think she likes children much."

Mrs. Cooper raised a hand to cover her amusement. "Some old folks don't."

"You're not that kind of old person, are you?"

"There are many kinds of old ladies just as there are a great variety of young ones."

"I'm neat like you. I'll probably be old like you too."

The patterns appeared on the woman's face again. "Your Flowerman tells me you do your job in less than an hour."

"Yes, ma'am, sometimes. When I'm finished early I help Miss Parsons in the kitchen until my time is up and I have to leave."

"Then you do like being here?"

"Oh, yes, very much."

"Do you wish to continue?"

"Yes, ma'am, I do."

"Very well," said Mrs. Cooper, and she leaned back and closed her eyes.

"Should I go now?" asked Kat.

Mrs. Cooper raised her lids and looked into Kat's eyes. "Do you wish to?"

"I can stay if you want me to."

"Have you begun reading *The Last of the Mohicans?*"

"Not yet. I'm going to the library tomorrow to get it."

Mrs. Cooper reached for the books on her table. "These are from my personal library. I will loan them to you if you promise to take very good care of them."

"Yes, ma'am, I will."

Mrs. Cooper handed *The Last of the Mohicans* to the child. Kat stroked the soft, worn leather cover with her hand, then put it up against her cheek. Mrs. Cooper smiled at Kat's spontaneous gesture of tenderness. "Yes, I see that you will. This other is a book of poetry. Do you read poetry?"

"I did once in school."

"It's time then. You may take this one also and learn to read songs."

"Songs?"

"Yes, child. A poem has rhythm and should be treated like a song. Be easy with it; don't try to sing it. Let it happen."

"Thank you. I'd like to try."

Mrs. Cooper turned and faced the window. It was meant as a dismissal. Kat watched the old woman for several moments, then rose and left without another word.

70

Each of the rooms on the second floor of the boardinghouse had a corner sink, but the residents on the floor shared a toilet and tub. Above the common bath was Mrs. Cooper's bath and below was the Eisenbergs'. Because the plumbing followed this direct line down from the third story, all the plumbing problems in the house ended up in the Eisenbergs' pipes. David Webb was summoned on such occasions. Today was one of those times. On his way into the house David stopped to talk to Francis, who was repairing the porch steps.

"If you ask me, Francis, you should pour a cement foundation under that. You've got no support there. As soon as it rains, that step'll sink again and crack."

Francis looked up from where he sat on the ground, his forehead beaded with sweat and his headband slipping down. He wiped his brow with his arm and complained, "I haven't got any cement. I haven't got the money to buy cement. And even if I did, do you think it's easy to get cement these days?"

"What the hell's eating you?" asked David.

Francis didn't bother to answer.

"If you'll let it be, I can get my hands on some cement this afternoon."

Francis glanced up at David and refused the offer of a cigarette.

"I've gotta go in there and clean out the Eisenbergs' toilet again. Twice this week," David added, taking a drag on his cigarette. "This goddamned house. The Mississippi is a fresh mountain spring compared to the water that flows through this place."

Inside, Sarah Eisenberg rocked back and forth as she watched Kat water her plants. "Not too much there," she warned.

"Yes, ma'am," answered Kat. "But it looks awfully thirsty."

"Moderation," mumbled Sarah. "Don't you know moderation?"

"I'm sorry, Mrs. Eisenberg, I didn't hear what you just asked."

"Who listens anymore?" Sarah stopped rocking and adjusted the satin cushion at the small of her back.

"I listen. It's just sometimes I can't understand what you say."

"Have your parents news from Andrew?" Sarah asked as she resumed rocking.

"Yes, ma'am. We hear from Andy at least once a month and sometimes twice." Kat pinched off a dead geranium blossom and several leaves with her finger and thumb nail as Francis had shown her.

"We didn't get a single letter," Sarah said, mumbling again.

"Mrs. Eisenberg, I have a hard time hearing you. Did you just ask me something?"

"Who listens?"

"Mrs. Eisenberg, I'll listen."

"Just the telegram saying Ira was gone," Sarah went on.

"Who's Ira?" asked Kat.

Sarah repeated aloud the litany that rolled over and over in her mind every day. "Ira Eisenberg, second lieutenant, shot and killed by enemy forces March twenty-fifth, nineteen hundred and eighteen, in the Battle of the Somme."

"Was he a relative of yours?" Kat asked in a soft voice because Sarah was acting strange and Kat didn't want to excite her.

"He was my son." Sarah stopped rocking.

Kat looked at the woman's eyes, magnified behind her thick glasses. No one had told her Sarah had had a son who died. Suddenly Kat saw something in the woman's eyes she'd never seen before—a kind of sadness without tears.

The rocking started up again. "I like my things left as I put them."

"Yes, ma'am," Kat answered, then left the room and closed the door softly behind her.

Before going up the stairway to water the plants on the second floor, Kat sat down on the bottom step to allow what Sarah had said to sink in. She could hear the creaking of the floorboards beyond the closed door and could imagine Sarah rocking with that faraway look in her eyes. Why hadn't anyone told her about Ira? Didn't they know? They had to know because they were grownups. Maybe it was one of those things no one talks about because it makes everyone too sad. Or maybe since it was a long time ago people had forgotten. Just then David stepped into the hallway, and Kat rose and went upstairs to continue her work.

Each time Kat stepped into Eva Parsons's room she was impressed by how tidy it was. Nothing was ever out of place. Kat went to the flower stand by the window. Eva had given her careful instructions: never use cold water on the Saintpaulia and see that the water never touches the leaves or flowers. Kat knew the violets were important to Eva, so she did just as she was told, glad to be trusted. When she finished watering the violets, Kat went over to Eva's bureau to admire the smooth ivory comb and brush. She felt the stiff bristles of the brush with her forefinger, then picked up the comb. It was cool against her cheek. Suddenly it occurred to Kat that Eva might not like her things touched any more than Sarah. She put down the comb and went on to Miss Renee's room to water the lipstick plant there.

How like Miss Renee to have such a plant, thought Kat, as she tipped the spout and watched the water trickle out onto the potted soil. The plant went with her red hair and painted nails and the brilliant red dress which Kat thought too obvious, like Miss Renee's flirting with David Webb. In a small, brass-colored picture frame on the dressing table was a photograph of a man in Navy bell-bottoms, white tee shirt, and sailor's cap. He was standing with one arm flexed, a tattoo of a heart on the bulging muscle. Kat bent down and looked closely at the picture. She didn't recognize the man's face. Before leaving the room, Kat filled up her watering can from Miss Renee's corner sink.

As Kat walked down the hall to the men's rooms she passed the stairway and paused to look up, wondering what Mrs. Cooper was doing in the room above her.

Francis had a flowerbox outside his window in which he grew marigolds. Kat raised the screen and emptied the water from the green sprinkling can onto the dark soil, then watched the water seep in and smelled the moistened earth. It was like Flowerman to share his flowers with the outside world, thought Kat. Whenever she looked in the direction of the boardinghouse from a distance, Kat could see the golden blossoms. They looked like little suns to her.

David Webb didn't have any flowers in his room. He had green snake plants and a small philodendron like the one on the player piano. David's room was different in another way too. He had a large bed, like Kat's parents', not a small one like she and the other boarders had. A framed picture of Miss Holmes rested on the walnut chiffonier, and Kat stopped to gaze at it before leaving the room. Everyone had a picture, she thought. The Eisenbergs had one of a soldier who Kat now realized was Ira. Miss Parsons had one of Judge Lionel Parsons standing next to a lady Kat assumed was his wife. Flowerman had a picture of a man who looked like Ronald Colman in the *Tale of Two Cities* movie; he'd told her the man was a friend from a long time ago. And Miss Renee had the sailor picture. Except for Miss Holmes and Judge Parsons, Kat had never seen any of the people in these pictures. People who are missing someone live in boardinghouses, thought Kat. That's why they get together. Except David. He was the exception to the rule, as Miss Holmes would say, not about David but grammar.

Kat left David's room. When she reached the stairway to go down to the first floor, she looked up again and wondered if Mrs. Cooper had a picture. Maybe she had one of Mr. Cooper. Then Kat remembered how the stairway turned and continued to the fourth floor. She started up to the third-story landing to take a peek at it again. When she got to the landing she held her breath, turned left, and continued tiptoeing up the stairs in the pitch-blackness.

On the fourth-story landing Kat saw a crack of light under a door before her. She touched the door lightly and it opened. A moment later she was standing in the middle of a large, nearly empty room with a skylight, the noon sun pouring in on her. Beside her was an artist's easel, a canvas with splashes of green and blue paint resting on it. Next to the easel was a straight-backed chair and a paint chest on which there rested tubes of paint, brushes, and a palette. At the far reaches of the room where the ceiling sloped down was a small studio bed covered with a persimmon quilt. On one wall was a small, round window with leaded glass. Kat had seen this window from outside the house and thought it must be in an attic. Surrounding Kat on all the other walls were brightly colored paintings. Kat turned round and round, trying to take them all in, then stopped before a painting of a woman seated in a chair with an ocher shawl around her shoulders the same color as the tiger cat in her lap. The woman had a long neck and loose, dark hair and eyes the color of chocolate; they looked directly at Kat and for several moments held her captive. Next to this canvas was another painting of the same woman, but in this one she was lying down with no clothes on. Kat had never seen a woman painted like this, with her breasts and hair showing. She'd seen breasts in paintings before, but there always was a cloth covering the stomach and legs. The woman's creamy skin looked so real Kat felt an urge to reach out and touch it. Just as she stretched her hand toward the painting someone shouted, "No!" and she jumped around, frightened, dropping the watering can she was holding.

"Explain yourself!" Mrs. Cooper commanded.

Kat could feel her heart thumping in her throat. "I—I can't."

"You must!" The old woman's eyes glared at her, and Kat began to tremble.

"I wasn't going to touch," Kat tried.

"You don't belong here."

"I'm sorry," Kat said, and tears flooded her eyes and her chest started to heave. Unmoved, Mrs. Cooper stood and watched her. Kat stammered, "I—I—I'm sorry, M—M—Mrs. Cooper. I—I—I didn't mean t—t—to do a bad thing."

Mrs. Cooper took Kat's hand, led her to the studio bed, and sat her down on it. Taking a hanky from her sleeve, she offered it to Kat and said, "Calm down, child."

Kat wiped her face, then whispered, "I don't know why I did it."

"Think!"

"I'm trying," Kat whimpered.

Mrs. Cooper turned her back on Kat and waited. After a long silence the old woman said in a low voice, "This is my place."

"Yes, ma'am," said Kat. "Like my tree fort."

Mrs. Cooper turned around and faced Kat on the bed. "Then you do know what you have done?"

"Yes, ma'am. I'll never do it again."

"You may go now."

Kat rose. As she started toward the door the old woman pointed to the green sprinkling can on the floor. Kat bent over and picked it up, then left.

When Kat stepped off the boardinghouse porch on her way home, she kicked a chunk of loose cement and it tumbled down the steps. Her chin on her chest, she kicked the piece of stone with first one foot, then the other, until she reached the sidewalk and it leaped off the walkway onto the grass. Looking back over her shoulder at the small, round window at the top of the house, Kat wondered if she would ever see Mrs. Cooper again.

≈§14§≈ George Howard and Sheriff Frank Kramer stood at the front of the Fourth of July parade supporting the white banner with "Marching For Victory" painted across it in large red letters. Behind them marched Philip Cox, Hawthorn's mailman, carrying Old Glory, and behind him, with trumpets, were Joe Riley and his drinking buddy Johnny McGee, Lloyd Nichols, and Judge Lionel Parsons. Nichols and Parsons had toy trumpets from Nichols' Five and Dime. David Webb marched along wearing a red clown's nose and playing a kazoo, while Kat paraded in a Browns' baseball cap and carried a jew's-harp. Francis wore flowers around his crown, Jesse James sported a daisy chain collar, and the Reverend Paul Wiley, the best-dressed member of this circus, wore an Uncle Sam costume and held a placard advertising war bonds. The Red Cross contingent carried handbells and colorful basket lunches to be auctioned later, and Daniel Brooks played the cymbals behind them. At the end of the procession marched four volunteer firemen carrying a ladder broadside, with red, white, and blue balloons tied to each rung. Those marchers who were not playing some relic retrieved from an attic and dusted off for the occasion sang; those who were not marching stood alongside the road waving American flags as the parade wound its way from Hawthorn High to Defoe Park.

As the parade passed the boardinghouse on Steuben Place, the band was playing "When Johnny Comes Marching Home Again," and Kat took the jew's-harp out of her mouth and sang at the top of her lungs, substituting the name "Andy" for "Johnny" in the lyrics. The Eisenbergs waved from the porch swing as the parade went by, and Kat looked up to Mrs. Cooper's window. If Mrs. Cooper had been there, perhaps everything would have seemed in order. Kat's trespassing the day before loomed large in her mind again. She had been to work that morning and had gone about her dusting without anyone mentioning the preceding day. Evidently, Kat thought, she was to continue her job but be cut off from Mrs. Cooper.

When the parade reached Defoe Park, most of the children ran off in one direction to play and the adults in another to sit in the shade and visit. On a grassy spot near a large maple Kat asked Francis, "Why wasn't she in the window today?"

Francis studied Kat, then lay back in the grass and said, "Look! That piece of blue sky through the branches looks just like a dog."

"Aren't you gonna answer my question?" asked Kat.

"What makes you think I can?"

"Because you know her best."

"Maybe I don't know her that well."

"Do you know why she never comes out?"

"Is your fort in a tree as old as this one?"

"How come you keep changing the subject to this tree?"

"Because it's more important."

"I did something bad." Francis turned his head and looked at Kat closely. She had taken the baseball cap off her head and was now bending the visor back and forth. "I went to the room at the top of the stairs and saw the paintings."

"Kathleen Howard!"

For the first time Francis addressed her by her full name and like a parent—and for the first time Kat felt the difference in their ages and sensed her friend's disapproval. But she had to tell someone.

"Does anyone else know what you've done?" Francis asked.

"Mrs. Cooper. She was real mad."

"Did you tell her?"

"No, she found me. I said I was sorry, but I was so scared I didn't do it well."

Francis saw Kat's lip quiver, and he sat up and put his arm around her. "Don't worry, Kat. It's not a terrible thing."

"I was afraid she'd take my job away."

"Nonsense."

"And now I'll never see her again."

That was possible, Francis thought, but said nothing.

"She's an artist, Flowerman. Did you know that? Or is it supposed to be a secret?"

"I know. I don't know if anyone else does."

"I just told you because you're her true friend."

Francis took the baseball cap from Kat's grip and put it back on her head.

"I'd be her true friend. I wish she could be here with us right now, but she wasn't even in her window today. Do you know, when I leave she turns her head?"

"Maybe she prefers not to see you go."

Kat thought of Andy and remembered her papa didn't look at Andy when he got on the train to go to the war. "I just hope she's not so angry she doesn't like me a little."

"She likes you, Kat."

Kat lay back in the grass and cupped her hands under her

head. "There's gonna be a three-legged race this afternoon and Daniel Brooks asked me to do it with him, but I said I was doing it with you."

"We are?"

"Would you like to?"

"You'd have a better chance with Daniel."

"I want to do it with you, but you don't have to. I'm not forcing you."

Francis sat up. "Of course you are. What a lawyer you'd make."

"No, I'm going to be a baseball player in the major leagues . . . It does look like a dog."

It was an unwritten rule that husbands and suitors weren't allowed to bid on the basket lunches of their wives or fiancees. In one instance, to protect the vanity of a maiden lady, this rule was overlooked: Roy Mulqueen won his uncontested bid to share Eva Parsons's basket lunch. When Daniel Brooks won his bid on Marjorie Holmes's basket, Kat turned away, disheartened. It didn't sit well with her when Daniel won something she couldn't compete for. This was why she burned so to defeat Daniel whenever she could.

For his part, Daniel never quite understood why Kat delighted in her victories over him. He wanted to be her partner, not her opponent. Sitting cross-legged on a red-and-white-checkered picnic cloth with Miss Holmes, Daniel asked, "Are you going to run in the three-legged race with David Webb?"

"I don't think so, Daniel."

"Kat's gonna with Francis."

"Who are you going to race with, Daniel?"

"I wanted to do it with Kat."

"I see."

"But she's mad at me."

"Why do you say that?"

"She gave me a horrible look at the auction when I asked her."

"You'll just have to give her time to discover you."

"How will she when she doesn't play with me anymore? She's always at the boardinghouse with Francis. I don't see why he's so special. He's too old to be a boyfriend."

"I tell you what, Daniel, I'll run the three-legged race with you."

Daniel looked surprised.

"What kind of face is that?" asked Marjorie. "I realize I'm not Kathleen—"

"In one way you're better. You're a real lady."

Marjorie smiled, then pursed her lips in a slightly provocative expression, which Daniel missed altogether.

At a picnic table in another section of Defoe Park, Janet Howard sat stiffly, her hands clasped on the table in front of her, keeping a comfortable distance from David Webb.

"Cheer up, Mrs. Howard. This is just a once-in-a-lifetime event." David pinched his red rubber nose to humor Janet, whose expression remained serious.

Janet's cheeks were flushed, and her forehead glowed with perspiration. Her embarrassment had not yet subsided from her ordeal on the auction platform. David Webb had been bound and determined to outbid everyone for her basket lunch. Now he had the gall to expect her to warm up to him.

"I know you don't trust me, Mrs. Howard. That you don't approve of me. I don't think your daughter does either." Janet looked at him quizzically. "High standards. She gets them from you, no doubt."

"Have you been giving her a hard time?" Janet asked, concerned.

"No, ma'am, I wouldn't tangle with that one. I'm sure she packs a mean wallop!" David laughed, and Janet's smile was nearly a laugh. "That's better. You've got a hell of a family, Mrs. Howard. Marjorie and I want a family like yours." Janet couldn't imagine that. "I know what you're thinking," said David, removing his clown's nose. "I love her, Mrs. Howard."

Was it his removal of that ridiculous nose, his changed attitude, or his words which forced Janet to regard him more seriously? "I hope so," she said in earnest. David held his eyes on Janet, so that for an instant his penetrating glance reminded her of George's. "Anything's possible, I suppose."

David laughed. "Gets her mean wallop from you, too, I guess."

"And I always thought she was her father's child."

Seven couples were tied together with strips of bed sheets for the three-legged race: Daniel and Marjorie; Francis and Kat; Annie and Betty Lou; Joe and Johnny; Eva and Roy; David and Miss Renee; and a most unlikely pairing, Ralph Quinn and Reverend Wiley.

Judge Lionel Parsons boomed, "Are you ready? Get set! Go!"

They were off and running. Before any couple had reached the first marker Eva Parsons jerked up her leg to avoid a gopher hole, and Roy Mulqueen hollered, "No, Eva!" The two fell like stiffs to the ground. The crowd hooted, and when Betty Lou turned around to see the cause of the laughter, she and Annie bit the dust, narrowing the challengers to ten.

Somewhat inebriated, Joe and Johnny were stumbling toward the first marker when they saw that the other four couples already were well beyond the second. Shrugging their shoulders, the two men plopped down on the ground, giving in to certain defeat. Then, at the third marker, Kat lost her sandal, and the others passed Francis and her by.

Miss Renee was in near ecstasy with her leg tied to David Webb's. At the fourth and last marker before the finish line, David put his arm around Miss Renee's waist to support her, she squealed, that startled him, and the two fell, Miss Renee tangled and giggling in David's arms. Marjorie and Daniel, too close to maneuver around these two fallen soldiers, crashed right into them. The crowd roared with laughter, then cheered as the Reverend Wiley and Ralph Quinn crossed the finish line to victory. Behind them tottered the runners-up, Francis and Kat.

Kat and Daniel watched the award presentation together.

Ralph accepted the gold-colored wooden Olympian figure, and Reverend Wiley made a short acceptance speech, ending with, "It helps to have the Lord on your side."

Kat whispered to Daniel, "If you ask me, it was the devil and Reverend Wiley who won."

This tickled Daniel silly. His mouth wide open and full of dirt from his tumble, he shook with laughter. Kat laughed with him, then looked down at her friend's dirty white bucks. "Brooks, your feet look ancient!" A flash of concern crossed Daniel's pug face, and then Kat showed him the sandal in her hand. It cheered him up considerably to see she wasn't in any better shape.

After everyone had recovered from the three-legged race, the three swings competition was organized. Anyone who could swing a bat was invited to compete and would get three chances each time his turn came up to hit the ball.

By the third go-round Johnny McGee's hip flask was empty and he couldn't get a single pitch in the strike zone, so Philip Cox relieved him as pitcher. Most of the contenders had been eliminated by then also. The four remaining were David Webb, Daniel Brooks, Ralph Quinn, and Kat Howard.

David was at the top of the batting order. He swung and missed twice, then lambasted the ball on the last pitch. Daniel followed him and struck out.

It was Kat's turn next. She left her father's side and took the bat from Daniel.

"I hope you whip 'em, Kat," said Daniel.

"Thanks, Brooks."

Her eye on the pitcher, Kat pulled back on the bat, swung, and missed. Stepping aside, she wiped her hands on her backside, then planted her feet firmly once again. Her eyebrows pulled together in fierce concentration, she raised the bat off her shoulder and hit the ball dead center. Philip Cox hit the dirt, narrowly escaping her line drive.

Ralph Quinn was up next. On the first pitch he hit a high fly over left field.

David began at the top of the batting order once again. With Daniel eliminated, there were only three batters left. David swung and missed on the first, then on the second, and again on the third good pitch.

"Strike out!" shouted the judge. "Next batter."

George Howard leaned down and whispered in his daughter's ear. Kat nodded and stepped forward.

"Go get him!" said David as he handed Kat the bat.

The first pitch was low and outside. Kat swung at it, and it glanced off the top of her bat foul.

"Strike one!" hollered the judge.

Kat took in a deep breath and shook the nerves out of her legs. Philip wound up for the throw.

"Strike two!" She was late on the second pitch.

Turning to her papa on the sidelines, Kat saw his confident smile. Francis stood beside Kat's father, holding his breath and looking as though he were about to be sick.

A coiled spring, Kat pulled herself in, bent low over the plate, and held the bat back, her knuckles white around the handle. She lifted the bat as Philip released the ball, then swung and connected. *Crack!* The bat broke, and the ball sailed over the heads of the crowd.

George Howard leaped into the air, and Francis breathed again, the color returning to his pale cheeks.

On his way to the batter's box Ralph Quinn cursed Kat under his breath. The crowd hushed as Ralph crouched into position. His face was tight and his neck red in furious determination. On the first pitch he swung too hard, pulling the bat down. Grumbling that there was something wrong with this new bat, Ralph let go of it, grabbed some dirt, and dusted his sweaty palms. The second pitch was a fast ball in the strike zone, and Ralph swung late.

"Strike two!" yelled the judge.

Ralph spit to the side and rubbed his right hand on his thigh before taking a firm hold on the bat again.

Kat was standing beside her father, with Daniel on her other side. The next pitch might decide the contest. Philip Cox wound up and released a slow pitch. Ralph swung early, expecting another fast ball.

"Strike three!"

"She won!" someone in the crowd shouted. "The girl won!"

Ralph threw down the bat. As he passed Kat he spit on the ground, missing her but getting Daniel's left buck. "No stupid girl is gonna get away with that!" Ralph swore as he marched off.

Daniel shook his foot as a cat does when it accidentally steps into some water. "Gee whiz, I didn't do anything," he muttered and started off. "I don't ever get a trophy, just dirt and spit. That's all I ever get."

Kat looked up at her father.

"You're the champ," he said proudly.

"I did what you said, Papa."

"Half of winning is inspiration," George answered with a smile that matched his daughter's.

Trophy in hand, Kat, her father, Francis, and Frank Kramer—who also had been on the sidelines—headed toward the picnic grounds to join their friends and family. When Betty Lou and Annie saw Kat coming toward them, they leaped up and ran to her.

"What'll you do with your trophy?" asked Annie.

"Put it in my fort with my other things."

"I think you should put it on the mantel in your house so everyone can see it," said Betty Lou.

"That would be bragging," Kat replied.

George and Frank joined the women at the table, and Francis began to head toward Steuben Place. "Bye, champ!" Francis called over his shoulder.

"Wait up, Flowerman!" Kat hollered back. Turning to her chums, Kat said, "Be back in a sec'."

As Kat started off with Francis, Annie put her arm around Betty Lou's shoulder and said, "Let's play jacks. She's going off with him."

"Boy, she doesn't ever play with us anymore."

"Shut up, Betty Lou. You're starting to sound like Brooks. You got a crush on her too?"

"You're stupid, Annie. How could I have a crush on Kat? She's my girlfriend."

"Girlfriends can have crushes."

"Not on their girlfriends."

"Then how come you get so jealous and gushy whenever she looks at you?"

"I don't."

"Do so. Everyone knows you're in love with her."

"Am not!"

"Are so!"

Betty Lou folded her arms across her chest. Only yards away, Frank Kramer slapped his hand down on the picnic table and said with a hardy laugh, "She's a chip off the old block."

"Hell, no!" countered George. "You saw me strike out on the first round."

"I'd keep a close eye on the Quinn boy," Frank warned.

"What do you mean?" Janet asked him.

"Kat's asking for trouble from him."

Janet turned to her husband. "Is Kat all right?"

"Happier than a lark. She'll probably have difficulties with Ralph, though."

"What happened over there?"

"She beat him," answered Frank, "and he was none too pleased."

"Don't worry, sweetheart. Kat can take care of herself."

"Where did she go?" Janet looked around for her daughter. She needed to see for herself that all was well.

"I think I saw her walk away with Francis," said Marge Kramer.

"Now there's a peculiar one," commented Charlotte Ferrand. "A grown man with a child for a friend." All adult attention turned to Charlotte. "Well, I'd be a little suspicious is all."

"You'd be suspicious of Ma Perkins." George got out his pipe and filled it with tobacco.

Charlotte was annoyed by George's remark and his attitude.

85

She wouldn't go into open battle with him, but she did ask him a question which sounded more cross than curious. "Why does she call him Flowerman?"

"Because he's a blooming friend." George was the only one to smile. Tension showed on everyone else's face, especially Janet's.

"I hear she's getting friendly with that Mrs. Cooper too," added Charlotte.

"Is that a problem for you, Charlotte?" Janet asked.

"Now, Janet, I wasn't meaning there was anything wrong with your child. But that old woman . . . She left the church, you know, and her family when she was young. There was some scandal, and she went off to New York City unescorted. Came back to St. Louis but her family wouldn't have her, so she moved here."

"I don't think Kat's friendship will do the lady any harm," Janet said softly.

Content with his pipe and willing to let his wife handle this matter, as she was better skilled than he to deal with Charlotte, George turned to the Kramers and asked if they were attending the concert later.

Sitting on the hard-packed ground several yards away, Betty Lou and Annie could catch only snatches of the grownups' conversation.

"Hey, Annie," whispered Betty Lou, "what do you suppose is going on? Mrs. Howard and my mummy look like they're having an argument or something."

"I don't know, and who cares anyway. It's your turn. You're up to threesies."

"Wait a sec'. I think I heard Mrs. Cooper's name."

"Betty Lou, what do you care what they say about an old lady no one ever sees?"

"That's just it. Maybe it's juicy."

"Do you want to play jacks or not, Betty Lou?"

George Howard had managed to get only Marge Kramer's attention. Charlotte would not let go of the subject, nor Janet, and Frank Kramer was becoming an active listener.

"Ten-year-olds are very impressionable, Janet. That woman is liable to corrupt your daughter." Charlotte finally took a breath, thinking she'd made her point.

Janet didn't respond, so Frank grabbed the opportunity to say, "George is right. Kat can handle herself."

Charlotte turned on Frank now. "Well, Kathleen Howard certainly is everyone's darling, isn't she?" she said, then got up and walked off. Janet followed her.

Charlotte stopped beside a hawthorn bush, and Janet noticed how gray Charlotte seemed next to its bright pink blossoms. "Charlotte, are you all right?" Janet asked. Her friend turned around, surprised she'd been followed. "You're crying."

"No, I'm fine," Charlotte answered, turning away from Janet.

"Let's talk about it. Away from the crowd." Janet put her arm around Charlotte, and the two walked away from the picnic area. As they passed the pasture where the three-legged race had been held, Charlotte spotted several dirty strips of bed sheet that had been discarded there. They reminded her of the Red Cross bandages she rolled, and suddenly she was looking at a battlefield, not a pasture. "Janet, I'm scared."

"Of what, Char?"

"The war. I can't read the newspaper anymore. Part of me wants to know, but another part is so afraid."

"It's hard. I don't know how you do it, Char."

"Andy's there too. How do you manage?"

"Not well."

"But you look—"

"No, Char, if you could see inside me."

"I should be proud."

"And you're not?" asked Janet.

"I try."

"Oh, Char, I do understand—believe me."

Charlotte turned and looked into Janet's generous blue eyes. The two embraced. Janet's touch felt so good to Charlotte she was embarrassed and pulled away. The two women walked on.

Reverend Wiley, still in his Uncle Sam costume, was having a beer with several men under the old maple where Kat and Francis had had their talk earlier in the day. As Charlotte and Janet passed them, Janet said, "I've been questioning so many things lately. I don't like it when I do that. I feel selfish being so concerned with my family ... not supporting the war one hundred per cent in my heart. Of course, I don't tell George. I don't want to disappoint him."

"I try not to show Betty Lou. I've gotten so I hide from her whenever I'm ... it's black and white to her. Better that way."

"For us it can't be ... When you understand what the mother of the boy who shoots at your boy goes through, well ..."

Charlotte stopped to rest. The two women were beyond the throng of townfolk now. "I remember that first long night alone when Lou left. I don't know what I would have done if you hadn't come. It was like being in my mother's arms. I was a child again and you took care of me."

"It seems every generation has its war. I can stand a thing if I know it'll be over eventually, but we just get over one war and a depression and ... I'm afraid our daughters and sons will face the same."

"Kat would be okay."

"Kat has a way of making us feel she can handle all the hard luck that might come her way, but she's just a good little pretender."

"She's the spirit in this town. Isn't that why everyone looks out for her? Cheers her on? As long as she's well, something in each of us stays alive."

"I wonder if it isn't a terrible burden on her, everyone thinking that."

"Have you heard from Andy?"

"I hope you won't mind my not talking about him just now."

"Is something wrong?"

"No, I just do better when I think of one child at a time. Right now Kat's on top of the world and I'm up there with her. I'd like to stay up there a while longer."

Like a shy schoolgirl, Charlotte said, "I've never told you this before, but sometimes I think of you as an older sister. Is that strange?"

"No, Char, it's a compliment." Janet smiled tenderly at her friend.

The two women started back to the picnic grounds. There was no need to speak. The silence was comfortable.

Betty Lou looked up from her game and said, "Here comes my mummy walking with Mrs. Howard. I guess they've made up."

"I guess," said Annie. "It's your turn."

"You girls having fun?" asked Charlotte.

"Uh huh," they answered in unison.

"You get along like sisters, don't you?"

"Uh huh," said Annie, not taking her eyes off Betty Lou to look up at Mrs. Ferrand just in case Betty Lou was thinking of taking advantage of this interruption to cheat on her.

Blocks away, Kat and Francis were on the boardinghouse porch. Kat had set the Olympian figure on the handrail supported by the porch balusters and was sitting beside Francis on the porch swing admiring it. "Do you know that if it wasn't for General Eisenhower there wouldn't be any baseball this year?" Kat said.

"How's that?" asked Francis.

"He sent a letter all the way from Europe asking the majors to play."

"Mmm." Francis recalled the rumor.

"They were gonna skip this season 'cause most of the good players got drafted. But the soldiers didn't want them to, so General Eisenhower wrote a letter. And that was a good thing 'cause it may be the only chance the Browns have to win."

"I think I read that in the newspaper."

"Uh huh, you did. Pepper Martin—he used to be really something, but he's forty now—he's playing this year. And some managers are too. Did you know that?"

"Does forty seem old to you, Kat?"

"Yeah, but on you it seems young 'cause you have blond hair."

"How did you know I was that old if I don't look it?"

" 'Cause you know about a lot of things. Andy's got blond hair, too, and he looks young."

"Does he listen to the games overseas?"

"Sure, he's a baseball fan too." Kat got up, stepped off the porch, and moved a few paces down the walk.

"Still checking, huh?"

"She's there! She's back!" Kat ran to the porch, grabbed her trophy, and ran back down the walkway and held it up. "Do you think she can see it?"

Francis shook his head with delight at Kat's enthusiasm. He didn't remember ever being that full of himself.

Kat returned to the porch and leaned against a pillar. "If it wasn't for the war we'd have some swell fireworks tonight."

"The war's got a way of spoiling some things, doesn't it?"

"Uh huh, but there's gonna be a concert in the square tonight. Are you going to it?"

"No."

"I don't think I will either ... Will you be with Mrs. Cooper?"

Francis nodded yes.

"You could tell her something. Jesse and I are going to sleep in my place tonight and listen to the concert from there. And you could tell her ..."

"Yes?"

"Ah, nothing." Kat slipped off the pillar and started for the steps. "I guess I'd better get home now. Thanks for the three-legged race. I'm sorry I lost my sandal. We would have won otherwise."

"You're a born winner."

"Do you think so?" Kat asked, jumping off the porch step.

"I said so."

"I think you're right," she said as she turned, tucking the trophy under her arm and putting her two hands into her shorts pockets.

"You've got what it takes," said Francis as he got up from the swing.

"Inspiration!" Kat shouted without looking back.

"I suppose that's it," her friend answered loudly.

"Oh, yes, my papa and I know it is," Kat said to herself, as she was now too far away to be heard.

When Kat arrived home she took the gardenia toilet water off its shelf in her fort and put the gold-colored Olympian figure there.

"Do you want to smell pretty, Jesse?" Kat unscrewed the cap and dabbed some of the fragrance below each of her ear lobes and on her wrists, then reached for Jesse, who struggled in vain, and put some behind his ears. "It's okay to smell pretty, Jesse. Boys don't have to smell like boys all the time. Besides, you're a pussy cat." Jesse shook his head and began licking his right paw and circling his ear with it. "I don't know what you are really, but I love you."

Kat left Jesse in the fort when she went inside for dinner. After dinner she returned to the tree house. Lying on her back looking up through the open hatch at the dark blue sky, Kat cried out excitedly, "Jesse, there's Saturn right by the moon! Isn't that something!" Jesse was resting peacefully in the arms of Kat's calico doll. "I wish you understood these things, Jesse. It would mean so much to you."

Kat picked up *The Last of the Mohicans* and her flashlight and started reading. When she heard the concert begin, she put down her book and gazed once again at the stars overhead. Jesse crawled up on her chest and kneaded till he was content to lie quietly and dream with her. Kat imagined Mrs. Cooper waltzing with a man. They were in a ballroom with mirrors on the walls, and Mrs. Cooper was real happy. The patterns Kat loved showed on the old woman's face.

Francis was leaving Mrs. Cooper's room with her dinner tray when he heard the familiar strains of the "Missouri Waltz" and remembered his promise. "Kat asked me to tell you that she and Jesse were going to listen to the concert in her place tonight."

Mrs. Cooper looked at him and smiled.

"Does that mean something special to you two?"

"I don't know, Francis, perhaps."

"She missed you today."

"Hmmm."

"She told me she was in your studio."

The old woman motioned for Francis to put down the tray. When he did, she gestured for him to pull the desk chair over to her. Once he was seated beside her she said, "I caught her up there, standing in front of Thea."

"I think you scared the heck out of her."

"What was that contraption she was holding up?"

"Her trophy. She won the baseball competition today. Showed 'em all up."

"I can't allow her to become too familiar, Francis . . . Tell me, how have you been?"

"Good."

"My goodness, but that was a weak response."

"I'm fine."

"Not very exciting around here, is it, with an old woman like me?" Moments earlier Mrs. Cooper had motioned for Francis to stay, thinking he wanted some company. Francis had understood her gesture to mean she wanted company.

"Why did you take his name?" Francis asked.

"Why out of the clear blue are you asking that?"

"It occurs to me often. Just now you did something that . . . No, it wasn't what you did, it's what you looked like. What was it?"

"I'm old, that's what it is."

"No. Independent, that's what I saw."

"Because it's a good joke on him," Mrs. Cooper answered his question finally.

"That's what you say, but—"

"And why do you ask if you know better?"

"The three times I've asked in the last thirty years you've said that very thing, and never have I been convinced."

"You're quite patient, aren't you, dear Francis?" Francis

looked at her closely and waited. "Oh, all right. I did it to confuse people."

"I'm not certain I understand."

"Few people really want to know the truth. The deception, the joke, is easier, or more interesting perhaps ... Would you like to go to St. Louis one weekend, Francis? I can get on for a few days without you."

"You're evading me."

"A privilege of age, Francis."

"I may take Kat to St. Louis for the World Series."

"That wasn't what I meant."

"I know. I can do a sidestep too."

"Ha! So she whipped them all today."

"Sure did. She told me she was going to play in the major leagues."

"Yes, she told me that also."

"Well, she made a believer out of me today."

"An artist will do that."

Francis watched the old woman rub her thumb and forefinger together. It was a gesture he'd seen her make many times. What was she thinking when she did this? he wondered. In the years he had known her she frequently puzzled him—never bored him.

15 Eva Parsons didn't wear a regular apron; instead she wore a large piece of muslin sheeting which she tucked into her waist and which hung down the length of her long skirt.

Kat watched Eva move about the kitchen from stove to cupboard to ice box to drainboard, shuffling in her slippers but keeping her back straight. Her movements were so quick and abrupt at times that it could make a person dizzy just watching. In less than an hour Eva had lunch ready: the soup cooked; the muffins browned and buttered; the tea steeped, cooled, and poured with ice cubes, lemon, and a spearmint leaf; and Mrs. Cooper's tray set with one fresh flower in the blue-and-white porcelain bud vase.

"It's a cornflower," Eva answered Kat's inquiry as she snipped off the very end of the stem, placed the blue flower in the china vase, and wiped her hands on the front of her apron sheet.

"Does it smell?" asked Kat.

"I couldn't say. My nostrils are full of sweet basil and dill weed."

"Are you pretty strong?" asked Kat.

Eva turned and looked at Kat, who was sitting atop the step stool squeezing the daylights out of the oleo margarine. "Doubtful as strong as you."

"Do you think we can move the player piano?"

"Can, perhaps, but shouldn't you ask if you may first?"

"It's in a bad place—too close to the big chair. I think it'd look better on the other side of the room."

"The chair would move more easily," said Eva as she placed her hands at the small of her back and stretched to relieve the tension in her shoulders.

"I know, but then the two chairs would be together and look funny, and besides, if we moved the piano it would be the first thing you saw when you came into the room, and that would be real nice."

"For twenty years it's been as it is."

"I just know the change would be good for the room. It looks real lopsided the way it is."

"We'll take a look at it. Is that margarine ready?"

"Yep. It's that horrible yellow color. I'm getting good at this, did you notice? There are only two streaks in it and no white spots." Kat stepped off the stool and placed the margarine on the counter before Eva.

At that moment Francis appeared at the kitchen door, his shoes, socks, and pant legs soaked with water. Kat was the first to see him. "You look like you fell into an awful big puddle," she said.

"The basement in the courthouse flooded last night. I'm looking for David. Anyone seen him?"

"It's Saturday," said Eva. "He's probably still in bed."

As Francis turned to go, he spotted the white wicker tray. "Kat, take Mrs. Cooper's tray up to her, will you? I'm a mess."

Kat was slow to say yes. Surprised by the request and Francis's off-handedness, she wasn't certain at first she'd heard him correctly. Kat hadn't seen Mrs. Cooper since her blunder nearly two weeks earlier and had resigned herself to never seeing her again. She thought about the old woman and the paintings often. She looked for her in the window each day when she arrived and left after work, but refrained from waving. Now she would see her again, and Mrs. Cooper wouldn't be expecting her. That detail disturbed Kat. It would be different if Mrs. Cooper had asked for her—then she would know she was welcome.

Kat went into the dining room and examined herself in the mirror over the hutch. There was a spot right in the center of her pale blue tee shirt. She pulled her shirt out of her pants and sucked on the spot, then tucked her shirt ends back in her shorts, smoothed down the wet spot and the wrinkle she'd just put in it, and blew on the spot. It showed just as bad, but it was the best she could do, and she returned to the kitchen for the tray.

Carrying the tray up the stairs, careful not to spill anything, Kat's heart beat fast and her mouth became dry. When she got to Mrs. Cooper's door she set the tray down on the floor and knocked on the door lightly.

"Yes, Francis, come in."

Kat swallowed, then spoke up, not daring to open the door before she announced herself. "It's not Francis, Mrs. Cooper. It's Kat. Francis is a mess, so he sent me." Kat waited and listened for a response. There was none. Should she say it again or just go in? She decided to wait to a count of ten.

On six, the voice within said, "Come in, Kathleen."

Kat opened the door, picked up the tray, and stepped into the room. When she looked to the place where Mrs. Cooper always sat, in the chair at the window, and saw the chair was empty, she stopped in her tracks.

"I'm over here," a voice said from behind her.

Kat turned around and saw Mrs. Cooper seated on a settee behind a low table, nearly hidden from view in an alcove off the room.

"Bring the tray here, Kathleen."

Kat did as asked, then looked up at Mrs. Cooper. What was it she had planned to say if she ever saw the old woman again? Her mind was a blank.

"Kathleen, pull the desk chair over here and sit down, please."

Again Kat did as she was told. Once seated, she remembered what she was going to say. "You're a wonderful artist, Mrs. Cooper."

The old woman leaned back, closing her eyes. Kat watched her carefully. When Mrs. Cooper didn't move for a long time Kat got scared. She'd never seen a person die, but her papa told her it was like falling asleep.

Mrs. Cooper's eyelids raised slowly, startling Kat. "I had a hunch you were going to disrupt my life."

"I don't want to disrupt your life, Mrs. Cooper. I want to be your friend."

"Perhaps that's what a friend does." Mrs. Cooper took up the napkin. Kat watched as she unfolded it and placed it across her lap, then took up the soup spoon.

Should she say something or just watch? Kat wondered. Her mama told her she should never talk with her mouth full—but she wasn't eating, Mrs. Cooper was. Just the same, maybe it wasn't polite. Kat followed the soup spoon up to the woman's mouth and watched her blow across it, closing her eyes as she did. When the old woman puckered her lips to sip from the spoon, lines like rays of the sun fanned out from her mouth. The amethyst lavaliere clinked against the soup bowl as Mrs. Cooper leaned forward. She held it against her bosom with one hand, then set down the spoon and tucked the stone and chain inside the open neck of her shirt and looked up at Kat.

"You mean it's all right if I disturb you?" Kat had waited until now to ask.

"Pardon me?"

"You said that's what a friend does."

"Did I say that?"

Didn't she? Kat didn't know now what Mrs. Cooper had said. The old woman took a bite off a roll, chewed, then swallowed and said, "I've seen two kinds of trouble. There's the kind that jumps out at you without warning. Often you don't know where it comes from or why." She took a sip of soup and swallowed. "You do the best you can to overcome it or live with it ... Then there's the other kind of trouble. It creeps up on you. You see it coming, know where it comes from and why, and you might well have prevented it but didn't." She paused to wipe her mouth with the napkin. "Why?"

"I don't know, Mrs. Cooper. Which one am I?"

Mrs. Cooper was looking directly into Kat's eyes, but, Kat realized, the woman's gaze went well beyond her to some distant place where Kat had never been. "I saw you coming," Mrs. Cooper said finally.

Did Kat imagine that Mrs. Cooper's cheek trembled? She was pretty sure she didn't understand what the old woman was saying, but it sounded important—like when someone tells a secret to a friend.

Mrs. Cooper took two more sips of soup. "When two strangers meet, it is as if they were blind. They must feel their way to one another. And often they're clumsy at it. Have you heard the expression 'stepping on someone's toes'?"

"Yes, I think."

"It describes the sort of clumsiness I'm talking about. You stepped on my toes when you went to my studio uninvited."

"I promise never to step on your toes again."

"Careful, child. It may be more difficult than you think to keep your promises, and relying upon the good will of others to forgive you could be as costly a mistake."

Kat bowed her head. "What should I do?" she asked.

"Make your promises to yourself alone and let your actions speak for you." Mrs. Cooper sat back and waited until Kat raised her head. "And forgive yourself, child. It does no good to go through life full of regrets. You cannot march forward while you're weeping over the past." She pushed her lunch tray aside.

Kat's face was a study in sincerity as she strained to understand Mrs. Cooper's meaning. It was apparent to the old woman that this dedicated soul would find her way, and she felt a gentleness toward the child, knowing the cost of that. After a moment, Mrs. Cooper stood up, went to her bookcase, and stretched for a book of Elizabeth Barrett Browning's poetry.

Kat watched as the old woman walked slowly to the window, eased down, her hand searching for the arm of the chair, and at the last second dropped into the chair, her feet lifting off the floor a few inches and coming to rest side by side on the hardwood floor. Mrs. Cooper pulled out a pair of eyeglasses from the pocket of her skirt and wiped the lenses on the front of her shirt before placing them on her nose. When she had done that, she looked up and beckoned for Kat.

It felt good to Kat to sit on the stool again, by the window, and see the light on the old woman's face. Mrs. Cooper held the book open in her lap with one large hand. The other hand trembled slightly as it patted the air beside her:

> You see this dog. It was but yesterday
> I mused forgetful of his presence here,
> Till thought on thought drew
>   downward tear on tear;

Kat listened and watched in awe as the old woman sang the song and told the story with her hand:

> When from the pillow, where wet-cheeked I lay,
> A head as hairy as Faunus, thrust its way
> Right sudden against my face, — two golden-clear
> Great eyes astonished mine, — drooping ear
> Did flap me on either cheek to dry the spray!
> I started first, as some Arcadian,
> Amazed by goatly god in twilight grove:

But as my bearded vision closelier ran
My tears off, I knew Flush, and rose above
Surprise and sadness; thanking the true Pan,
Who, by low creatures, leads to heights of love.

When she finished, Mrs. Cooper turned and looked out the window. Kat turned also to see what it was the woman was gazing at. She saw the top branches of the oak trees in the square and the blue sky and a wave of red that was the flag.

"Did you have a dog once?" Kat asked the old woman.

"I had a cat once," Mrs. Cooper answered, turning back to Kat. "He was a tiger and had large, round eyes as golden as a maple leaf in autumn."

"Like the one in the painting upstairs?"

"That was he."

Tucking her hands under her fanny, Kat asked, "Who's the lady?"

"I called her Thea." Once again Mrs. Cooper's gray eyes looked directly into Kat's eyes.

"What did she call you?" Kat asked in a much softer voice, not taking her eyes from the old woman's.

Mrs. Cooper removed her glasses and turned her head to the window again. Kat could see in her soft profile that she was far away.

As Kat left she wondered when she would see this woman again. This woman with the journey eyes.

16

The next day after church Kat went to her tree fort, got out her tablet and crayons, and put a pinch of catnip under Peggy Sue's calico dress. Jesse didn't go wild over catnip; he just liked to lie on it. So while Jesse lay still in the lap of her doll, Kat made an outline drawing of him; then, with her yellow and brown crayons, she made every-other stripes on the body, turning Jesse into a tiger. Once that was finished she wrote a note below the picture, printing instead of writing because Mrs. Cooper wouldn't be as familiar with her handwriting as Andy was. Kat practiced different ways of signing on another page from the tablet and finally settled on "Clumsy Kat" because it was a joke Mrs. Cooper might smile at.

On Monday Kat gave her note to Eva Parsons, explaining she'd asked Mrs. Cooper if she and Eva could move the player piano. Eva agreed to put the note on Mrs. Cooper's lunch tray that day, right next to the flower vase.

When Kat arrived at work on Tuesday, Eva had a note for her. It said, "Come see me Wednesday at one o'clock," and was signed with the letter *C.*

Kat stayed in the kitchen with Eva Parsons after delivering the Wednesday groceries, but her attention was not on Eva. She stared at the turquoise wall clock; it was taking forever for the noon hour to pass. Eva made Kat a sandwich, but Kat took only a couple of bites from the center of each half and passed up the offer of a cookie.

"When you don't want a cookie I know something's wrong," said Eva, shuffling over to the table to take a closer look at Kat.

"It's my stomach," said Kat.

"Are you coming down with something, child?"

"No. It's just that there's no room in it 'cause it's full up with butterflies."

"What are butterflies doing in it?"

"I'm going up to see Mrs. Cooper at one."

"That woman makes you more nervous than a bunch of gnats buzzing round." Eva returned to the cutting board, where the pastry cloth was lying out, and slapped the ball of dough with her floured-white hands.

"Doesn't she ever make you feel that way?" asked Kat.

"No, child. I mind my own business and leave her to mind hers."

"If I did that . . ."

"Yes?"

"I don't know."

As Eva rolled out the dough with the red-handled rolling pin, she said, "You just behave now. Remember what I told you about not getting yourself entangled."

"Miss Parsons, sometimes a person's got to—just a little."

"Not this person," Eva said firmly. "I do just fine by myself, and that woman upstairs does also."

"Is that why you don't live with the judge?" Kat asked, peering through the space between counter and cupboard at Eva.

"Mmm hmm," Eva responded, glancing at the clock. "It's one o'clock, child. As long as you're making her your business, you better be on time."

Kat jumped up from the kitchen table, stopped, and then looked at Eva with a worried face.

"Go on now—you look just fine," said Eva. Kat gave her a grateful smile and hurried off.

Mrs. Cooper was reading at her window when Kat arrived and took a seat on the small footstool. "Are you reading *The Last of the Mohicans?*" she asked Kat, closing the book in her lap.

"Yes, ma'am, but it's not very easy. I have to look up a lot of words."

"When do you read?"

"In my tree fort after work and sometimes at night, too, but then it's hard 'cause I have to hold my flashlight. In the morning's the best. Jesse sleeps in the fort, and I play with him first thing and sometimes I read to him."

Mrs. Cooper set down her book by the glass candy jar on the table beside her. The green-striped spearmints inside the jar didn't look so appetizing to Kat at that moment. Her stomach was still a bit unsettled, though she could feel the room starting to have its calming effect. "Why do you want to move the player piano?" asked Mrs. Cooper.

"Because it's crowding the chair, or the chair's crowding it. If the piano was on the other wall, it'd balance better, and it'd look nice to walk in and see it first." Kat thought a moment, then added, "It would make the room proud."

Mrs. Cooper smiled broadly and said, "I understand."

"Then it's okay to move it?"

"Do you think you and Miss Parsons can?"

"I think so, and there are plenty other bodies if we need them."

"You have my permission."

"Thank you. Should I go now?"

"You don't want to?"

"No, ma'am. I like visiting this room. It's a little like a library."

"Did you want to look at the books?"

"I'd like to sit at your desk."

Mrs. Cooper nodded her approval.

Kat stood up and went to the rolltop desk in front of the bookcase, pulled the desk chair up close, and sat down. Resting her palms on the soft green blotter, she examined the small drawers with brass fittings, the pigeonholes filled with paper clips, rubber bands, and stamps, the maroon fountain pen and ink well, and her drawing and note lying under a glass paperweight. Mrs. Cooper watched as Kat took in everything in a furious manner and marveled at the child's restraint in touching only with her eyes. "Can I shake this?" Kat asked, pointing to the glass weight.

"Yes," answered the old woman.

Kat picked up the glass and shook it hard. The white snow swirled, then settled on the Christmas tree and ground. Mrs. Cooper watched Kat and wondered how the snow beyond the glass managed not to melt from the intensity of the child's gaze. "I've seen one of these before—at Annie's," said Kat. "Only the Kramers' doesn't have a tree. It has a Santa Claus. I don't have a desk."

"Do you write at a table?"

"No, I write where I read, in my fort. I hold my paper up like this," and Kat demonstrated for the bemused old woman.

"Where is this fort of yours?"

"In back of our house. In the oldest tree in Hawthorn. I'll show it to you sometime. You'd like it because it's way high up."

Mrs. Cooper leaned back and listened to the child's clear voice in a room where most times the only other voice came from her own imagination. There were those occasions when Francis visited and when Sarah used to come to complain, but this child's voice was special. Was it the innocence of the conversation or the celebration of life on the child's lips which made the room come alive?

Kat placed the glass paperweight a little to the right from where she'd found it and got down from the chair to take a closer look at Mrs. Cooper's old victrola in the corner beyond the bookcase. She'd seen the phonograph on her last visit, but now she could really study it.

"Keep talking," Mrs. Cooper urged.

"Should I tell you about me?"

"Describe your fort."

Kat told the old woman about the hatchway and how the sun burst through it, and how at night she could see the stars and sometimes the moon when it was in just the right place. Mrs. Cooper could see it all; then, for some reason, she saw Van Gogh's *Starry Night* and her heart trembled, and she opened her eyes with a start, searching for Kat. Kat had walked into the alcove on the other side of the room and was admiring the kaleidoscope on the coffee table.

"Is this new?" Kat asked, not recalling having seen it before.

"No, it's very old," Mrs. Cooper replied. "You may," she added, recognizing Kat's curiosity.

"Oooh, my gosh!" Kat sighed as she twirled the kaleidoscope toward the light.

The old woman rubbed her knees with her hands, looked out the window at the clear sky, then rose slowly and walked toward Kat. Against the wall extending into the alcove was an iron stove used to heat the room in the winter, and beside it a small rosewood end table. Mrs. Cooper picked up the stereoscope and cards which rested on the small table and motioned for the child to join her on the settee. While Kat held the apparatus against her cheeks, the old woman slipped a card in place in front of the viewer. A city scene with cars and people and buildings jumped out at Kat.

"Oh, wowee, this is really something!" Kat exclaimed. "It's three-dimensional. It feels like I'm right in the picture!"

Mrs. Cooper removed the card and put another in its place.

"Is that . . . ? It is! It's Sportsman's Park!"

"And your favorite underdog," added Mrs. Cooper.

"The Browns?"

"Back in 1885 they were called the St. Louis Maroons. At the turn of the century they became the Browns and moved from the National to the American League."

Not taking her eyes away, Kat said, "You sure know a lot about baseball." Kat was delighted at this discovery.

"The pitcher on the mound was called One-Arm Daily," Mrs. Cooper said excitedly, caught up in Kat's enthusiasm.

"How did he pitch with just one arm?" Kat asked, her face still hidden behind the stereoscope.

"With his heart," answered the old woman.

Kat lowered the stereoscope; the outline of it remained on her forehead and cheeks. "I know what you mean," she said with great feeling. Mrs. Cooper patted Kat's knee, and Kat looked into the old woman's filmy gray eyes and asked, "How come you never come out?"

Flustered by the child's directness, Mrs. Cooper sat back. After a moment she said, "While most birds fly in flocks, one does not." Then she rose from the settee, returned the stereoscope and cards to the rosewood table where they belonged, and went to her chair by the window.

Kat started for the door. Before leaving, she turned and asked, "Do you think I could come here regular?" Mrs. Cooper did not respond. "Sunday maybe?" asked Kat. "Sunday is a visiting day."

"Every Sunday?" asked Mrs. Cooper.

"That would be swell," Kat said, knowing in her heart the old woman had asked a question of her, not offered an invitation.

"We shall see," Mrs. Cooper answered, facing the window.

"Does that start this Sunday?" asked Kat.

"Bring *The Last of the Mohicans* with you."

That evening Kat searched through her picture book of birds and flowers for the bird that does not fly in flocks. It was the dipper, a dark gray bird the size of a bluebird whose white eyelids gave it a sage appearance.

Kat read aloud to Jesse, who looked very naughty with his head under Peggy Sue's dress:

The *Cinclus mexicanus*, or dipper bird, lives along the cold mountain streams as far north as Alaska, south through Alberta, Canada, northern central Montana, and southwestern South Dakota to southern California, Mexico, and Central America. It bobs its head in and out of the water as it walks along the bottom of shallow creeks searching for aquatic insects and fish eggs. The dipper gets its common name from its characteristic dipping for food as it dauntlessly wades through frigid torrents on its long legs, facing the full force of the current as it plunges into the water—a remarkable feat since it cannot swim.

The American dipper is a nonmigratory bird; it flies parallel to a stream while skimming the water's surface, venturing only as far as the stream's tributaries. It builds its nest out of small sticks, grass, mud, and moss near the water's edge, between craggy rocks or behind a waterfall hidden from view, and lives in seclusion or in pairs while it is raising its nestlings. It does not leave the territory where it was hatched and reared unless it is forced to by water contamination or human intrusion. Once the dipper does abandon an area it never returns.

During the hard winter months when most birds are struggling to keep alive, the dipper, a song bird thought to be related to the wren or thrush, can be found perched on an icy rock or the butt of a waterlogged tree, singing brightly and melodiously, its shrill, piping notes in defiance of the frosty air and snowy banks. However, when spring arrives, the song of the dipper cannot be heard over the roar of flood waters and the snapping of timber, and it is believed that the frequent bobbing of its dark head is what draws a mate's attention.

Admired for its courageous, free spirit, the dipper will tolerate human presence if the observer does not become too pressing.

This is really something, thought Kat. Does Mrs. Cooper know she's a dipper? Kat put down the nature book and took up another, whose soft, yellowed pages smelled of lavender.

~§ 17 §~ The room had an entirely different atmosphere. It was not quiet like a library; music was playing. Though Kat had never been in a Parisian salon, that was the mood of the old woman's room this cloudy Sunday.

Mrs. Cooper was sitting on the settee working a puzzle while the voice of Edith Piaf whispered, trilled, and hummed in the cozy room. The old woman tapped two fingers on the edge of the table, and the fine white hairs of her eyebrows flicked in response to the vibrating strings under the rich voice of the singer. Mrs. Cooper had invited Kat to join her with a hand gesture, then without looking up at the child had placed a finger to her lips, expecting Kat to see and respect her wishes.

The child was content to sit silently at the old woman's side. Being with her was enough—there needn't be conversation. Mrs. Cooper was the only person Kat knew who was comfortable being watched. The gray eyes had a light source of their own in this shady room; the large-knuckled hands worked slowly but deftly, with no false moves, even though they trembled from time to time; and the woman's soft lips pursed now and again when the singer paused. Kat was moved by the old woman's subtle, natural sensuality and remembered what the woman had said about a poem—that one should treat it like a song. The old woman was a song.

When the record was over, Mrs. Cooper tapped Kat's hand, and Kat understood what she should do. When she returned to the settee, Kat saw that the puzzle also was finished. She was surprised to see it was a picture of the boardinghouse. Not expecting it to be that, she hadn't caught on until it was complete.

Mrs. Cooper sat back with her hands on her knees and sighed.

"Is that . . . ?" Kat asked in a whisper.

"Yes, do you like it?"

"Oh, yes, but how can that be?"

Mrs. Cooper scratched some paint off a puzzle piece with her thumb nail, then handed the piece to Kat. Beneath the scratch was the original puzzle picture. "Once I finish a puzzle," the old woman explained, "I paint my own picture over it. That way a single puzzle can be a pleasure for years."

Kat shook her head in amazement and said, "Mrs. Cooper, you're a genius!"

The statement was said with such sincerity it tickled the old woman, and she patted Kat's hand once again—this time as a thank you rather than a please.

"I've never known anyone like you," Kat added. "You're a new person."

"I'm an old person, Kathleen, with wrinkles and stiffness to show for it."

"Not to me. To me you're bran' spankin' new."

The patterns appeared on the woman's face, then disappeared, and she said, "Did you bring the book?"

"Yes, ma'am."

"And how is it going?"

"I finished it," Kat said proudly.

"You finished it so quickly?"

"I stayed up real late last night to do it and got in trouble twice."

"Trouble?" Mrs. Cooper asked, concerned.

"Papa caught me first, then Mama."

"In your tree fort late at night?"

"No, with my light on in my room."

"What do you have to say about Mr. James Fenimore Cooper?" the woman asked, slapping her hands on her knees.

"Is he a relative of yours?"

"No, child," the woman chuckled.

"I'm glad 'cause . . ."

"Yes?"

"Well, I liked the parts when Uncas was searching for Cora and Alice, but I didn't like the scalping so much and I wish Uncas and Cora didn't have to die in the end." Kat looked away from the woman to the puzzle.

"Yes, I can understand that."

Raising her eyes, Kat said boldly, "I don't like war."

"Do you suppose anyone does?"

"I think men do," answered Kat.

"Why do you think that?"

"Because they do it and women don't."

"You may be right, child," said Mrs. Cooper, leaning back.

"Do you think Americans took America from the Indians?" asked Kat.

"You mean the colonists? The English, French, Spanish, and Russians?"

Kat nodded.

"No," answered the woman.

"But they did."

"No, child, they did not."

"But we've got it, and they don't anymore. That's what happened."

"That's what it looks like to some."

"You mean the Indians still own it in secret?"

"No, Kathleen. No one owns land."

Kat looked at Mrs. Cooper as if she were a bit cracked.

"Generations come and go, but the land remains. The Indians never owned America. No one owns America. Those who try to own land seem always to end up covering it with their blood for believing they can."

Mrs. Cooper peered into Kat's doubting eyes. The child obviously was giving her idea some thought, but was not convinced.

"That tree where you have your fort—will it be there when you are old like me?" asked the old woman.

"Yes, if no one cuts it down."

"And when you die?"

"Uh huh."

"And someone else will make it their place?"

"I suppose."

"For the moment it feels like you own it, but you really don't, do you? It owns itself."

Kat's eyebrows pulled close together. "Could anyone take it and make it theirs?"

"They could try. And if you insisted it was yours and the other insisted it was his, you might have a war over it, and no matter who won or lost the war the tree would never be owned by either of you."

Kat was confused. She'd never heard anyone say these things before. Everyone knew the tree fort belonged to her.

"What need do you have to own the tree?" Mrs. Cooper asked in a gentle voice. "It is enough to love it. You can take things in and make them yours in your heart. Then, no matter where you go or what goes from you, you'll never be without your treasures."

"I have to think about that to see if it'll work."

"Don't think about it—try it. Next time you come upon a woodland thrush, let its song inside your heart and it will be yours forever. You can do the same with a sunset, a tree, a kitten, a person. Especially do it with people. It is a grave mistake to think we can own another person. And it is a mistake to think someone cannot be ours if we make the person ours in the only way we rightfully can, by taking his or her song into our heart."

"Does that go for family too?"

"Especially family."

"But family belongs to each other."

"We belong to ourselves alone. We can only share ourselves with others. It is no different with land, which can be shared, never owned, dear heart."

"You make it all sound right, but I think I still have to think about it some more."

"Yes, Kathleen, you must do that." Mrs. Cooper leaned back and closed her eyes.

"I don't want Andy just in my heart. I want him in the flesh." The old woman nodded.

"Do you think I'm like the colonists because of that?"

Mrs. Cooper lifted her eyes and said, "It's very hard for all of us."

In the silence that followed, Kat longed for the good feeling she'd had before this talk. "Can I put on the record again?" she asked.

"Did you enjoy it?"

"It makes the room a song," said Kat, and as she uttered the words, she suddenly experienced a breakthrough.

The old woman saw the startling awareness on the child's face and said, "Yes, my sweet, this is your room now also."

⇜ 18 ⇝ From where Kat sat cross-legged on the floor of Sarah Eisenberg's room she could see Marjorie Holmes's reflection in Miss Renee's cheval mirror, which had been brought downstairs for the dress fitting. Kat watched the sunlight dance on a wave of Marjorie's brown hair, then noticed the pulsing vein in Marjorie's neck and followed the blue line down to the jewel neckline of the ivory satin dress she was wearing.

Kneeling beside Marjorie, Janet Howard put straight pins in the kick-pleat train at the back of the wedding dress, recalling the day a generation earlier when she stood in the dress looking at her own reflection in a mirror. She had felt that day, as she had at each turning point in her life, that the moment was larger than life itself and she small. Looking back now, she couldn't think why she'd felt melancholy nor what on earth she'd thought she was saying good-bye to.

As Kat's mother took one pin after another from the pin cushion on her wrist to mark the dress hem, Marjorie gazed at Janet's profile in the mirror. She'd always dreamed her mother would share this time with her, but Mrs. Holmes had died before Marjorie's second year of college and her father was her only family now. Mr. Holmes was taking a train from his home in Birmingham, Michigan, to be with Marjorie on her wedding day.

Seated in the swan's neck rocker in the window light, Sarah Eisenberg took fine stitches in the crêpe de chine garment on her lap. Once the trousseau was finished, she would begin work on the Juliet cap and shoulder veil. For the first time in years Sarah seemed almost happy. She was caught up in her task, her attention outside herself.

"Marjorie, raise your arm now . . . Yes, that's it." Janet took a pin and marked where she would take in the waist.

"What's the something blue?" asked Kat, unfolding her legs.

"The bouquet," Marjorie answered.

"The dressing gown's finished," Sarah announced.

The three generations of women looked to the fourth and oldest. "Hold it up!" Kat cried excitedly.

"Oh, my, it's lovely."

Sarah swelled with pride at Janet's remark.

"How can I ever thank you—"

"Nonsense, Marjorie," Janet interrupted. "It's wonderful of you to let us share in this."

"You're going to carry blue flowers?" asked Kat.

"Yes, Kathleen, forget-me-nots."

Up on her knees, clapping her hands together in excitement, Kat asked, "What's the something old gonna be?"

"My grandmother's chemise," answered Marjorie, tickled by Kat's enthusiasm and recalling how excited Kat got in class whenever something burst into her understanding. In this, she and Kat were alike. But that was all she and Kat had in common, Marjorie realized, looking at Kat's scraped knees and dirty elbows and remembering how she'd hated to wear anything but dresses and preferred being home with her mother to going off on wild adventures. It wouldn't have occurred to Marjorie to go to a baseball game in a large city by herself, and everyone knew Kat would take off tomorrow if she had the means. Coming to Missouri from Michigan had been frightening to Marjorie at twenty-two.

"What's the something new?" asked Kat.

"The veil," Sarah answered.

"And the something borrowed is this dress," Marjorie added, anticipating Kat's next question. Marjorie's mother hadn't worn a traditional wedding dress, and neither had her grandmother. Janet Howard had discovered this somehow and had offered Marjorie her own wedding dress for the occasion.

Kat rose. Pretending she had a bouquet of flowers in hand, she twirled around the room singing to a made-up melody, "Something old, something new, something borrowed, something blue."

"Be careful, child," warned Sarah. "Don't go knocking things over with your wild dancing."

Janet looked up and smiled at her daughter.

"I'm glad you're happy, Kathleen," said Marjorie.

"I'm not happy," announced Kat. "I'm exuberant! You're the prettiest person who ever lived. Wait till David sees you. He'll explode!" After a pause, Kat asked, "What's he gonna wear? What does the man wear, Mama?"

Before Janet could answer her daughter, Sarah said, "A soldier's uniform."

"But David's not a soldier," objected Kat.

The room fell silent. Janet looked about her, then said softly, "Your papa wore a navy blue suit, Kat, and he was the handsomest man in all of St. Louis."

"How old were you when you and Papa married?"

"Seventeen."

"I have seven more years."

"You have as long as it takes to meet the right man and fall in love," her mother assured her.

"Do you think I will?" Kat asked her, standing beside Marjorie so that she, too, was reflected in the full-length mirror.

"Yes, indeed!" Janet answered, taking the pin cushion off her wrist.

"I'm glad I've got seven more years because I haven't got breasts."

Marjorie blinked at Kat's immodesty, and Janet looked in the mirror at her daughter's face. Kat was oblivious to the effect of her remark.

"Betty Lou does, though," Kat went on innocently, then flew away from the mirror to twirl some more. "I think she'll marry before me. But I'll have breasts someday, I know."

"In God's good time," Janet answered, amused.

"It's strange, though. I'm three inches taller than Betty Lou, but I haven't got breasts yet. Did you have breasts when you were ten, Mama?"

Janet looked toward Sarah, grateful that the old woman was engrossed in her sewing. "No, Kat, I did not."

"Were you as tall as me?"

"Not quite."

"Does that mean I'll be taller than you when I'm grown?"

"Can't say. We'll just have to wait and see about that and breasts. Okay, Marjorie, you can step out of the dress." Janet stood up. "Lord," she groaned, "I'm stiff."

"Mrs. Cooper's got stiff knees," Kat interjected. Dizzy from twirling, she stopped and focused on the sewing box on the floor.

"Let me get those for you," Janet said to Marjorie, and Kat watched as her mother unbuttoned the back of the dress. "Be careful of the pins as you step out," Janet cautioned.

Kat looked at Marjorie's shapely legs and remembered the painting of Thea in the studio above. When Marjorie stepped into her own dress and went to Sarah for a veil measurement, Kat remembered she still had work to do. "I'm going to go change the other beds now," she announced, picking up the pile of sheets she'd set down an hour earlier and running out the door.

Eva Parsons's room was next on Kat's rounds. After she finished making Eva's bed, Kat took one of the sheets to be laundered and, draping it around her like a sari, posed in front of Eva's mirror. Not quite satisfied, she picked up her pigtails and held them on top of her head with one hand, tilted her head, and squinted her eyes. Disappointed, she let the braids and sheet fall. Cotton didn't compare to satin, and off she went to the next room.

Before leaving Miss Renee's room, Kat sat down at the dressing table. Looking at her face in the mirror, she tried a beguiling smile. If she couldn't even pretend to be beautiful, how would she get Miss Holmes to notice her? As Kat left, she wondered if Miss Renee felt the same about David Webb marrying as she did about Miss Holmes marrying.

Next, Kat placed a set of clean sheets on Francis's bed, then went to his window to admire the marigolds. Was Miss Holmes carrying forget-me-nots because she had given her a painting of them? Kat wondered. "I hope you will forget me not, for I shall not forget you," she whispered in a low voice. Miss Holmes had promised she wouldn't forget, but Kat had a foreboding that that promise would be broken.

After making Francis's bed, Kat added his dirty sheets to the pile at the top of the stairs and took the last set of clean sheets and a pillow case to David's room. As she opened the door she heard sounds from within, but it was too late to knock. The door open, she stood facing the unmade bed, where two naked men lay, the fanny of one and the hairy chest and black eyes of the other confronting her. She dropped the sheets.

"Jesus Christ!" cried David.

Francis turned and saw Kat bolt from the room. "Oh, my God!" he gasped. Grabbing the towel from the bed, he ran after her.

Kat fell blindly into the pile of sheets at the top of the stairs. Regaining her balance, she tore down the stairs.

Francis called out to her, "No, Kat, wait! Damnit, wait!"

Kat burst out the front door. Her legs pumped like steel pistons as she fled across the square.

Francis stood on the landing, his arms hanging limply at his sides. His friend had run scared from him. Looking down at himself in the towel, he turned and walked slowly back to David's room.

David was standing at his window looking out. When Francis entered, he turned around. His broad chest glistened with perspiration; a trickle of sweat flowed down the hairline of his torso. Francis looked at David's naked body, then glanced away, and David turned as quickly to the window again. His back to Francis, David stood facing out for a broodish moment, then slammed his fist against the wall.

Francis knew that his lovemaking had given David pleasure. It hadn't mattered that David would not desire him beyond the moment. Francis hadn't expected more; he hadn't asked for more. But now, looking at David's angry back, he felt a terrible disappointment and a loss.

"An attack of conscience?" Francis asked in a gentle tone.

David stretched his arms out wide, a hand on each side of the window frame. Sweat trailed down his spine between his sharp shoulder blades.

Francis looked at the taut tendons at the back of David's knees, then went to David's closet, reached for his robe, and took it to him. "You don't have to worry about me, David. I won't return."

"She was running across the square . . . to Marjorie."

"No, David."

"She's gone to tell Marjorie."

"For chris'sake, she doesn't even know what she saw. What are you really afraid of?"

"I'm not afraid of anything!" David shouted.

"What is it then? Seeing yourself with another man?"

"Man?" David said with a bitter laugh.

Francis had been around too long to be hurt by such obvious defensiveness, yet there he stood, stunned once again by that familiar insult. "Very well, David," he said in a quiet voice.

David turned and faced him. His sturdy composure was gone. His shoulders hung, and his dark eyes were pleading. He walked over to the bed and sat down on it, his head in his hands.

Francis reached for his trousers on the chair, stepped into them, and said, "Listen, David, I don't think Kat will go to Marjorie. She's probably off by herself trying to sort things out. I'll go to her and explain."

"What will you say?"

"Not much. Kids trust simple explanations."

David ran his hand through his wavy black hair. "I don't know what's the matter with me," he said in a stricken voice.

"Nothing," Francis chuckled, "you were glorious."

David wrapped his arms around himself, then said, "I feel like shit."

"Stop punishing yourself."

"I'm a goddamn joke to you, aren't I?"

"No, you haven't been awfully funny." Francis started for the door.

"Wait, can I ask you something?"

"Yeah."

"Why did you come here? Did you know I would . . . did you think I was a—"

"Say it."

"I can't."

"Goddamnit, say it."

"A faggot?"

Francis stood looking at David for several moments. "What the hell does it matter what I think?"

"I'm not!"

"I came here for recreation, David—don't get psychological about it." Francis opened the door, glanced at David before leaving, then stepped into the hall and closed the door softly.

Kat huddled in the corner of her tree fort staring at the picture of Andy beside her July calendar. Her best friend was far away in a place she couldn't even imagine, and she ached for him. David had spoiled her friendship with Miss Holmes and now with Flowerman. She hated David. How could Miss Holmes love him? And Flowerman, did he too? Kat didn't

116

know what the two men had been doing, but she'd sensed their intimacy and was shocked and jealous.

"I haven't got anyone but you, Jesse," Kat moaned. "Jesse? Jesse, where are you?" He wasn't in the fort. "Jesse! Jesse!" she called out the door.

A small white form leaped over the hedge at the side of the Howard house, then loped to the tree.

"Oh, Jesse, I need you!"

The wayward cat stretched his paws up against the tree trunk and meowed.

"You're impossible, Jesse! I've got to come to you even when I need you to come to me." Kat climbed down her rope ladder, then back up with her cat clinging to her. Inside the fort, Jesse stretched out on his side, pawing the air while Kat petted him.

"I'm always the one who does the scratching while you do the purring," Kat complained. She stopped petting Jesse and sat back in the corner of her fort with her knees against her chest.

Jesse looked over his shoulder at Kat and meowed.

"No, I'm not doing it anymore. I don't like you. You're not reliable."

Jesse got up lazily and went to her. She ignored his coaxing against her leg, so he raised up on his hind legs and butted his head against her cheek.

"Do you really love me, Jesse?" Kat asked through her tears.

Jesse purred loudly.

"What am I gonna do, Jesse? I can't get rid of it unless I tell someone, and there's no one I can tell." She lay down on her back and Jesse curled up in a tight ball on her chest. The two fell asleep.

When Francis finished cutting the grass on the library green behind the courthouse, he put the mower in the tool shed beside the jailhouse, wiped his hands and face with his neckerchief, and started down Elm Street. What would he tell Kat when he found her? Would she listen to anything he had to say? She'd been like a little sister—no, he felt like a parent more than a brother. And it was because of that assumed responsibility that he was feeling so low. As he took slow steps toward the Howard house, he told himself that he must first show Kat that he cared for her, and he must not rush her. Francis walked up the Howards' drive to the back of the house, hoping to find Kat in her fort.

"Kat! Kat, are you up there?"

Inside the fort, Kat opened her eyes. Asleep for over an hour, she was awakened by the sound of her name. Disoriented at first, she wondered where she was and what time of day it was, and it took the recognition of Francis's voice calling her a third time for her to recall the trauma of her morning. She peeked out one of the fort windows and saw Francis standing beneath the old oak straining to look up.

"Kat, if you're up there, I'd like to talk to you . . . We need to talk . . . Please don't hide."

Kat had crouched down in a corner of the fort doing just as Francis suspected. Janet Howard, hearing Francis, opened the screen door and walked over to him.

"Hello, Mrs. Howard. Have you seen Kat?"

"Not since this morning, Francis. Is something wrong?"

"No, nothing's wrong."

He's a liar, thought Kat. He's lying right through his teeth. She poked her head out of the fort and called down, "Something is too wrong."

Francis looked up at Kat.

"I'm not talking to him, Mama."

"I'm sorry, Mrs. Howard. I guess I better go."

"I don't know what's happened between you two," said Janet, "but I do hope you work it out."

"I hope so, too, Mrs. Howard. Thank you."

When Francis left, Janet asked her daughter, "Are you okay?"

"Yes, Mama."

"Did you have any lunch?"

"I wasn't hungry."

"Well, it's three, so if you're going to eat anything before dinner it had better be now or you'll spoil your appetite."

"I think I'll just stay up here."

"Suit yourself."

Kat stayed put until it was time to do her paper route. She delivered the *Post-Dispatch* in record time, returned home, had a quiet dinner with her parents, then joined them in the living room to listen to "Major Bowes' Amateur Hour" on the radio. It was unlike Kat to sit hunched over in the corner of the couch, wiggling her way into the cushions and huddling there like a troubled spirit. Her father watched her closely, then glanced at his wife with his eyebrows raised. Janet returned a puzzled look to her husband and asked her daughter if she was feeling all right. Kat gave an ambiguous nod. When Phil Spitalny and his All-Girl Orchestra came on the radio, George looked at Kat expectantly. If anything could perk her up, Evelyn and her magic violin would. But instead of getting up and miming for her papa, as she always did, Kat rose and went off to bed.

The next day there was little change in Kat's behavior. She went to the boardinghouse, accepted the grocery list, coupon book, and her wages from Francis without comment, and did her chores. Eva Parsons, surprised by Kat's distance, questioned Francis. He confided nothing.

That night, when George and Janet went to bed, George told his wife his intentions. "Tomorrow, if this continues, I'm going to have a talk with Kat. It isn't like her to be so moody."

Janet turned out the light and crawled into bed beside her husband. "I wonder if this has anything to do with the wedding."

"Why do you think that?" asked George.

"She was with us yesterday morning when we were working on the dress."

"And? . . . My God, Janet, how can your legs be cool? It must be eighty out."

"She's had a crush on Marjorie for some time. Remember how she was when Andy was getting ready to go away? . . . Do you want the window fan on?"

119

"No, it makes a racket . . . Yes, I remember. She was pouty for a couple weeks. But what does Francis have to do with Marjorie and David's wedding?" George ran his bare foot along Janet's leg, enjoying the feel of her cool, smooth skin.

"Honey, if I knew the answer to that . . . I thought I'd understand her better than Andy, but she's a tough one to figure."

"I'll talk to her tomorrow," George said as he cuddled closer to Janet.

Nuzzling with him, Janet whispered, "You'll do all the talking, no doubt."

The following day was Sunday. Janet stopped to talk to Charlotte Ferrand after church, and George seized the opportunity to be alone with his daughter.

"Something's up, Kat. Your eyebrows are hanging over your eyes."

Kat walked beside her father, her braids wagging but her tongue still.

"Cat got your tongue?" George kidded her. The corners of Kat's mouth turned up slightly. "I've missed that smile of yours," he said, taking her hand in his and giving it a gentle squeeze. "Want to walk some?"

"I've got my Sunday meeting."

"Are you happy there?"

"Yes, Papa," Kat answered softly.

"You don't have to keep up a brave front."

"I know, Papa."

"You want to continue there?"

"Yes, Papa. I want to go to the World Series."

"Are you going to ask Francis to be your escort?"

"I haven't decided."

"Mama tells me you and he had a difference."

"Yes, Papa. I've gotta go now."

George bent down and kissed his daughter's forehead. "Those are powerful worry lines pulling at your forehead. If you want to talk, just let me know. I'll wait on you."

"Thanks, Papa. Bye."

George tapped Kat's bottom and watched her walk off toward the square. A mind of her own, he thought.

Mrs. Cooper was sitting at her desk writing a letter when Kat tapped on her door. She turned around as Kat entered and said, "Here comes the sunshine."

When the old woman got up to ring for Francis, Kat stopped her, saying, "No!"

"Is it the cookies or Francis you've got no taste for?" asked Mrs. Cooper.

Did she know? Maybe Francis told her. No, Kat decided, he couldn't tell her the truth—that's for sure. Maybe he lied to her.

Mrs. Cooper walked over to Kat and put her hand under Kat's chin, raising the set jaw to her. "You look like you've got a nasty taste in your mouth—perhaps you should spit it out. This old woman won't mind."

Kat started to tremble.

"Heavens to Betsy, child!" The old woman took Kat into her arms. "Been holding onto something too long." Kat hid her face in the body of the woman. "Yes, yes, I know about these things," Mrs. Cooper sighed as she patted Kat's back. "Let's go sit in the sunny window. You aren't too old to sit on my lap, are you?"

"Jesse's fourteen in animal years, and he sits on my lap," Kat sniffled, wanting desperately to be held now, ready to let go of the hurt she'd been carrying for two days.

Mrs. Cooper sat down in her chair and helped Kat onto her lap. "Now, you just sit here in this old lap, and we'll rock until those miseries let go their hold on you." Kat's cheek rested against the woman's soft bosom. "Now, aren't you a sight for sore eyes! You've got the handsomest face I ever saw." Mrs. Cooper took her finger and marked a line down Kat's nose, then took the child's hand and held it in one of hers.

The woman's familiar lavender scent was comforting to Kat, and she opened her eyes and looked up into Mrs. Cooper's face. "What's a person supposed to do when they see something bad?" she asked.

"That depends upon who the person is," answered Mrs. Cooper.

"I don't understand," confessed Kat.

"One rule doesn't fit all."

"But I need a rule."

"Yes, I suppose you do," said the old woman, but she felt in no hurry to offer the child one. For the time being they would rock. The old woman knew the importance of waiting for the right moment to speak about difficult things. When she felt Kat relax, then take in a deep breath and sigh, she spoke tenderly, saying, "Kat, when something happens to me that hurts, I get a lonesome feeling, and I know I've got to take care of that lonesomeness before I can wrestle with the problem—so I look for company. It's not always another person, though that can be a good place to find comfort. Sometimes a puppy or a kitty is as good. For me, a tree, song, or painting do as well."

Kat looked into the old woman's eyes and said, "I tried Jesse."

"He didn't want to rock you, is that it?" Mrs. Cooper asked with a smile.

"How'd you know?"

After a gentle hug, Mrs. Cooper said, "I don't know it so much as I feel it . . . Are you ready to wrestle with your problem now?"

"I don't think I can tell it."

"Try drawing a picture with words."

Kat bit her lower lip, trying to get up the courage to say it, then blurted, "His fanny was sticking up, and the other man was looking at me."

"Yes?" the old woman said calmly.

"They were naked."

"And that's your problem?" Mrs. Cooper asked.

"It wasn't right!" Kat insisted.

"Why?"

Kat closed her eyes tightly and put her cheek back against the woman's breast. She didn't want to see it again. "I-I-I can't," she stammered.

The two rocked, and Mrs. Cooper said quietly, "You've seen

nakedness before?" Kat nodded. "And I'm guessing it didn't hurt you."

"No," Kat whispered.

"Maybe that wasn't it. Maybe something else is bothering you."

"No, I saw it!" Kat objected. "I saw David and Francis touching."

"You're touching me," the old woman said gently.

"This is different."

"Yes, it probably is. But because the other was different doesn't mean it was bad ... Shall I tell you a story about me when I was a little girl?" Kat nodded. "I was younger than you when I saw a baby being born. I wasn't supposed to go into the room, but when I heard my mother's voice I went uninvited. There I saw my aunt holding a little pink baby upside-down and spanking him hard enough to make him cry. I thought that was a very bad thing, and I ran out of the room. For several days I tried to erase the sight of my aunt hitting my little baby brother and couldn't talk to anyone about it. Finally my mother called me to her. She told me something I've never forgotten." Kat adjusted herself in the old woman's lap. "Why don't you sit down there, Kat." Mrs. Cooper pointed to the stool. "We don't need to rock anymore."

Kat got down, and the old woman leaned back and closed her eyes for a moment. Kat understood that she was collecting her thoughts.

"When we don't see what comes before or what follows an event, the little we do see can be frightening. I hadn't seen my aunt's strong, gentle hands lift my baby brother from my mother. And I ran out of the room and didn't see my aunt wash the baby and place him in my mother's arms. I only saw the spanking part and ran scared because I didn't know the spanking was needed to get my brother breathing on his own. My aunt hadn't done a bad thing; she'd helped my brother take his first breath of life ... What I'm trying to say, Kat, is that when we see something for the first time and don't know or see what came before and what follows, the little we do see may make no sense or bad sense. It's like hearing a half-truth."

"But David and Francis weren't having a baby."

"No, child, but you don't know the whole truth of what it is they were doing, do you?"

"No, what were they doing?"

"You said they were naked and touching," Mrs. Cooper answered matter-of-factly. "If you want to know more, you'll have to ask them."

"I've never seen *men* naked and touching," said Kat.

"I realize that. But you have seen women naked and touching?"

"I did once with Betty Lou."

"Did you think that was bad?"

"No, but we aren't grownups."

Mrs. Cooper laughed out loud. "Isn't that something! Grownups are always telling children what they can't do because they're children, and you, child, are telling me what grownups can't do because they're grown up. I wonder if we all aren't a little of both."

Kat liked it when Mrs. Cooper laughed because her whole being laughed. "You can be a child if you want to, and do whatever you want," Kat said, smiling broadly.

"I'm glad you said that, because I like being ten once in a while."

"I wish I were grown up sometimes." Kat got up and twirled around the room singing her song, "Something old, something new, something borrowed, something blue."

Mrs. Cooper leaned back in her chair and hummed.

Kat stopped to listen, then said, "I know that song. That's the 'Missouri Waltz.' "

Nodding to the child, Mrs. Cooper lifted herself from her chair, then walked slowly to the door beside the iron stove at the far side of the room. When she opened the door, Kat could see into an adjoining bedroom. This explained the door to the left of the stairway which Kat had wondered about—it was the hallway entrance to Mrs. Cooper's bedroom. The old woman disappeared into the room. When she returned to the sitting room a moment later, she was wearing a purple hat and carrying a cosmetic bag. Taking a seat at the window and beckoning to Kat, she said, "Come, let's play pretend. Who would you like to be?"

"A clown," Kat bellowed, then changed her mind. "No, I want to be a soldier."

"All right, my sweet. You can be a soldier and I'll be a clown." Mrs. Cooper licked the tip of a black eyebrow pencil and drew a mustache above Kat's lip, then clipped Kat's pigtails on top of her head with two pins she pulled from her hair. "Hold still now," the old woman scolded playfully. "There!" she said and began singing, "This Is the Army, Mr. Jones."

Kat ran to look at herself in the round mirror over the rosewood table where the stereoscope rested.

Mrs. Cooper got out a pot of rouge and painted red circles on her cheeks, then colored her lips a ruby red and powdered her nose white. When Kat turned and saw the woman's comical face, she was alarmed. She couldn't decide if the old woman behind the strange face was funny or scary. Seeing that Kat was caught between a laugh and a cry, Mrs. Cooper got down on her knees, stretched her arms out wide, and sang her heart out for the child: "Toot, toot, tootsie, don't cry . . ."

Tears of joy streamed down Kat's cheeks as she watched the old woman perform for her. Screeching, Kat grabbed herself.

"What's wrong, child?" Mrs. Cooper asked with sudden concern.

"I think I peed in my pants," Kat giggled.

"Good heavens!" The old woman laughed and sneezed white powder.

Kat wanted to run to the funny clown and proclaim her love, but the old woman's words intervened. "Come here and help me up, child. I've just grown back into an old lady."

~§ 19 §~ **B**y August, St. Louis was
playing believe-it-or-not baseball. The Cardinals had a firm hold
on first place in the National League, and the league's batting
title seemed safely in the hands of Cardinal Stan Musial. Luke
Sewell's Browns, the season's Cinderella team, were in first place
in the American League, and, though ranked seventh as a team
in batting, were managing to score more tallies per hit than any
other big-league club. A trolley-car World Series was becoming a
real possibility. As excitement over the pennant races raged, Missouri sweltered under a no-let-up August sun, and Hawthorn's
sticky grownups sought relief by running under garden hoses
with their children.

There seemed no remedy for Kathleen Howard's discomfort.
Her predicament clung to her as the humidity clung to Hawthorn's days and nights. Having spurned Francis for nearly a
week, she didn't know how to be his friend again. Francis was
aware of Kat's dilemma and tried to show that he considered
her, as before, his friend. Kat turned away, as if embarrassed by
his kindness. She had to find her own way out of the woods, out
of the corner she'd backed herself into.

On a sleepy, sultry Friday afternoon, the first week of August,
Kat pulled her Red Flyer up Waller Street toward the town
square. Jesse sat atop the stack of newspapers howling like a
coyote.

Kat finally stopped the wagon and gave Jesse a stern look. "If
you don't stop your bellyaching, Jesse, I'm gonna leave you
home from now on," she scolded.

Jesse flattened his ears against the cross sound of Kat's voice,
but once they were rolling again he resumed his howling. Kat
turned around fast and gave him a threatening look. Jesse gave
one final protest, then circled in the wagon until his tail faced
Kat.

It was either the cessation of Jesse's whining or nature's gasp
for air that caught Kat's attention, and she noticed that the sky
had turned a peculiar yellowish color and that not a blade of

grass nor leaf was moving. A moment later the stillness was broken by a swift westerly wind. The gust caught one of the newspapers in the red wagon and sent it flying across the courthouse lawn. Kat ran after the paper. A thunderbolt cracked open the now darkened sky, and everything below was drenched in a sudden burst of rain. Kat forgot the lost newspaper and ran lickity-split back to her wagon, gathered up an astounded Jesse, who was hiding under the Flyer, then dashed for cover under the Hannibal House canopy. She found little protection there as the wind began whipping up a frightful storm and sheets of rain slapped against the sides of buildings and shot up from the sidewalk. As Kat opened the door of Hannibal House to throw Jesse and the newspapers into the foyer, Jesse leaped from her arms and ran across the street to the square. Kat took off after him, hollering, "No, Jesse, wait!" Just as she reached the square, a bolt of lightning struck one of the oaks not more than five yards ahead of her. The tree cracked down the center of its trunk and fell. Kat halted, fear-struck, and Jesse leaped into the bushes for cover.

Francis was closing the front windows of the boardinghouse when he saw Kat standing in the center of the storm. "Oh, my God!" he gasped and ran for the door. Bolting across the street, he whisked Kat up in his arms and raced into the courthouse.

"Jesse! Jesse!" Kat cried as Francis put her down.

"Where?" asked Francis.

"Out there," she pointed and started for the door.

"No, Kat!"

Kat paid no attention to Francis. She lurched for the door.

Francis caught her by the seat of her wet pants and stopped her. "I'll get him."

Sheriff Kramer heard the commotion and came running into the hallway. "What's going on?" he asked.

"Frank, stay with Kat. I'll be right back."

When Francis let go of Kat, she jumped for the door, and he stopped her again. This time, looking her squarely in the eyes, he said, "Kat, trust me."

Kat gave Francis an anxious stare, and he put his hand on her shoulder and gave it a firm squeeze before turning toward the door.

Just outside, Francis heard a cat's hiss and looked to the right of the courthouse steps. Huddled against the brick near the entrance of the building was Jesse. Francis reached down and scooped up the rain-soaked bundle that neither looked nor sounded like a coyote or a cat, but more like a drowned rat. Once Jesse was safely indoors in Kat's arms, he let out a blood-curdling yeow, and Kat and Francis looked at one another and laughed.

The storm appeared to be quieting, and Francis went to take a look outside. Kat followed him to the door. Ruby streaks of light flared across the horizon.

"Ooh, I've never seen a storm so beautiful!" exclaimed Kat. "I'm going out." She handed Jesse over to Sheriff Kramer, who wasn't thrilled with his custody, and followed Francis outside.

"It's magical," Kat whispered in awe. "It's absolutely, positively—"

"Magical," Francis said, grinning.

Kat remembered what Mrs. Cooper had said about seeing what comes before and what follows an event. "I'm sorry I ran from you," she said, looking up at Francis.

"A summer storm can be a scary thing."

"I mean the other day."

Francis looked down into Kat's eyes and said, "Yes, well, I didn't blame you for running then either."

"I want to be friends again," Kat was able to say.

"We have been all along, Kat."

Kat looked up at the rain running off the end of Francis's straight nose and said, "I jumped to conclusions, I think."

"Hush," Francis said, bending down and brushing her wet bangs off her forehead.

"You saved me and Jesse."

"Some friend I'd be if I hadn't tried."

"Doesn't the rain feel good on your face, Flowerman?"

"Sure does," Francis agreed, opening his mouth at the same moment Kat did to drink in the rainwater.

Kat giggled when she saw her friend's impulse had been the same. "It unburdens me!" she rejoiced, with all the largeness of spirit she was feeling.

⋙20⋘ Taking Andy's jackknife carefully in hand, Kat made a three-inch incision down Peggy Sue's back and removed the doll's stuffing. Her savings would be safe and sound here—no one would think to look in a doll, not with a piggy bank present. Thirteen dollars and fifty cents was tucked inside Peggy Sue and fifty cents in Piggy Blue, perchance to fool a trespasser. After today, payday, she would have sixteen dollars—that was more money than she'd ever had. Kat imagined all she could buy with the money. Other than the World Series tickets, only a paintbox like Betty Lou's was attractive enough to consider. Her savings stashed, Kat closed the incision with a piece of tape and put the brown-and-yellow calico dress back on her doll. When Peggy Sue was given to her several Christmases earlier, she was wearing a pink dress which Kat thought ordinary, so her mother had fashioned the calico dress out of leftover material from her sewing closet.

Kat left Jesse in the tree fort when she departed for the boardinghouse. Jesse didn't accompany Kat on Wednesdays and Saturdays, the days she did the shopping, because Barney's twenty-two-pound tomcat rested on his haunches by the front door of the grocery, claws retracted but at the ready, prohibiting any feline from coming within sight or smell of the butcher's raw kidney and liver scraps.

Francis was having a cup of coffee with Eva in the boardinghouse kitchen when Kat arrived at a quarter past ten. He gave her the shopping list, coupon book, and twelve dollars. Ten dol-

129

lars went toward the groceries, and the two remaining dollars, folded and clipped together, was Kat's salary for the week. Kat put the ten in her left pocket and the two in her right before leaving the boardinghouse with Francis. As her friend turned and headed toward Defoe Park to weed and water the flower gardens that morning, Kat turned in the opposite direction toward Barney's to do the grocery shopping.

It wasn't quite noon when Kat placed the two grocery bags in the wagon and left Barney's. As she started up Steuben Place paying careful attention to her load, Ralph Quinn came out of nowhere, jerked the handle of her wagon from her, and raced up the street with it. The wagon bolted over a rough spot in the sidewalk in front of the boardinghouse, and the grocery bags fell over. Ralph picked up two eggs from the opened carton, heaved them at a pursuing Kat, and yelled, "Let's see ya hit these!"

The eggs struck Kat in the stomach and chest, raw egg yolk and white dripping down to her bare knees. In spite of the onslaught, Kat ran after Ralph to rescue her wagon and what there was left of the groceries.

"Let's see ya hit a home run now," Ralph mocked her, throwing two more eggs that found their target on her forehead and cheek. Blinded by the egg and stung by the impact, Kat stopped her pursuit. Ralph jerked the wagon farther up the street, the groceries now garbage on the sidewalk. When a back wheel broke off the Red Flyer and sailed into the street, Ralph kicked the wagon over and ran off, hollering, "Serves you right, Kat Howard, for smart-alecking on the baseball field. You're just a stupid girl with egg on your face."

Kat wiped the raw egg from her brow and eyes and recovered her wagon.

Daniel Brooks had turned the corner on roller skates in time to see it all. "We'll get him," Daniel promised, catching up to Kat. "We're gonna get him once and for all."

"It's no use, Brooks," said Kat. "Look what he's done."

"I can fix the wagon for you. Look, I've got the wheel. I got it when it flew into the street."

"Thanks, but you can't fix up the groceries."

Meanwhile, David Webb had been working on the Eisenbergs' toilet and heard the commotion. He reached the boardinghouse porch in time to see Ralph Quinn run off and Daniel comforting Kat. David picked up the spilled groceries from the sidewalk in front of the boardinghouse, as well as the grocery list Kat had dropped.

"What are you gonna do, Kat?" asked Daniel.

Kat searched her pockets. "Did you see a piece of white paper around here, Brooks?"

Daniel looked about, then shook his head no. "Is it something important?" he asked.

"It's the grocery list," said Kat, and she started away.

"Where are you going?"

"Home to get some money . . . I'll just have to remember."

"I don't understand, Kat."

"I want to go to the World Series," she cried as she ran off toward home, tears streaming down her face.

Back home, Kat washed her face with the garden hose, then climbed up to her fort, took the tape off Peggy Sue's back, and got out eight dollars. That and the two in her pocket would pay for another load of groceries. Putting the eight in her pocket, Kat realized there was no way she'd be able to make up the loss before the World Series. She had worked it out exactly—she needed every cent—and now she was ten dollars short. She'd be short a lot more, she figured, if she were fired from her job for not doing the Saturday shopping.

When Kat returned to Steuben Place, Daniel was standing proudly beside the Red Flyer, his roller skates still strapped to his white bucks. "I did it just like I promised, Kat."

"Thanks, Brooks. I'll take it now. I've got to get new groceries."

"I'll come with you just in case Ralph comes back."

"If I see his ugly face," Kat swore. "I'll spit in it."

Excited by her passion, Daniel yelped, "I'd like to see that. Would I ever!" as he followed Kat down the street.

When Kat and Daniel arrived at Barney's, David Webb was coming out, loaded down with groceries. "Where are you two going?" he asked.

"Brooks is helping me grocery shop," explained Kat.

"I'm her bodyguard," said Daniel.

"Yeah, I saw what happened."

Kat looked at David, surprised. "You did?"

"Brother, he sure got you, didn't he?" said David, noticing the mat of egg in Kat's hair.

"And he's gonna pay!" Kat said as she reached for the door.

"Wait!" said David. "I've got the groceries here."

Kat glanced back, confused.

"I found your list on the sidewalk," he explained.

"You mean you bought those for the boardinghouse . . . with your own money?"

"We'll keep it our little secret, okay?"

"But—"

"No buts."

"But where did you get the coupons for them? I've got the coupon book—oh, my gosh, I clean forgot! How am I gonna make up for the coupons? That takes more than money."

"Calm down, Kat," David said in a low voice. "I've taken care of the matter."

"But how?"

Daniel moved in close to catch this one.

"You kids promise not to squeal?"

"Yes, sir," promised Daniel.

"I can't promise till I hear what you say."

"Hell, Kat, you'd cut off your nose to spite your face! Just between us, I made a deal with Barney. I have a friend who works for the War Production Board, and Barney could use a favor, so . . ."

"Sounds unscrupulous to me," said Kat, looking up at him past her thick brows.

"Un-what?" asked Daniel.

"Unlawful," replied David. "Just bending the law a bit, for a good cause."

Kat hesitated for a moment, then smiled and said, "Thanks, David."

"You're welcome, kid. I figure I owed you one."

"Owed! Oh, I almost forgot." Kat pulled out her ten dollars and offered it to David.

"Put that back in your pocket."

"No, it's my job. I've gotta give this to you."

"I don't understand you, Kat."

"Me either," said Daniel.

"I promised Mrs. Cooper I could do the job. If she found out someone had to help me do it she'd think I wasn't fit for it and she'd fire me."

"And how is she gonna find out?" asked David.

"Papa says lies always get found out," Kat replied. She handed David the money, and he accepted it.

"Kathleen Howard, you're gonna amount to something. Maybe you'll be our first woman president."

"I'm gonna be the first woman major-league baseball player."

David and Daniel stared at her point-blank. She was as serious as a heart attack, and they knew it.

"I hope Ralph Quinn lives to see the day," chuckled David.

"He will," Kat said with confidence. "He will!"

David put the groceries in the Red Flyer and the ten dollars in his pocket, and the three began walking back to the boarding-house together.

"Kat, when you're through, do you want to play some catch?" asked Daniel. "It'll make you feel better."

"Yeah," Kat said absently, her mind on the ten dollars she would have to make up.

That evening when Janet Howard looked in on her daughter before going to bed, she found Kat awake, sitting upright in bed, with her arms folded in front of her and a stern look on her face.

"Having trouble sleeping, Kat?"

"My mind's not sleepy."

Janet cradled her child's head in her lap and combed her fingers through the waves of light hair.

"Mama, is it wrong to want to get back at him?"

"If you're planning to, that's probably why you can't sleep. It's hard to rest when anger storms in you."

"Does anger storm in you ever?" Kat asked.

"Oh, yes. But it's never done me any good."

"Ralph's stealing from me didn't do me any good."

"It won't help to do yourself injury on top of his."

"But I can't let him go on stealing from me whenever he wants."

"Maybe you should talk to him."

Kat raised her head from her mother's lap and said, "He hates me—he'd just throw more eggs at me. Besides, I'd like to beat him up." Kat lay back down.

"There'd be no end to it then," said Janet. "He'd just get himself a rock instead of an egg. Why don't you outsmart him?"

"How do you mean?"

"Show him what you've got up here," said Janet, tapping on Kat's forehead. "Then perhaps he'll take a step back and consider you more seriously. He knows he can whip you with his muscle . . . but, Kat, brawn can most always be outclassed by brain."

Kat sat straight up in bed. "I bet you've done that."

"Sure have."

"I could tell by the way you said it, with real feeling."

Janet wore a girlish grin on her face. She looked away from her daughter to the two socks pulled over the bedposts at the foot of Kat's bed and, gazing beyond them to the pine dresser with its white porcelain drawer knobs, stared at the photograph of the Howard family set in the white porcelain picture frame Kat had selected because it would go with the knobs.

"Will you tell me?" asked Kat, curious to know what thoughts pulled the corners of her mother's mouth upward.

Turning back to her daughter, Janet answered, "I'll think about it . . . Is your mind getting sleepy yet?"

"Starting to."

Janet kissed her daughter on the cheek, then put her cheek

against Kat's and purred. She was the only human being Kat knew who could purr.

The next day after church Kat passed the word to Annie to meet her at Betty Lou's at two o'clock that afternoon. Annie assumed Betty Lou knew what was up, but Betty Lou told her all Kat had said was that she should be ready for an adventure by two. Daniel overheard Annie and Betty Lou whispering and, putting two and two together, guessed that Kat was about to make her move on Ralph Quinn.

By quarter to two Daniel was on the steps of the St. Pierre Inn with his scaling knife in a leather sheath attached to his belt, his slingshot sticking out of his tee shirt pocket, his bow and arrow strapped over his shoulder, and his bat in hand.

At precisely two o'clock Kat skipped around the corner of Elm Street and Waller in her white shorts and orange-and-green-striped tee shirt, singing "This Is the Army, Mr. Jones." When she saw Daniel she waved.

Daniel jumped up. "Hi, Kat, I'm ready!"

"For what, Brooks? And what's all that you've got hanging on you?"

"Armaments."

"Daniel Brooks!"

"I heard Annie and Betty Lou talking about an adventure at two, and I brought these 'cause I know girls don't have them."

"Well, if you wanna come along, you'll have to leave that stuff behind."

"Gee whiz, Kat, I was just trying to help. You don't have to be so mean."

"Okay, you can keep your knife, but not that other junk."

"How about my slingshot? Can't I bring my slingshot?"

"We won't need it, but you can bring it if it'll make you happy."

"What are you gonna do, Kat?"

"You'll see," Kat replied, grinning broadly and shoving her hands deep into her shorts pockets.

Annie and Betty Lou stuck their heads out of the window above the two. "Hey, is Brooks coming on our adventure?" asked Betty Lou.

Kat and Daniel looked up. "Yep, I invited him." Daniel grinned, revealing his darkened front tooth. "Bring a Mason jar of water with you when you come down, Betty Lou," Kat hollered.

"A what?"

"A Mason jar full up with water," Kat repeated.

"Why?"

"Just bring it."

"Okay, okay, we're coming down," called Betty Lou, and the two girls pulled in their heads.

"What's the water for, Kat?" asked Daniel.

"In case I get thirsty," Kat giggled.

"Kat, you're sure hard to figure."

"That's my plan."

As the small French clock on Mrs. Cooper's desk chimed twice, the old woman reached for the buzzer, rang five times, then stood and began pacing her room. When Francis arrived at her door she barked, "Come in, come in!"

"What's wrong?" asked Francis. He looked about the room. "Where's Kat? Isn't she usually here on Sunday afternoon?"

"Exactly. Where is she?"

"I don't know. I just asked you . . . so that's it."

"Francis, do you know what happened yesterday between Kat and the Quinn boy?"

By the look and sound of his questioner, possibly more than he'd been told. Francis hadn't seen the old woman this upset in years. "David said something about a chase."

Mrs. Cooper rubbed her backside with her hands and said, "It wasn't a chase, dear heart, it was an assault. I saw it from up here." She pointed to the window, then started pacing again and waving her arms.

Francis was more alarmed by the old woman's frenzied behavior than by the event of the day before. "Please, don't; you're racing your heart. Won't you sit?"

"I don't feel like sitting, my boy. Stay clear of my path."

Francis stood to the side and watched silently. Caught by a twinge of pain in her chest, Mrs. Cooper stopped pacing, and Francis, now angry with her for the scare she had given him, said sharply, "Can I do something for you?"

"Yes, you can go over to the Howards' and find out if she's all right."

"Just exactly what happened yesterday?" he asked.

Mrs. Cooper described the scene, and Francis cursed, "That bully! He's twice her size! Good thing for him I wasn't around or he'd be a dead bully."

Hearing Francis's rage and aware she'd triggered it by her own, Mrs. Cooper said quietly, "When you see the Howards, please make certain they understand I'm not disturbed that Kat missed our meeting. I'm only concerned about her welfare."

"Would you like to telephone? I'll help you with the stairs."

Mrs. Cooper shook her head. "I didn't put a telephone on this floor for a good reason. Words from black boxes are words only. You go show them your face and they'll catch your meaning."

Francis looked at her, baffled by her inconsistency. Mrs. Cooper never showed her face to the world outside. But she was an old woman, after all, and he could certainly do what she asked without question.

As soon as Francis left, Mrs. Cooper went to her bedroom, took a small white pill from the prescription bottle on her nightstand, placed the pill under her tongue, and sat down on her bed to rest. For some reason Thea's face flashed before her. The old woman's throat tightened and her heart gave a shudder. "No," she whispered aloud. "I can't allow that. Dear God, why? Why Thea?" she groaned. That child, she realized. I let that child in and now I can't close the gate. All it takes is one unguarded moment. Mrs. Cooper shook her head violently, as if she could, by doing so, shake herself loose of her thoughts. It was no use—Thea was there and the old woman's eyes stung.

By the time Francis returned and knocked on her door, Mrs. Cooper had washed her face and was reading at the window in her sitting room. "Come in," she said in a low voice.

"She's just fine," Francis beamed. The old woman studied him carefully. "She's just fine, I tell you."

Mrs. Cooper put her hand to her mouth, but Francis saw the sudden emotion in spite of the old woman's effort to conceal it.

"Mrs. Howard said Kat has gone over to the Quinns' with a couple of her friends. She said you needn't worry, Kat would handle herself well. Then she thanked you for being concerned and apologized for Kat not keeping her appointment with you."

Mrs. Cooper motioned for Francis to come to her, and she patted him on the arm several times.

"I'll go now and let you rest. I see you were reading."

The old woman turned to the window, and Francis slipped out.

Ralph Quinn stepped out onto the porch of his home, surprised to have visitors.

"Ralph Quinn," Kat said, shoulders back and chin up, "I'm going to give you a chance to beat me fair and square, once and for all."

Ralph looked askance at his company. "What are you getting at?"

"You've been holding a grudge against me for winning three swings. I don't like being the victim of your grudges, so I've come to propose a contest. If you win fair and square, you won't have any reason to hate me. If I win, you have to promise in front of witnesses never to bully me again."

"What kind of contest?" Ralph asked, looking to Kat's left and right at the others and expecting a trick.

"Arm wrestling."

Daniel's eyes opened wide in surprise. "No, Kat, he'd win. He's older than you, and he's got bigger arms."

"Shut up, sissy," hollered Ralph. "What are you doing here anyway? Ain't you got nothing better to do than tag along with stupid girls?"

Daniel took a step back.

"Daniel Brooks is our friend," Betty Lou spouted. "And you can like it or lump it."

Annie turned to the side to suppress the spontaneous giggle she felt erupting inside her.

"Will you accept my challenge or not?" Kat asked.

"Yeah, Ralph," taunted Daniel. "Maybe you're afraid she'll beat you again."

"You just keep your trap shut, tag-along, or I'll shut it for you."

Daniel swallowed and put his hand on his knife.

"Ralph, if you think arm wrestling isn't fair, we could do three swings again," suggested Kat.

Ralph looked at the solemn faces before him, thought a moment, and said, "Okay, we'll arm wrestle."

Kat could taste sweet victory but remained poker-faced. Annie tapped her on the shoulder, then whispered in her ear, "I think you've gone nuts. You can't beat him at that."

"What's she saying to you?" asked Ralph.

"She asked if she could be the judge."

Annie's heart quickened. She didn't want to be a part of any lie that involved Ralph Quinn.

"We don't need a judge," Ralph said as he rolled up his sleeve, revealing his well-developed bicep and large purple arm veins.

"Then who will say, 'Are you ready, get set, go'?" asked Annie with a coolness that surprised everyone. Annie rarely was bold, but her mind was quick. She knew Kat wouldn't offer a challenge she couldn't meet and that a lie wasn't a casual thing for her.

"I'll say it," offered Daniel.

"No!" yelled Ralph.

Kat stepped between Ralph and Daniel to prevent a certain clash. "Wait a sec'," she said to Ralph. "Has your pocket watch got a second hand?"

"Yeah."

"You pick someone to call out 'ready' on ten, 'set' on eleven, and 'go' on twelve; that should be fair."

139

Ralph wavered for a moment, then reached into his pants pocket, pulled out his watch, and gave it to Betty Lou, who swelled with indecent pride.

A second after Ralph and Kat got into wrestling position on their bellies on the porch floor, Kat leaped up and grabbed the watch and Mason jar from a bewildered Betty Lou.

"Hey, what's going on?" Ralph shouted, jumping to his knees.

"Shut up and listen," Kat bellowed, "or I'll drop this watch in the water!" Everyone stood agape.

Ralph got to his feet and made a move toward Kat.

"I'll drop it, kerplunk, if you move one step closer to me," she threatened.

"That's mine. Give it to me," Ralph demanded. "You give that back."

"I'll give it back. If you don't watch it, you'll get it back in the jar."

Daniel was so excited he jumped up and down, yelling, "Hooray for Kat! Hooray for Kat!"

Ralph went for Daniel, and Kat snapped, "That goes for my friends too. You touch any of us and I drop it."

Ralph had no choice. If the watch dropped into the jar it was ruined, and when his father found out he'd get a whipping.

Poised, cool as a cucumber, Kat held the watch over the water. "Better sit down, Ralph. I've got a speech to make." Ralph lowered himself to the porch floor, not taking his eyes off the watch and Mason jar. "I want three things and then the watch is yours. The first thing is an apology for bullying all of us. Not just for yesterday, but for all the times before too. That's why my friends are here—to hear your apology and your promise. That's the second thing. We want to hear you promise never to bully any of us again. And the third thing is the ten dollars you owe me."

Words were one thing, but money was quite another, and Ralph stood up. "I haven't got ten dollars."

"This watch is worth more than that," Kat said, unruffled.

"It's my father's. It's not fully mine till I'm eighteen."

"The groceries weren't mine either," Kat began, "and you destroyed them. I had to take money from my savings to buy them again. You can thank Daniel for fixing my wagon or you'd have to do that too," she added, without a hint of arrogance or anger in her voice.

"But I told you I haven't got any money."

"That's a problem for you to solve. I'll give you till ten o'clock tonight to come up with it. If you don't, kerplunk. You get my message?"

Ralph clenched his teeth.

"Have you gotten my message?"

"You're a cheat, Kat! A lying cheat!"

"Watch your mouth, Ralph Quinn. I'm running out of patience."

"That's kidnapping and it's against the law, Kat Howard."

"Nope. I'm simply offering you a chance to clear your debts and your conscience. I haven't taken your watch permanently, and I'm not asking for anything you don't owe me. Now, before we go, you have two things to do. First, say you're sorry."

Ralph snarled at Kat and her friends, then whispered low, "I'm sorry."

"To each person—and loud enough so they can hear you."

Ralph's mouth twisted as he said, "I'm sorry, Annie; I'm sorry, Betty Lou; I'm sorry, tag-along."

Daniel looked to Kat, and Kat turned to Ralph. "Do it right or I'll—"

"Brooks!" Ralph shouted.

"And one more," said Kat.

Ralph could not get the "I'm sorry" out, but he did manage to say her name, and she let it pass.

"Now promise not to bully us ever again."

"I promise."

"Your word had better be good."

"Or what?" Ralph challenged.

"Or you'll tell time by the sun. See you tonight."

The four walked off, leaving Ralph to stew on his porch.

When Kat and her friends reached the square, Daniel asked

Kat if she was going to hold the watch over the jar all night long.

"Don't have to," said Kat.

"How come?"

"Ralph will see it there just the same."

"That was really something, Kat," said Annie. "I've never seen Ralph so scared."

"Dumbfounded was more like it," whooped Betty Lou.

"How'd you think it up?" asked Annie.

"I was inspired," Kat replied.

"Think he'll show up tonight?" Betty Lou asked.

"I'd bet my ten dollars on it."

"Would you really have dropped it, kerplunk?" asked Daniel.

"Ralph thinks I would have."

"Yeah," Daniel hooted. "Boy, oh boy, you're really something!" Unable to contain himself, he began jumping up and down.

Betty Lou covered her mouth. "Don't anyone breathe— Brooks just farted."

"You don't need to hold your breath," Annie sighed, "just your nose."

"No," Betty Lou insisted, "everyone knows you can get TB from breathing farts."

Mr. Quinn and his son had not spoken to nor looked at one another on their walk. Standing beside one another at the Howards' front door, each was feeling humiliated by the other. For as many years as anyone could remember, Pat Quinn and his son had not gotten along.

As George Howard opened his front door, Mr. Quinn began a speech rehearsed earlier. "I've brought my boy to apologize to your family." George nodded for the two to enter and saw that Ralph had a cut at the corner of his right eye and that his upper lip was swollen to his nose. "There's no excusing him," Mr. Quinn went on. "We ain't here for that."

George looked at Ralph's numb expression and said gravely, "Please have a seat. I'll get Kat."

On his way to the backyard, George passed through the kitchen, where his wife was drying the dinner dishes. Janet saw the meaning in her husband's eyes: their expected company had arrived.

When the Howards joined the Quinns in the living room, Mr. Quinn yanked Ralph up by his shirt collar. His eyes lowered, Ralph said, "I'm sorry," and his lip started to bleed.

Kat winced and put out her hand to shake Ralph's.

"Shake her hand, boy!" shouted Mr. Quinn.

Kat waited with her arm out, wishing she hadn't made the gesture because it had only made things worse.

"You're damn lucky she's offering it. If it were me, you'd get a fist—not a handshake." It was obvious to everyone that Ralph already had gotten a fist.

Ralph shook Kat's hand but could not look at her.

"I took a strap to him, George. Whipped him good for what he done. I don't stand for bullying, and he knows it."

Janet left the room and went to the kitchen, where she dabbed cool water on her brow and cheeks. Although George kept his eyes on the Quinns, his mind was on his wife. He knew why she'd had to leave. He'd felt her brace herself when Mr. Quinn said he'd beaten his boy.

When Janet returned to the living room she was carrying a tray of iced tea. She offered Ralph a glass, but he didn't respond. What went on in the room affected him only remotely. It was as if a large part of him had tuned out. After a moment Ralph stood, reached into his pocket, and pulled out some bills, which he handed to Kat. In turn, Kat took the watch from her pocket and gave it to Ralph. The exchange seemed unfair to Kat somehow. She thought when this moment arrived she would feel victorious. Instead, she felt shameful, as though she'd done the wrong, not Ralph.

"Give that to me," Mr. Quinn barked at his son. "That ain't never gonna be yours now." Ralph handed the pocket watch to his father without hesitation or expression. "The ten bucks was mine too," Mr. Quinn shouted. Mr. Quinn had been shouting all along. Kat gritted her teeth, wishing she could flatten her

143

ears as Jesse did in defense of harsh, piercing sounds. "And that's the last time I reach into my pocket for that boy," Mr. Quinn continued. "He'll work at the station till he pays me back, then he gets on the next train . . . time he was on his own."

Kat's mother had been gazing at the Chinese ginger jar on her mantel but had been hearing it all. "Mr. Quinn, he's only a boy."

"It's time he was a man."

Janet looked at Ralph, who sat staring into space, and recalled an incident that took place when he was seven. There was nothing she could do for him this time.

Mr. Quinn lifted his glass and emptied it, then set it down hard on the coffee table. "Thanks for the refreshment, Mrs. Howard." He stood up. "There'll be no more trouble from him, I guarantee that."

Kat was ushered off to bed by her mother while her father said good night to the Quinns. Ralph was out the door first and away. He didn't wait to walk home with his father.

"See how he does at the station, Pat," George prevailed upon Mr. Quinn. "The boy will improve himself. We don't need to lose another young man. The war's claimed too many."

"Improve himself?" Mr. Quinn sneered. "You don't know that boy like I do."

"No, but we weren't much good for anything at fourteen either." George shook Mr. Quinn's hand and saw by the man's expression that Ralph would get no understanding from his father.

Seated beside Kat on her small bed, Janet began unbraiding her daughter's hair.

"I'm sure glad I sleep in this house," said Kat. Her mother was unable to say anything. "Are you crying, Mama?"

Janet nodded yes.

"You don't cry loud, like me. It's hard to tell, but I thought you were going to."

Janet looked into her daughter's eyes and saw the concern.

"Are you crying for Ralph because he can't?" asked Kat.

How could a ten-year-old have such wisdom? Janet wondered.

"I felt it, too, Mama. And Papa's cheek did that little thing it did when Andy went away."

Her mother lifted the covers, and Kat slipped under them and slid down.

Janet looked about the room and, after several moments, sighed deeply and began, "One summer night, years ago, your papa was called out on an emergency. It was around midnight. Roy Mulqueen's wife was sick with pneumonia . . . she died the next morning. Andy was asleep in his room, you were in yours—you were very small then—and Ralph was with me in Papa's and my room. He was seven years old. He'd been at our house all day; he liked to play in the tree fort. His father had gone off the night before, and no one knew where he was. Ralph was left alone—"

"Where was his mama?"

"She died when Ralph was born . . . Around one in the morning there was a terrible banging on the front door and hollering. I don't think I'll ever forget the hollering. It woke everybody up but you. I went to the window and looked out. It was Mr. Quinn, and he was demanding that his son be turned over to him. He must have guessed Ralph was with us. I was as scared as I've ever been in my life."

Kat looked closely at her mother. Could it be that her mother got scared like her? Did grownups get scared?

"Your papa away and that crazy man trying to break in . . ." Janet continued. "I told Andy to take his jackknife and climb above the fort in the old oak, then hold real still and wait for me to turn on the kitchen light. That was his signal to climb down to the fort, cut the rope ladder free, shinny down, and run back into the house. I'd be watching out and hold the door open for him. Well . . . I made Ralph stay in our bed, and I went to the kitchen. When I was certain Andy was safe above the fort, I yelled out to Mr. Quinn that his boy was sleeping in the tree fort. It took him about half an hour to climb the rope ladder. It was pitch-black out and he was drunk. He stumbled and fell once, and I was afraid he wouldn't make it, but finally he did. As soon as I could see he was in the fort, I turned on the kitchen light, and Andy cut down the ladder and high-tailed it in. Then I got you out of your bed, and all four of us slept together. Mr. Quinn was stuck up there, too drunk and too scared to climb down. The next day Papa got him out."

Two tears fell silently from Janet's eyes, and she wiped them away with her hand.

"That was real smart of you, Mama." Kat took her mother's hand in hers. Her mother was so good at comforting, she wished she knew how to do it as well. "Was that the time you out-smarted someone?"

Janet nodded yes and smiled. It was one of those smiles that sits on top of sadness.

"I hope his papa doesn't send him away."

"I never thought I'd feel this way, but I think he'd be doing Ralph a favor."

"Do you think Ralph will be safe tonight?"

"Night after night I used to worry about him. A couple of years passed, and I got to telling myself he'd survived all those nights I worried and he'd keep on surviving. Some do, you know. I don't know if God protects them or they protect them-selves, but some survive."

"I'm gonna make a promise for the future and then he'll sur-vive," said Kat, her mind suddenly made up about something. "I'm gonna ask Ralph to go to the World Series with me."

Janet's lower lip quivered as she tried to smile at her daughter.

Kat bunched up her pillow, plopped her head down on it, closed her eyes, and waited for her mother's kiss.

Before going to bed, Janet went back to the living room, sat in the dark, and thought about Andy, asking God to protect him that night also.

T^{he} following week when Kat arrived for her Sunday meeting, she found Mrs. Cooper seated at her desk cutting an article out of the newspaper. The old woman was wearing one of her tailored shirts with fine blue stripes and a long, navy blue skirt. Peering over Mrs. Cooper's shoulder, Kat watched the sure hands work, the right hand holding the stainless-steel sewing scissors with thumb and second finger because, Kat observed, the woman's first finger was too large at the first knuckle to fit into the little scissor loop. Kat studied the hand; she'd try to hold her scissors like that later, in private.

"Do you keep a scrapbook?" the old woman asked as she trimmed the edges of the article.

"No," answered Kat. "Do you?"

"When I was young I did. I cut out pictures and stories from the periodicals and pasted them in a book along with birthday cards . . . and my dance cards."

Kat stepped around the corner of the desk so she could see Mrs. Cooper's face. She put down the book she was holding so she could lean on the desk with her elbows, her chin in her hands. "What kind of dances?" she asked once she was situated.

"Ballroom dances."

"Were there mirrors on the walls?" Kat was looking at the old woman's face with great interest. The fine white eyebrows flickered, and the lashes as delicate as an insect's wings blinked.

"Are there supposed to be mirrors on the walls?" Mrs. Cooper asked.

"I dreamed you danced in a ballroom that had mirrors." Mrs. Cooper put down her scissors and looked into the intense fawn eyes before her. "I dreamed it in my fort on the Fourth of July when I was listening to the 'Missouri Waltz.' "

Aware of the child's passion, the old woman flushed and looked down at the article she had trimmed. "How about this?" she changed the subject.

"That's Pete Gray," said Kat. "Is that from the *Post-Dispatch?*"

Mrs. Cooper nodded. "I was gonna tell you about him, but I forgot. I forgot nearly everything last week."

"The second man in history to play with one arm."

"Do you think Memphis will trade him to the Detroit Tigers?" asked Kat.

"They say he's the miracle man of '44."

"I tried to catch like he does. To see if I could do it. I'll show you." Kat backed into the center of the room and pretended to catch a fly with her left hand; then, continuing to mime, she tucked the illusionary glove under her right arm and threw the make-believe ball with her left. "It's real tricky, and when it's a grounder he flips his glove in the air and catches the falling ball for his throw. It's really something, isn't it?"

"You're really something," Mrs. Cooper answered.

"I heard he was asked to give an exhibition, and he said he was a ballplayer, not an exhibitionist."

"Good for him!" laughed Mrs. Cooper.

"Can I look at your stereoscope again?"

The old woman nodded her approval and asked, "What is this you brought?" not recognizing her own book.

From behind the stereoscope, Kat answered, "That's Amy Lowell, remember? *Pictures of the Floating World.*" Mrs. Cooper nodded. "One-Arm Daily is missing his left arm."

"What made you decide to be a baseball player?" Mrs. Cooper asked, gazing at the book of poetry.

"Amelia Earhart," Kat answered.

"You've got me," Mrs. Cooper chuckled, turning to look at the child behind the stereoscope. "I don't understand."

"I want to be the first woman to do something too. Like Amelia Earhart and Mrs. Roosevelt."

"Mrs. Roosevelt may be the First Lady of the land, but she's not the first to be that."

"But she's different," Kat said, not taking her face from the contraption. "I like different people."

After a moment the old woman said, "Not everyone takes kindly to those who are different."

"Dorothy Thompson does."

"And what does Dorothy Thompson say?"

Kat lowered the stereoscope. "She wrote in the paper that First Ladies don't have to all be the same because presidents aren't all the same. And I agree with her. She doesn't think they should spit on the floor, though, even though some presidents have." Kat returned to the stereoscope.

"How do you feel about that?"

"I don't think anyone should spit on the floor—yuck! ... If Pete Gray does get traded, maybe I can see him next year when the Tigers play the Browns." Kat lowered the stereoscope again and looked at Mrs. Cooper. "Are you gonna vote for President Roosevelt?"

"Phew, it's not easy following your train of thought. First politics, then baseball, then politics again."

"They're a lot alike."

"How's that?" asked Mrs. Cooper.

"They're both American pastimes." Kat giggled, knowing she'd said something funny.

Mrs. Cooper laughed. "You may be right. Who would you vote for?"

"I'd vote for Mrs. Roosevelt."

"I'm with you."

Kat changed the card in the stereoscope and continued, "My papa says we shouldn't change horses in the middle of the stream. I think he means because of the war. That's what the papers say. Besides, Senator Truman is from Missouri, so it's double loyalty. But I'm more interested in who's gonna win the pennant. What are you gonna do with that clipping?"

"I was going to give it to you."

Kat took the stereoscope from her face and set it down on the table. "I don't have a scrapbook, but I could put it up on the wall in my fort. That's where I put all my special things ... I wish you could visit my place once."

Again the old woman felt the child's intensity and was rattled by the kindling of her own emotions, by her passionate response to the youngster. She got up and went to the buzzer to ring for Francis.

"Is that for cookies?" asked Kat.

"Yes, don't you want any?"

"Sure. Can Flowerman stay and have cookies with us?"

"If he'd like to."

When Francis arrived he moved the desk chair to the settee, and Mrs. Cooper seated herself in it across from Francis and Kat, who sat down next to each other on the small couch. After several moments Kat asked in a conspiratorial whisper, "Do you want to know what I did last Sunday?"

Mrs. Cooper and Francis looked at one another, remembering their Sunday.

"I challenged Ralph Quinn to an arm wrestling contest and then fooled him. I was real cagey. I got him to turn over his pocket watch to Betty Lou for the 'get ready, get set, go,' and then I grabbed it quick and held it over the jar . . . Oh, I forgot to tell you, I had this Mason jar of water. I held it over the water and told him to apologize and promise never to bully anyone again, and if he didn't, I'd drop the watch in the water, kerplunk."

Her audience laughed loudly, and Kat giggled. Mrs. Cooper was so tickled she began rocking back and forth in her chair. Then Kat remembered the whole truth of the previous Sunday, and a frown replaced her grin.

Mrs. Cooper saw the sudden change and asked, "Is there something else, Kat?"

"It didn't turn out to be funny," Kat murmured. "I took Ralph's watch home with me as a kind of ransom for the money he owed me. See, he turned over my wagon and ruined all the groceries, so I had to buy more—and then I was out ten dollars. When Mr. Quinn came to our house with Ralph to get the watch, it was real bad. He shouted a lot, saying mean things about Ralph in front of everyone, and Ralph looked sick, and his face was cut."

Mrs. Cooper was following Kat's story closely, and her face became a reflection of Kat's. Francis's forehead creased also.

"Mr. Quinn said he was gonna send Ralph away," Kat continued. Then she looked up at Francis and whispered, "Would you be mad if I asked Ralph to go to the World Series with me?" Francis didn't answer immediately, and Kat tried to determine what his worried expression meant. "I was going to ask you to be my escort, but I'm afraid Ralph will have to go away if—" Something suddenly occurred to her. "Maybe Ralph won't want to go with me, after what happened, but he likes baseball a lot."

Mrs. Cooper's head was bowed. No one saw the tear that fell from her eye. In a voice louder than usual she said, "Kat, I have something for you in the studio," and she started to get up.

Somewhat bewildered, Kat turned to Francis, who said, "I'm glad you're going to ask Ralph. I'll be your relief escort." Then he lowered his voice to a whisper and said, "I think she wants you to follow her."

Kat looked to the door. Mrs. Cooper stood with her hand on the door, her eyes glowing, and said, "Bring Miss Amy Lowell and you can read to me upstairs."

Kat followed the old woman's skirt up the stairs. It waved to and fro slightly as the woman moved slowly upward, sliding her hand along the smooth wood handrail. Kat felt her heart quicken, not from the climb—though it was steep—but from the excitement of this journey and where it would take her. Although she had been in the studio once before, this time she had been asked there—invited to this very private place.

It was afternoon, so the sun didn't pour into the studio as it had the time before, and because her image of the room was of that time, Kat was taken aback by the difference, and in an odd way she felt disappointed.

Mrs. Cooper walked to the easel in the center of the studio under the skylight, where the indirect light from above created a soft-edged spotlight on the canvas and floor. "Come," she said to Kat, and Kat walked to the center of the room into the light.

The canvas with the blue and green splashes which Kat had seen her first time in the studio had changed also. Before Kat was a painting of a baseball diamond with nine players in

Browns' uniforms, and under each cap hung two braids of light hair. It took Kat a second, then suddenly she raised her hands to cover her mouth.

"I remembered what you said about liking all the positions," the old woman said shyly.

"You painted me!"

"Nine times," Mrs. Cooper added, waiting for appraisal from this young critic.

"It's beautiful," Kat said, not disappointing her.

"I watched you from the window and worked on it a little each day." There was still some apprehension in the woman's voice, making her sound young and vulnerable. "It's for you."

Kat ran her fingers over the numbers 1944 and the letters *AD* in the lower left corner.

"Adeline Dupre," explained the old woman. Kat looked up, her eyes large and innocent. "I'm glad you like it."

"I'm in love with it," said Kat, and it was obvious she meant much more than that.

Mrs. Cooper was overwhelmed with joy. Her heart racing, she eased down onto the chair beside the easel while Kat lowered herself onto the floor.

"Were you an artist when you were my age?" asked Kat.

"I don't know."

"I think you were. You were a born artist."

Kat had spoken the words with such conviction that the woman smiled with amusement, then said, "So are you, my sweet."

"Oh, no, I can't do it good at all."

Mrs. Cooper looked at the painting and said, "Whatever position you decide to play, you will be an artist at it . . . It isn't the part but the passion that makes the artist." Saying this—no, owning up to it, to her own passion—was taking a risk, and the old woman knew the price and was frightened, more frightened than she had been in years, in all her years alone.

Kat, aware of the charge in the room, for it energized her, did not, however, understand this. She turned her gaze from the canvas to the painter's chest, and in particular the flat wooden box on top of it. "Is that your paintbox?"

Mrs. Cooper sighed as she put her hand on the smooth lid and opened it. Small tubes of oil paint lay inside the mahogany-stained box.

"Betty Lou has a paintbox that's real nice. Annie gave it to her. Did someone give that to you?"

"I gave it to myself."

"I've never seen one like it."

"It came from Paris."

"Paris, France?"

"*Oui.*"

Kat smiled at the lips and the French word they formed. "How did it get here?"

"Why don't you read me a poem, " Mrs. Cooper suggested.

"Can I take off my sandals? I do better in bare feet."

Mrs. Cooper chuckled, "*Oui, mademoiselle.*"

"You said that like a real French lady." Kat unbuckled her sandals and slipped them off.

"*Tes orteils ressemblent á des petites saucisses.*"

Kat giggled, and Mrs. Cooper translated the words for her: "Your toes look like little sausages."

"Do you talk French a lot? I never heard you before."

"Only to myself . . ." the woman's voice trailed off.

Kat looked down at the book she held, then up at Mrs. Cooper. "I practiced the one that had the ribbon marking it because I figured it must be a favorite of yours."

Mrs. Cooper looked down at the book, interested, then turned her face away, afraid of giving away the feelings that suddenly surged in her. Why had she given Kat the book Thea had given her?

Kat began reciting in her clear voice, and the old woman stared off into the room.

MADONNA OF THE EVENING FLOWERS

All day long I have been working,
Now I am tired.
I call: "Where are you?"
But there is only the oak-tree rustling in the wind.

The house is very quiet,
The sun shines in on your books,
On your scissors and thimble just put down,
But you are not there.
Suddenly I am lonely:
Where are you?
I go about searching.

Then I see you,
Standing under a spire of pale blue larkspur,
With a basket of roses on your arm.
You are cool, like silver,
And you smile.
I think the Canterbury bells are playing little tunes.

You tell me that the peonies need spraying,
That the columbines have overrun all bounds,
That the pyrus japonica should be cut back and rounded.
You tell me these things.
But I look at you, heart of silver,
White heart-flame of polished silver,
Burning beneath the blue steeples of the larkspur,
And I long to kneel instantly at your feet,
While all about us peal the loud, sweet
　　　Te Deum of the Canterbury bells.

Kat looked up from the book and saw that the old woman
was looking at the painting of Thea and that her cheeks were
moist and glistening. She lowered her head and asked in a soft
voice, "Is the madonna Thea?"

A hand reached down and patted Kat on the head. "To me
she is."

"You painted her like the poem."

Mrs. Cooper closed her eyes.

"What happened to her?"

Now it was happening . . . and what next? The gray eyes
looked at the young, inquisitive face. Get hold of yourself,
Addie, the old woman said to herself. She lives in St. Louis. She's
nearly as old as I.

"Does she ever come to visit?"

154

"No."

"Do you?"

Mrs. Cooper teetered getting up, then walked over to the paintings of Thea and said, "We were young then."

"She's so beautiful I want to touch her. Was she your best friend?"

"I loved her very much."

"Don't you still?"

Mrs. Cooper raised a hand and brushed back the fine wisps of white hair that escaped her bun. Then she walked over to the studio bed and sat down. Beginning to sense the old woman's emotional strain, Kat watched with concern and didn't dare to move or say anything more.

"Come here, child, and sit with me," Mrs. Cooper said with restored strength.

Kat climbed onto the studio bed and cuddled up beside the woman. Mrs. Cooper put her arm around the youngster and began to speak. "Thea and I were childhood friends. Our families lived in the French quarter of St. Louis."

"Did Flowerman's family live there too?" It was one of those intuitive guesses that seem to come from out of nowhere.

"Yes. His mother was a friend of ours. Her family was French also; their name was Genet ... When I was eighteen I became an illustrator." Mrs. Cooper hadn't talked to anyone about herself in years, and she felt unexpected pleasure telling Kat about her youth.

"What does an illustrator do?"

"Draws pictures for storybooks."

"What did Thea do?"

"She was an English teacher. She gave me that book of poems when she left St. Louis."

"Why did she leave?"

After a moment Mrs. Cooper answered, "She married a young banker ..." Funny to say "young," she thought, but she'd only seen him when he was young, so he remained so. "And they moved to New York."

"But she lives in St. Louis now?"

"Yes, she returned many years later."

"Did he too?"

"No," the old woman answered but did not explain—did not tell Kat that he killed himself in 1929. "I moved to New York a few years after Thea. I lived in a women's residence in Greenwich Village and worked for a calendar company. While I was in New York I took life drawing classes at New York University. I painted the large picture of Thea then." Remembering those years, she felt young again. "Another artist and I saved all our money, and a couple of years later we sailed to Paris on the *La Savoie.*"

"You went all the way across the ocean?" Kat was enthralled.

"Yes. We lived in a pension on the Left Bank. At night I scribed the menus for a small restaurant on the Boulevard du Montparnasse. They fed me and paid me a small salary. My friend painted theater posters. In the daytime we painted on the streets."

'Why the streets?"

"Ever since the Impressionists were thrown out of the Parisian salons, throngs of young artists have painted on the streets."

"Who were the Impressionists?"

"Monet and Renoir and Cézanne and Degas . . ." Again the woman's voice trailed off in a kind of reverie.

"Were they your friends?"

Mrs. Cooper smiled and patted Kat's arm. "Such great artists! So brilliant, so alive, so gay—like Paris. They painted what their eyes really saw."

"Is that how you paint?"

"Yes, Kat. Can you see that your arm is many colors? It only looks like one color because we are accustomed to blending color in our mind's eye. If you try not to think about it, but truly see it, you will see white and pink and brown."

"I can see it. I can."

"Yes, of course you can. When the Impressionists first painted this way they were insulted, laughed at."

"How long did you live in Paris?"

"Ten years. I returned just before the war but couldn't go back to work as an illustrator."

"Wouldn't they let you?"

"I'd had enough of city life, I suppose, so I moved to Hawthorn, bought this house, and had the skylight put in . . . Now I paint for myself."

"Was that the First World War?"

"Yes."

"Did you know Ira Eisenberg died in that war?"

Mrs. Cooper nodded yes.

"When did you marry Mr. Cooper?"

"I didn't."

Kat was mystified. If she didn't, how could she be Mrs. Cooper?

It was not difficult for the woman to explain. "I took the name thinking people would be more likely to take a room in a widow's house than a maiden lady's."

"Is that allowed?"

Mrs. Cooper cackled, "Yes, it's allowed, if you sign the legal papers."

'I think your real name is pretty. Will you say it again?"

"Adeline Dupre."

Kat said it softly to herself, then asked, "Can I call you by it?"

"You may call me Addie if you'd like."

Looking long into the gray eyes, Kat said in a low whisper, barely audible, "Addie." She took Addie's hand into her own two hands and held it. "Did you ever know someone named Mr. Cooper?"

"Yes," said Addie.

"Did you love him?"

"Heavens no!"

"I think you should have kept your original name then. I'm not going to change my name until I get married and have to. Do you think I will?"

"Most people do," said the old woman, wondering who that young man might be.

"How come you didn't?"

Addie looked down at Kat's turned-up face, and the two regarded one another for several seconds. She could feel the child's eyes on her like a caress, but the caress pained her and she shut her eyes. Kat put her hand lightly on the old woman's cheek. "I'm sorry, Kat. I left you for a moment."

"Are you gonna cry?"

"No, dear heart. I was just thinking about someone."

"It makes you very sad."

"Mmmm."

"Is it because the person you're thinking about went away?"

Addie patted Kat's knee and asked, "Would you like to read me another poem?"

"Yes, but I only practiced the one."

"I have a short one in mind," Addie said cheerfully.

Kat got up and went back to the easel, where she'd left the book of poetry. When she returned with it, Addie opened to "A Sprig of Rosemary," and Kat read:

> I cannot see your face.
> When I think of you,
> It is your hands which I see.
> Your hands
> Sewing,
> Holding a book,
> Resting for a moment on the sill of a window.
> My eyes keep always the sight of your hands,
> But my heart holds the sound of your voice,
> And the soft brightness which is your soul.

When Kat finished, the old woman began humming. As she hummed Kat talked softly to the music. "When Andy went away I was real sad. I keep hoping he'll come home soon. I haven't gotten a letter from him in a long time. He usually writes once or twice a month . . . When I read his letters I can hear the sound of his voice . . . it's been over a month. I think the hardest thing is when someone goes away."

Addie became serene, rocking and humming to herself. Kat placed the book in the woman's lap, then went to the center of the room, took the painting off the easel, and walked back to Addie. Tilting her head, she looked at the old woman, but the woman didn't see her; so she picked up Addie's hand, about to say, "Whenever I look at this picture I'll see your hands," when she changed her mind, laid Addie's hand down gently, and left without disturbing the old woman's dream.

◄§22§► Except for the time she spent doing her chores and paper route, Kat passed the next four days in her tree fort. Gazing at Addie's painting which hung on one wall of the fort, she floated in and out of day-dreams on a wave of fancy. She drew a picture of Jesse on Monday and one of a dazzling bluebird on Tuesday, and on Wednesday she tried to draw Addie. But Kat was frustrated each time because her pictures did not seem, to her, to do their subjects justice. She wrote Andy several letters, pouring out her feelings, but she didn't mail any of them because it was not Andy she wanted to say these things to.

Finally, on Thursday, Kat wrote Addie a letter thanking her for the painting. She began by telling Addie that no other gift had meant as much to her. Carried on a wave of emotion, she wrote several passionate pages comparing Addie to Mrs. Roosevelt and Stan Musial and even Tuesday's bluebird. At last, proclaiming her love, Kat told Addie that she loved her more than she loved—but she stopped herself before the word "anybody" because she suddenly felt disloyal to Jesse and Andy and Mama and Papa and Jesus. She couldn't tell Addie she loved her sixth—never mind that it wasn't true, for she loved her first in that moment—no one wanted to be sixth.

Anyone could see that Kat had fallen in love. But Addie was

more than someone the child had come to love dearly and deeply. Kathleen Howard was growing little green shoots of the artist she would one day be, and Addie was her Muse.

Those same four days Addie rose before dawn, restless to paint, and worked from dawn to dusk in her studio. She was happy thinking about Kat and for the time being not seeing the child. Her time alone was full of reflection as well as outward activity, and the days seemed much too short. The smell of linseed oil in her nostrils when she left her studio at night made her feel light as a child, and the smile she wore on her face all day was on her face in bed as well. It was a sweet joy to be in love. Now that she was not so near the flame, she also delighted in the physical stirrings. When her love for Thea had not been allowed full expression, passion had seemed to die in her, but the irrepressible child had changed all that. Delighted, Addie embraced this last romance.

Friday morning Addie awoke at four and went to her studio. She made tea for herself, then sat before her canvas holding the delicate Limoges cup in her swollen hands, paint pigment in her cuticles and skin creases, while she waited for the sun. From memory she had painted New York's Washington Square arch, a copy of the Arc de Triomphe, and the park beyond it, with students studying under autumnal trees and playing chess and dominoes at small tables. She had meticulously worked and reworked the three central figures: two young women and a man relaxing under a red maple. The man wore dark knee socks up to his navy blue knickers and a sleeveless sweater over his shirt. His head rested on the lap of one of the women, and his cap was pulled down over his face to shield his eyes from the afternoon sun, which angled down on the three. The woman who held his head wore a long, white dirndl dress. Her dark hair was caught back in a barrette, and her eyes were lowered on the book she held in one graceful hand. The other woman, seated beside the couple, was nearly obscured by the easel before her. Only her face was clearly visible, turned toward the dark-haired woman.

With the first light of dawn, Addie began to put the finishing touches on the canvas. By ten o'clock the painting was finished, and she was so tired she couldn't imagine how she would get down the stairs and to bed to rest. When she'd managed this, she rang for Francis and asked him to send Kat to her before she left for the day.

By the time Kat arrived Addie had taken a bath and was sitting on the chair next to her bed. Kat entered from the sitting room on tiptoe. She looked shyly at the unmade bed, then at Addie, who seemed small and frail in her apple-green chenille robe—and old, except for her gray eyes, which seemed brighter than usual.

The old woman spoke in a whisper. "My sweet, will you make my bed for me? I cannot do it for myself today."

Kat nodded and went to a small commode near the door to the hallway and returned with clean linen for the bed. The sheets smelled of lavender, and Kat was tempted to put her face in them to breathe in the soft fragance, but knew that would be a strange thing to do with someone watching.

The old woman gazed wide-eyed at the youngster making the bed, wishing the child would not hurry so. Kat wanted to go slowly but felt that would be cheating, and so worked faster than usual.

After the cotton brocade comforter had been tucked into the small, hard bed, the sheet turned back, and the three pillows fluffed and placed neatly at the head, Kat ran her hand lovingly along the soft edge of the sheet. Addie saw the gesture and felt as though her cheek had been touched. She was glad it was the sheet that had received the gentle caress, for had it been her cheek she knew she would have cried, and she didn't want to cry and confuse the child.

"Thank you, my sweet."

"Are you going to go to bed now?" asked Kat as she stepped aside.

"Mmm hmm."

"Are you sick?"

"No, I'm only tired."

"Do you want me to turn it down then? That's what my mama does."

"Yes, please," said Addie, and she stood to take off her robe.

Kat turned down the bedcovers, then looked up at Addie in her buff-colored satin nightgown—her bare shoulders and arms as pale and as delicate as white clover. When Addie leaned toward the bed her satin nightgown clung to her small, round fanny, and Kat turned her eyes away.

Once Addie was comfortably beneath the covers, her eyes closed, Kat turned to go. At the door she paused, then turned and said softly, "Addie?"

The old woman opened her eyes. "Yes, child."

"Good night, sleep tight, don't let the bedbugs bite."

23 David was up, dressed in blue jeans, and crouched under his sink tightening a pipe with his wrench. Hearing the clanking, Francis had gotten up, thrown on a pair of khaki trousers, and combed his hair back off his face with his two hands before knocking on David's door.

"Yeah? Who's there?" David called from under the sink.

"It's me—Francis. What the hell are you doing banging around at eight o'clock in the morning on your wedding day?"

"Come on in."

"My God, you're at that sink again."

"Hell, I couldn't sleep a wink. Damn dripping kept me awake all night."

"You sure it was the sink and not the wedding jitters?"

"For chris'sake, this is just another day."

"Ha! You say!"

"Don't come in here if you're gonna analyze me."

"You've got 'em, all right."

David stuck his head out from under the sink and said, "Beat it!"

Instead, Francis settled down in David's chair.

"Well, that'll have to do it. I can't turn the joint any tighter." David slid out from under the sink but remained on the floor. "What the hell do you care anyway? You won't be sleeping here any more."

"Can't say I'm sorry."

"You and Marjorie leaving today?" Francis asked, turning away from David and looking at the navy blue suit hanging on the dresser and the two suitcases on the floor below it.

"We're staying at Hannibal House tonight and taking the train to St. Louis tomorrow." David slid over to his bed and leaned against it, his head back.

"Sure will miss you around here." It hadn't been the banging that woke Francis. He'd been listening for David, hoping to see him alone before he left for the church. There was no special reason—at least there was nothing in particular he had in mind to ask or tell David. Francis looked around the room, wondering what the next tenant would be like. Marjorie's teaching replacement—a woman—would be moving in the next week, so he and Sol would be the only men in the place. "I'll be cursing you the first time the Eisenbergs' toilet backs up."

"That shouldn't be long," David laughed and looked at Francis.

"I can see you won't feel the least bit guilty."

There was a weariness in Francis's kidding. David turned away, saying, "Hell, no. I'll not miss it for a minute. You should see our apartment in the city. It's small, of course, but new. Built just before the war, and no one's lived in it yet."

"I miss the city," Francis said wistfully.

"It's not the city you miss!" David looked up to see Francis's reaction.

"You're a lost cause, David. You've got no sensitivity at all."

The two regarded one another for several moments before David said, "Been a crazy summer, hasn't it?"

"It's been a good summer, but it's coming to an end." Francis was thinking about Kat now, not David. "You leaving, and before long the kids will be back in school."

"The *kid*, you mean." David was glad to talk about someone else.

"Yeah, I suppose that's what I mean."

"She's going to be the first woman in the majors," said David.

"She told you that too?"

David smiled up at the ceiling. "You were right about her. Do you know she insisted on giving me the money for those groceries?"

"Was it you who bought the second load?"

"Yeah, only she caught me . . . No boy would have done that."

"I'm not sure."

"No, that's why I like women—they've got scruples."

"Well," said Francis, getting up, "I'm glad," and he stuck out his hand and helped David to his feet.

"Thanks." David shook Francis's hand, then said, "Here, you might as well have this," and handed him the wrench. "You're gonna need it."

"Yeah, sure as hell will."

The two stood facing one another. Francis smiled warmly at David, then put his hand to his rough cheek and chin and said, "Well, I better go shave. It's getting late." He turned and left.

David watched Francis walk down the hall, then closed his door, walked over to the pressed suit hanging on the dresser knob, and felt the lapel. Just then the sink pipes gave a bellow, and David laughed out loud.

Marjorie rolled over, reached for the clock beside her, and flicked the alarm button down, having wakened without it. She'd slept fitfully all night and was glad it was morning. But instead of getting up, she lay staring at the ceiling fixture over her head and thought about her father. Mr. Holmes had arrived the day before. When he stepped down from the Union Pacific in his blue seersucker suit he looked drawn. He waved when he saw his daughter, but his smile was thin and his eyes dull. It had been six years, and still Marjorie hadn't gotten used to seeing him without her mother at his side. She hadn't been able to bring herself to mention her mother, and when her father said, "Your mother would be proud of you," she had changed the subject. Marjorie turned and looked at the clock—her father would be waiting. She jumped out of bed, hurriedly brushed her hair and teeth, and put on a sun dress. On her way out, she took a single white rose from the bouquet her father had given her the day before, to give to him for his lapel.

George Howard tiptoed into his daughter's room and over to the window to listen to the birds' pretty prattle. Kat was asleep in her bed, breathing in a slow, even rhythm. She stirred, and George held still, waiting to see if she was waking. She wasn't. He glanced at Kat's bureau and the clean undershirt, panties, slip, and socks folded neatly on top. Janet had laid them out for Kat the night before. Hanging on the doorknob of the closet was Kat's yellow chambray dress with its starched sash. In a year that dress would be not only too small, but too girlish, for his daughter. Kat was growing up fast. Andy would see a big change in her when he returned—and Andy would be changed also.

The small form stirred again, and this time Kat turned over on her stomach with her fanny in the air. How does she sleep that way? George wondered. Kat groaned, and George walked over to the bed.

"Hi, Papa," Kat said sleepily.

"Hi, Kitty Kat."

"Is it time for me to get up?"

"Uh huh."

"Were you watching me sleep?"

"And listening to the birds."

"Where's Mama?"

"Downstairs fixing breakfast." George sat down on the bed. "Do you ever wonder what the birds chirp about?"

Kat rubbed her eyes and said, "They talk to the flowers and the trees."

"I thought I heard them chattering about us."

Amused at the thought of this, Kat smiled broadly, her four front teeth appearing extraordinarily long beside her baby canines. "What did they say?"

"They said, 'Isn't it a shame humans can't soar.' "

"But we can run and they can't." Then, smelling breakfast, Kat added, "And they can't have bacon and eggs."

Laughing, George said, "And they're wrong about you because you do soar."

"Papa, do you think the birds can tell the difference between people?"

George raised his thick eyebrows and sighed, "They've been around longer than us. I suspect they could tell us humans a thing or two."

"Do you know that you've got a big white hair right in the middle of your eyebrow?"

"Time to get up and at 'em."

Kat padded down the hallway to the bathroom to brush her teeth.

Outside the old First Methodist Church, purple zinnias, yellow nasturtiums, white poppies, and wild honeysuckle were arranged in baskets around two poplars whose upper branches met in an arch, their leaves dancing in the sunlight. The church's upright piano had been moved outdoors under a rain tree which provided a natural canopy for Eva Parsons, who sat poised on the piano bench in her blue lace dress.

The wedding guests were seated on folding chairs on the green lawn. George, Janet, and Kat were on the bride's side beside the empty chair reserved for Mr. Holmes. Two schoolteachers and the principal of Jefferson Elementary sat behind the Howards. Betty Lou, her mother, Annie, and her parents sat behind the faculty, and behind those five, in the last row, were

Daniel Brooks and his mother. In the first row on the groom's side were Miss Renee and Francis. The Eisenbergs sat in the second row, with Roy Mulqueen and Judge Lionel Parsons behind them. Compared to the bride's side, the groom's side looked rather gloomy, with Sarah Eisenberg and the men dressed in somber shades of blue and brown. Thank goodness for Miss Renee in a peach chiffon dress, her brilliant red hair done up in a fashionable snood—she was a flame among the dying embers.

At precisely twelve o'clock Reverend Wiley motioned to Eva Parsons from the side, and she raised her wrists high and began the wedding march. Kat put her hands on her chair seat, raised herself up an inch, and watched as David took his place under the poplars. A basket of honeysuckle on the piano attracted a honey bee and Eva Parsons's eye. Eva began twitching her nose and shaking her head this way and that to ward off the insect. Soon her jerking movements caught everyone's attention. Finally, Eva paused, put her hat veil down over her eyes and nose, and began playing again. Reverend Wiley sighed as Eva raised her wrists high and launched into "Here Comes the Bride."

Kat turned around and looked down the aisle. The sight of Marjorie took Kat's breath away. She looked like Snow White. As she walked slowly down the aisle, one hand holding a bouquet of forget-me-nots and the other resting on her father's arm, she nodded to each of the guests and smiled. When she got to Kat's row, she turned instead and looked at David, and Kat's spirits dipped. As Kat watched the backs of the bride and groom and listened to them say their vows, she felt a terrible tugging inside her. It was happening so fast and sounded so final. David put the gold ring on Marjorie's finger and they kissed. Everyone cheered—everyone but Kat, who managed a smile as the wedding couple led the small party of friends across the street to the library green, where tables and chairs were arranged with lanterns and baskets of flowers for the reception. Kat ran and joined her friends.

"Did you see them kiss?" Betty Lou asked Kat as they skipped across the street.

"Of course I saw them kiss. I was there."

"We get to kiss them now."

"What are you talking about?" Annie asked, looking up from her mary-janes to Betty Lou's curls.

"Everyone gets to kiss the bride and groom at the party. My mummy told me."

The thought of kissing Marjorie seized Kat, and she blushed.

It was Daniel Brooks who came running over and announced in one breath that the reception line was forming and everyone was getting in line to take turns kissing the bride and congratulating the groom.

"You look real nice in your suit and tie," Annie complimented him.

Daniel grinned and rocked back on his heels, almost losing his balance.

"Yeah, you're pretty as a picture," Kat added.

"Girls are pretty," corrected Daniel.

"Suit yourself," Kat twinkled, amused at her pun.

Standing in the reception line, Kat watched the women and men kiss Marjorie on the cheek. She heard Marjorie laugh and saw her throw her head back when one of the men complimented her. Kat had seen Marjorie do this in class and had tried, in private, to imitate the coy gesture but had felt foolish, not enchanting.

"Kathleen, you look like a lovely buttercup."

Kat was standing in front of Marjorie now and could feel the heat crawl up the sides of her neck till her ears burned. Marjorie bent down to kiss Kat on the forehead, but her lips didn't touch, or touched so lightly that Kat couldn't feel them.

"Congratulations," Kat blurted as she ran off, embarrassed and disappointed, to join her friends, who were gathered round a large hickory tree.

Daniel folded his handkerchief into a blindfold and tied it around Annie's head, then turned Annie around twice and guided her to the trunk of the old hickory. "Draw a circle on the old man's back, put two eyes and a mouth, and who will put the nose?"

Betty Lou stepped forward and touched her finger in the center of Annie's back.

"Kat," guessed Annie.

"Nope," said Daniel. "You're 'it,' Annie. Count to fifty."

As she began, Daniel scooted off toward the table with the wedding cake and crawled under the tablecloth; Betty Lou found a bench and lay down flat on her belly, hidden from Annie's view; and Kat went to the far corner of the library lot and hid behind the olive-green mailbox.

"Fifty!" hollered Annie. "Here I come, ready or not!" She took off the blindfold and slowly ventured away from the tree in the direction of the benches. Betty Lou peeked her head around the bench and watched Annie approach, then pulled her head in and held her breath. Annie was two yards from Betty Lou when she changed direction and headed away. Betty Lou eased down off the bench and crawled away toward the library. She spotted the mailbox and made a dash for it.

"I've got this place," Kat whispered.

"Kat, I've gotta pee."

"Not here, Betty Lou. Not in my hiding place."

Betty Lou had a pained expression on her face. "I think I'm gonna burst."

"Betty Lou, how come you've always gotta pee when we play hide-and-seek?"

"I don't know," she whimpered.

"The library's open. Go in there."

Betty Lou scurried off, hunched over and holding her belly.

Meanwhile, Annie spotted Daniel's white bucks sticking out from under the tablecloth and tiptoed over to the table to tag him out. As soon as Kat saw this, she crept out from behind the mailbox and made a dash for the hickory, getting there without Annie seeing her and tagging home safe.

When Annie heard Kat call, "Allye, allye, in free," she turned around to see who it was. "Shucks!" she hollered.

Daniel, hearing Annie close to him, crawled out from under the other side of the table to escape. The tablecloth got caught on his head as he scrambled out, and he pulled it along with him. Miss Renee was standing near the table talking to Reverend Wiley when she saw the cake moving out of the corner of her eye. She grabbed for it in time, but the weight of it was more than she could handle and she lost her footing and fell flat on her bottom, squealing. Somehow she'd managed to hold the cake in an upright position, but her arms and lap were covered with white frosting, and one sugar rosebud stuck to the front of her dress like a corsage. All heads turned to her except Daniel's; he was high-tailing it out of there. Reverend Wiley took the cake from Miss Renee and put it safely back on the table while George Howard helped her to her feet. When she saw the state of her dress—sugar-frosted peach chiffon—Miss Renee looked around, trembling. The crowd began applauding and saved her from tears.

Daniel, meanwhile, was hiding behind a tree while his mother hunted him down. Too scared to move, he soon was discovered.

"Daniel Brooks!" his mother cried in a shrill voice and reached for his ear to pull him up. "What were you doing under that table?"

"Hiding from Annie," he said sheepishly.

"Hiding from Annie!"

"We were playing hide-and-seek."

"This is a wedding reception, not a playground."

"I know."

"You don't know. Do you know you almost ruined Marjorie and David's cake?"

"I'm sorry."

Mrs. Brooks lowered her voice to a whisper and said, in no uncertain terms, "You'll be good and sorry when we get home and you pull down your pants for a spanking."

Daniel looked around to see if anyone had heard the scolding he was getting. With the exception of Kat, who had been watching it unfold from home base, everyone's attention was on Miss Renee and the cake.

"You go sit over there," Mrs. Brooks pointed to one of the benches, "and stay put until I'm ready to go home."

Daniel slunk over to the bench and sat with his back to the party, his head against his chest.

"Are you in a lot of trouble?" Kat asked as she stole over to him and sat down.

Daniel concealed his face.

"I'm sorry you're in trouble."

Daniel lifted his head and looked at Kat. His wet cheeks told on him.

"You gotta stay here?"

He nodded.

"I'll sneak you some cake if you want some."

Daniel nodded yes again, and Annie approached the two of them.

"Hey, do you know where Betty Lou's hiding? We've got to find her and tell her the game's over."

"She went to the bathroom," Kat answered. "I'm gonna sneak Brooks some cake and then I'll help ya find her."

Annie stayed with Daniel until Kat returned with a piece of cake. Then the two girls headed for the library, promising Daniel they'd return when they found Betty Lou.

Betty Lou was sitting on the library steps with her arms clasping her knees, her face pinched.

"The game's over," announced Annie.

"How come you're sitting here?" asked Kat.

"I didn't make it in time."

"What do you mean?" asked Annie.

Betty Lou looked up at Annie but couldn't answer.

"I think she peed in her pants," Kat whispered to Annie.

"Is that what you did?" asked Annie.

"Uh huh." Betty Lou hung her head in shame.

"Did you take them off?" asked Kat.

"Uh uh."

"No? You mean you've got on wet pants?"

"Uh huh."

"Well, take them off!" exclaimed Kat.

"I can't."

"Why can't you?"

"I can't go around without pants on."

"Betty Lou, are you sitting on your dress with wet pants?"

Betty Lou showed them her dress was pulled out from under her.

"Well, at least that was smart," Kat said. "Come on, we'll go with you to the ladies' room and you can take them off."

"I can't."

"Betty Lou, don't be a ninny," Annie said impatiently.

"You take off yours, then, and give them to me," Betty Lou challenged.

"I'm not going around without pants on." Annie was not about to be Betty Lou's chump.

"See!" said Betty Lou.

Kat helped her friend up, saying, "Come on, I'll give you mine. I don't care if I've got pants on or not."

The three girls entered the library. Kat and Betty Lou went into a stall together while Annie stood guard by the door.

"What's taking so long?" Annie whispered, bending down and looking under the stall door.

"It's hard taking off wet pants," Betty Lou explained.

The two came out. Betty Lou was holding her wet panties at arm's length.

"Throw them away," said Kat.

"I can't do that."

Kat shook her head and said, "You gonna carry them around with you?"

"What if my mummy finds out they're missing?"

"You can say you left them at my house," said Annie, trying to be helpful.

Just then a woman came in, and Betty Lou threw her panties in the trash bin. The three girls walked out stiffly.

On their way back to the party Betty Lou asked Kat, "What's it feel like walking without pants on?"

"Real cool," said Kat.

"You got guts," said Annie.

"I just hope I remember not to do a cartwheel," Kat giggled.

"Especially not around Brooks," squealed Betty Lou.

"Brooks is being punished."

"How come?" asked Betty Lou.

"Oh, wow," said Kat, "you missed the excitement!" and Annie and she described the near catastrophe.

When the three girls reached Daniel, Kat sat on the bench beside him, and Annie and Betty Lou plopped down on the grass. Betty Lou started to giggle, and Kat gave her the evil eye as a warning.

"What's going on?" asked Daniel, feeling a conspiracy in the air and figuring he was about to be the girls' victim.

"Nothing," said Kat. "Betty Lou's just acting silly."

"Why don't you tell him, Kat?"

"Betty Lou, shut your mouth."

"Tell me what?"

"You asked for it, Betty Lou," said Kat, and she turned to Daniel. "Betty Lou peed in her pants."

"I'm wearing Kat's. She hasn't got any on."

Daniel looked at Kat. "Really?"

"Sure. What's wrong with that?"

"You mean you really don't have on any underpants?" Daniel was delighted but couldn't quite believe it.

"Nope," said Kat, holding her head high.

"Let's see. I don't believe you."

"You think I'm crazy? I'm not showing you my private parts."

"Just real quick. I won't stare. I just want to see if you're telling the truth."

"I'm telling the truth."

"You wouldn't go around without pants on under a dress."

"Yes, she would," said Annie. "Kat'll do anything."

"Show me."

"No. You're in enough trouble. You want me to tell your mama you asked me to show you my crack?"

"Okay, okay," Daniel gave in. "Only, can I ask you something?"

"As long as you don't touch while you're asking."

"Have you got hair by your crack?"

173

"Daniel Brooks!" cried Betty Lou. "You shouldn't talk like that."

"Do you?" Daniel tried again.

"How could I have hair down there if you don't?"

"How do you know I don't?"

"Because I have an older brother and I know."

"I've got one hair," Daniel said proudly.

"Show us," said Betty Lou.

"Not unless Kat shows me."

"Show him, Kat."

"Yeah, I'm from Missouri; I've gotta be shown."

"I'm not showing anybody anything. I'm not interested in Brooks's hair, and if you don't shut up, Betty Lou, I'll take my pants back."

"Did you work at the boardinghouse today?" Annie changed the subject.

"No. I did the grocery shopping yesterday so I wouldn't have to."

"How much longer you gonna work there?" asked Betty Lou.

"Two more weeks."

"That's good."

"Why is it good, Betty Lou?"

"Because two weeks is a short time."

"But I like working there. I'd rather do that than go to school."

Annie's hair was beginning to bristle from the tenor of the exchange. "Miss Holmes looks prettier than ever today. I wonder what our new teacher will be like?"

Betty Lou didn't hear Annie. "That's plain as anything to see, and don't think we don't know that, Kat. You've gotten uppity, and you're no fun anymore."

Kat looked at Betty Lou with steely eyes and said, "I'm interested in people who do something other than curl their hair, and that's what's plain as anything."

"Curling hair doesn't hurt anybody," Betty Lou declared.

Daniel and Annie had turned to look at Betty Lou, then Kat, then Betty Lou, and now rested their eyes on Kat, who chose passive resistance, turning her head away from everyone's glance and saying nothing.

"At least I never did anything bad in my life," continued Betty Lou.

At that, Kat turned sharply, and if looks could kill, Betty Lou would have been deader than a doornail.

"What do you mean, Betty Lou?" asked Daniel.

"Mrs. Cooper did something bad once."

"Like kill someone?" Daniel asked, his interest piqued.

"No, that's a lie!" Kat cried out in defense of Addie. "She couldn't have done anything bad ever."

"How do you know? She wouldn't tell you," said Daniel.

"I know."

"How?"

"Because she reads poetry and paints and sings."

"What does she paint?" asked Annie.

"People . . . She painted a picture of me that's hanging in my fort."

"Can we see it?" asked Betty Lou.

"Maybe."

"When?"

"I said maybe."

"Don't be stingy," Daniel grumbled.

"I'm not. I'll show it to Annie because she didn't say anything mean about Mrs. Cooper."

"I didn't say anything mean," Daniel was quick to correct. "I just asked."

"You were hoping—that's what you were doing. You were hoping she did something bad. You and Betty Lou always want to hear something bad about a person. I don't know why I gave my pants to you, Betty Lou."

Betty Lou began sniffling.

"See what you've done, Kat," said Daniel. "You made Betty Lou cry."

"She's not crying real tears." Kat got up and moved away from Daniel.

"Why'd you do that?"

"I don't want to sit next to someone with wicked thoughts."

"Everyone has wicked thoughts. Annie does, too, only she's quieter's all."

The sides were drawn up. Betty Lou got up and sat on the bench where Kat had been, and Kat sat down on the ground next to Annie.

"Admit it, Annie."

"I don't have wicked thoughts, Brooks."

"You're just saying that 'cause Kat picked you."

"Am not."

"Are too."

At this moment Janet Howard entered the battlegrounds and announced that everyone was gathering under the old hickory to watch Marjorie throw her bouquet. Annie and Kat got up together and started off. Betty Lou and Daniel did likewise; then Daniel remembered he had to stay put, and he threw himself down on the bench. Remembering the spanking he was sure to get, he kicked the dirt and whined, "This is the worst day of my life!"

Standing beside Marjorie before the small gathering, David made a short speech, which was answered with applause. Curiosity got the best of Daniel, and he crept close on his hands and knees, unnoticed by his mother and the others. Then, as Marjorie turned around to toss the bouquet over her shoulder, Daniel stood up, and, wouldn't you know, the bouquet was pitched to him. He dropped it like a hot potato and Kat caught it in time, before it hit the ground. Another round of applause filled the air.

Lost in thought, Kat stared down at the forget-me-nots as the party dispersed around her. She remembered once wishing she could hit a home run for Miss Holmes, but instead she had given her a hand-painted card. It was just as well because Miss Holmes hadn't been interested in the three swings competition at the Fourth of July picnic. Kat had hoped she'd catch the bouquet, but not by default. Nothing between Miss Holmes and her had ever turned out as she'd dreamed it might. Suddenly Kat realized it had gotten very quiet, and she looked up from the bouquet. Miss Holmes was standing nearby, David was well off to the side, and everyone else was heading for home.

"I'm glad it was you who caught it." Marjorie beamed. "I tried to aim it in your direction."

"Me too," murmured Kat.

"Someday you'll wear this dress."

"We never talked about *The Last of the Mohicans,*" Kat said, dispirited.

"Did you finish it?" asked Marjorie. She could see Kat was upset about something but couldn't imagine what it could be.

"Uh huh."

"Did you enjoy it?" Marjorie asked cheerfully.

"Kind of," replied Kat, looking into Marjorie's face. "It's all right. I talked to someone else about it." But in Kat's heart it wasn't all right. If Marjorie could forget that promise, she could forget another—the promise not to forget Kat.

"I'm glad, Kathleen. If you keep up your good work you'll be a fine teacher one day . . . Good luck."

Kat couldn't look at Marjorie any longer. She didn't want to be a teacher and she didn't want to see Marjorie go away. She could tell Marjorie was pulling away by the way she had said good luck. "Good luck to you too. Bye."

"Good-bye, Kathleen." Marjorie touched the top of Kat's head lightly, then walked over to David.

Kat swallowed deliberately. When she was certain Marjorie and David would be out of sight, she turned and walked swiftly home, hoping no one would notice her along the way. When she reached her driveway she slowed down, and the tears began running down her cheeks. She sat at the back door, the forget-me-nots grasped in both her hands, and watched some ants crawling along the step. Then she stood up, went inside, and put the bouquet in the ice box.

Janet heard the screen door slam and knew Kat was home. "Kat, you downstairs?"

"Yes, Mama."

"Better come up and change your clothes."

"Yes, Mama." When she got to her mother's room Kat asked, "Where's Papa?"

"Next door. Norma delivered her kittens while we were at the wedding."

Without a word Kat dashed into her room, threw off her dress, jumped into a pair of shorts, and tore down the stairs and out the back door, which once again slammed behind her.

"He's in the cellar, Kat," Mrs. Bennett directed, catching her screen door before it slammed shut. "Be quiet when you go down there so you don't frighten Norma."

Kat tiptoed down the dark stairs to the cool cellar. She called out softly, "Papa, where are you? I can't see anything."

"Over here, Kat," George answered. "Not too close now."

As Kat approached her father her eyes adjusted to the dark, and she could see Norma and her clowder in a cardboard dress box. "Oh, Papa, they're so tiny!"

"I think Norma was about to sacrifice one of them."

"What do you mean?"

"When a mother cat sees one of her babies is too weak to survive, she'll reject it."

Kat's full attention was on Norma, who was nursing the tiny kittens. "Did you do something to stop her?"

"I think it's okay now."

"Which one was she gonna sacrifice?"

"The smallest one." Norma was a tiger. Three of her five kittens were tigers, the fourth was a black-and-white, and the runt was all white.

"It looks just like Jesse. You've got to save that one."

"I'm doing all I can."

"Can you tell if it's a boy or a girl?"

"Too small, but let's hope it's a girl. Girls are stronger at birth."

"They don't look like kittens. They look like little mice." Kat got down on her stomach on the cool cement floor. "Can I pet Norma?"

"No, Kat. She almost scratched my eyes out when I was working on the littlest one."

"You should've told her you're a doctor."

"She'd have told me to mind my own business." Just then one of the blind little tigers got pushed off his mother, and Norma returned it to her with her rough tongue. "We'd better let her be now."

"She won't sacrifice the littlest one when we leave, will she?"

"I don't think so."

"You've gotta know so, Papa, else I'm not going."

"Oh, yes, you are," George coaxed softly.

"Can I come back a little later, after I do my paper route, and check just to make sure?"

"You can come back with me in the morning, before church."

"That's too far away. The little one could be sacrificed by then."

"Let's go." George patted his daughter's arm.

Kat leaned over the dress box and whispered to Norma, "Jesse was pitiful when he was a baby, but he turned out to be a real nice cat, didn't he? And Pip's gonna be too—you can believe me."

George took his daughter's hand, and the two found their way out of the cellar.

"What did you mean by 'Pip'?" George asked.

"It's short for Pipsqueak, Papa."

◄§ 24 ຮ► T he next morning when Kat returned home from her paper route she and her father looked in on Norma and her brood. George was disturbed by the listlessness of the runt and sent Kat home with the message that he would not be joining his wife and daughter for church. On her way into the house with her message Kat determined she would stay home also. Her mother was of another mind.

"No, Kat, you may not stay home from church."

"I've already been to church once this week. Isn't that enough?"

"No, and don't fight me on this."

Kat pinched the skin around a festering splinter in her hand and said, "I've gotta stay and help Papa."

"He doesn't need your help," said Janet, taking her daughter's hand and removing the splinter from the sore finger. "Go on now and get dressed."

Kat tugged on her tee shirt. "If I leave, Norma may sacrifice Pip." Janet didn't look up. "Mama, it's important!"

"Going to church is important."

"Not so much," Kat said obstinately as she thrust her hands into the pockets of her shorts.

Janet turned and glared at her daughter. "I don't know what gets into you sometimes. You are not going to spend the morning in the Bennetts' cellar. You are going to church."

"No, I'm not!" Kat cried as she ran out of the room and down the stairs.

"Kathleen Howard, come back here this minute!"

Kat was out the back door, slamming it hard, and up the oak tree.

Her mother followed after her. Standing below the fort, Janet hollered up, "Kathleen Howard, get yourself down here!"

Kat pulled the rope ladder in, then sat with her arms crossed stubbornly in front of her.

"I'm asking you one more time to come down here." When Kat didn't, Janet stalked off toward the garage and returned with a ten-foot extension ladder, which she propped up against the tree and mounted in her spectator heels.

"You can't come in here," Kat said when she saw her mother's angry face staring at her from the doorway of her fort. "This is my place!"

Janet crawled in on all fours and sat down across from her daughter. "If you think I wouldn't tear this place down, board by board, before I would allow you to bar me from it, you are sadly mistaken, young lady."

Kat was astonished at her mother climbing up and into her fort, then sitting there cross-legged in her dress and high heels. "How did you get up here?" she asked.

"Look for yourself."

Kat leaned out of the fort and saw the wooden ladder leaning against the tree trunk.

"You're such a miss smarty pants you don't give others credit."

Intimidated by her mother's resourcefulness, Kat slumped down in a corner of the fort.

"The world does not revolve around you, Kathleen Howard."

"You don't care what happens."

"You dare say such a thing?"

"It's true," Kat whimpered, though she knew better.

"Look at me, Kat. Your father and I have given you a great deal of liberty, which you have taken badly for granted."

"If you saw Pip you'd understand better."

"I understand you ache for that little kitten. That does not excuse your behavior toward me."

"You were gonna make me go to church."

"Yes. I'm your mother. When you were three I made you eat your vegetables."

"That's not the same."

"I recall that it was—you spit out your vegetables."

"Did you get mad at me?" Kat asked in a quiet voice.

"Yes. I once took a mouthful and spit them back at you."

Kat couldn't keep from smiling at the thought of her mother doing such a thing.

"I was exasperated with you . . . like now."

"How did you carry that ladder all the way here from the garage?"

"You're not the only determined spirit in this family," Janet declared.

"Are we gonna go to church now?" Kat asked.

"It's too late now."

"Are you real mad at me for making you miss it?"

"I'm more upset with you for going beyond your bounds. If that kind of behavior continues, you'll lose some of your privileges."

Kat bowed her head.

"And this fort was not built as a hiding place for naughty children. Hiding is no escape, Kat. Only a very young child believes things go away when she covers her eyes."

"I know."

"Now, let's see how you manage to get the ladder back to the garage."

"Can I go see Pip after I do that?"

"You may go see the kitten at noon, when you would have had you gone to church. And before you do that, find the commandments in the Bible and read the fifth."

As Janet backed out of the fort, Kat said, "It's real nice up here, isn't it?"

Janet looked up at the sky through the tree branches overhead. "The closest thing to heaven," she replied, then descended the ladder with Kat close behind.

Janet went inside and watched her child from the kitchen window. Finding the ladder too heavy to drag, Kat pulled her Red Flyer to the backyard and tried to lift the ladder onto it. After several unsuccessful attempts, she sat in the wagon and thought over her dilemma. Janet watched Kat struggle from inside the house.

Finally Kat managed to turn the cumbersome ladder on its side and began straddling it and urging it forward. It took her nearly half an hour to inch it back to the garage. When Kat returned to the backyard and glanced up at her tree fort, she saw she had forgotten to throw down the rope ladder; so she trudged back to the garage, Jesse in tow, and inched the ladder back to the fort. Janet had watched enough. She went out to help her daughter.

Kat looked up at her mother, humiliated. "I can't do anything right today."

"Don't lose heart, Kat. The day isn't over yet."

As George passed through the side hedge he saw Janet supporting the foot of the ladder for Kat, who was standing on the top rung reaching for the rope ladder. "What are you two up to? Didn't you go to church?"

"No, Papa, we went to heaven instead."

"What are you doing with that old ladder?"

"How do you suppose we got to heaven?" Janet asked.

George shook his head.

Kat climbed down to the ground. "Aren't you gonna ask what it was like?"

"It wasn't at all what you'd expect," Janet grinned, suppressing a giggle.

George looked from his wife to his child. "All right, tell me."

An impish grin on her face, Kat announced, "God is a woman!"

Janet gave a hoot, and George turned to her and said smugly, "I knew that."

Kat fell to the ground laughing, and her father reached down and gave her a playful tussle.

"How's Pip?" Kat asked when she'd caught her breath.

"Pip's doing just fine . . . purring like a little motor."

"Can I go see?"

"Don't you have something to do first?" her mother reminded.

Kat leaped up and ran into the house to find the Bible.

Addie had painted that Sunday morning. Flares of red, streaks of orange, and swirls of yellow. The canvas was a jolt of color, sunlight in a bleeding sky. It was wild and glorious. She had felt her genius and with lightning-like brushstrokes had given way to it till her brilliance gleamed back at her. Then, as often in passionate love, she'd had to retreat to keep from burning up in the flame.

Hours later, Addie sat in her chair by the window and read. Remnants of orange paint clung to the cuticle of the forefinger she held on the book before her. As she read, her finger moved down the right side of the poem:

The branches of the trees lie in layers
Above and behind each other,
And the sun strikes on the outstanding leaves
And turns them white,
And they dance like a spatter of pebbles
Against a green wall.

The trees make a solid path leading up in the air.
It looks as though I could walk upon it
If I only had courage to step out of the window.

She repeated the last line of the poem several times, then raised her head and looked out the window. The sun, bright on her face, made her skin look young, her eyes blue and translucent, and her white hair glisten like snow on a clear winter's day. She remained with her eyes opened wide, waiting. When she heard a soft rap on her door, she turned with a smile to welcome her guest.

Kat stepped into the room and stood at a distance, with her arms behind her holding onto something. When the old woman beckoned to her, Kat moved forward. Standing before Addie, Kat brought her arm around and offered the bouquet of forget-me-nots. The old woman caught her breath, then lifted her hand to accept the child's gift. Overcome with emotion, Addie looked down at the flowers, thinking, you're a crazy old woman; you didn't imagine such a thing and you don't know how to behave. Kat stood motionless, her heart trembling inside her. The old woman raised her eyes and looked into the child's, and a tear fell. She rose, walked slowly to the victrola, lifted the needle and placed it on the black disc, then walked slowly back to Kat. The Irish tenor voice of John McCormick filled the room.

Kat lifted her arms, and the two began waltzing, taking easy, deliberate steps. Soon they were dancing in perfect rhythm to the music:

We have been gay
Going our way
Life has been beautiful
We have been young;

> After you've gone
> Life will go on
> Like an old song,
> We have sung.
>
> When I grow too old to dream
> I'll have you to remember.
> When I grow too old to dream,
> Your love will live in my heart—
> So kiss me, my sweet—
> And so let us part—
> And when I grow too old to dream,
> That kiss will live in my heart—

As they twirled, the bouquet in their joint grasp, the fawn hair of the young one and the white hair and long skirt of the old one swayed as these things do in a gentle breeze. Kat opened her mouth and began to sing in her child's soprano voice, and the old woman joined her in a deeper voice:

> After you've gone
> Life will go on
> Time will be tenderly melting our tears;
> Yet will I find
> You in my mind
> Beckoning over the years.
>
> When I grow too old to dream
> I'll have you to remember.
> When I grow too old to dream,
> Your love will live in my heart—
> So kiss me, my sweet—
> And so let us part—
> And when I grow too old to dream,
> That kiss will live in my heart—

When the music stopped, the two stood still. Looking up with unwavering eyes at Addie, Kat asked, "Will you go for a walk with me next Sunday?"

"Yes," Addie answered, holding onto the child's gaze and smiling radiantly.

Kat lay on her back on the
roof of her fort, gazing up at a clump of oak leaves which looked
like the face of the wind she'd seen personified in storybooks.
The warm breeze blowing across her body was the wind's breath.
To Kat, there was no feeling in the world as wonderful as the
wind, and, as she lay resting, she imagined she heard Andy calling to her.

"Hello, Kat, I'm up here!"

"Hi, Raggedy Andy," she answered. "What are you doing in
the tree?"

"Taking a look at the world."

"It's the best place for that— Oh, Andy, there's so much to tell
you. Marjorie and David got married." Kat noticed what sharp
elbows Andy had as he leaned back against the branch above her,
cradling the back of his head in his hands. "Last Sunday when I
went to the station—Ralph Quinn's working there now—the
train for St. Louis was just pulling out, and I saw David and
Marjorie on the other side of the window. I waved good-bye to
them, but they didn't see me. And something else, I asked Ralph
Quinn to go to the World Series with me. I can't say for sure,
but I think he was glad. He tries real hard not to show how he
feels . . . You remind me of something, in the tree like you are.
Mama told me about the time you trapped Mr. Quinn. That was
real brave, Andy. I would have done it, too, but I would have
been real scared . . . Do people actually shoot at you in the war?"

Andy was looking up at the sky and didn't say yes or no.

"Norma is a mama now, and one of her baby kittens looks
just like Jesse. I named her Pip, and Mrs. Bennett says when
she's weaned she can come live with us. And Papa says when Pip
is old enough to be a mama, she and Jesse will have kittens.
Won't that be something?"

Andy looked down and smiled, and Kat saw the separation
between his two front teeth.

"And guess what else? Mrs. Cooper and I are going on a picnic today, and I got to decide what we're gonna eat."

Andy climbed to a higher branch and was almost out of Kat's sight.

"Don't go too far away," Kat called, her voice wavering. To keep Andy's interest she said, "Mrs. Cooper's real name is Adeline Dupre, and she lived in New York and Paris, and she's an artist . . . Andy, don't go so far up 'cause I can't see you. Andy, are you still there? Why haven't you written?"

The only answer was a rustle of leaves, and Jesse leaped down from a limb overhead, startling Kat. When Kat looked up at the clump of oak leaves again, neither the wind nor her brother was there. As Jesse purred in her arms she imagined Addie, whom she was sure to see soon.

Francis was waiting on the porch swing when Kat and Jesse arrived at the boardinghouse later that morning.

"I brought my wagon," Kat called out excitedly, "just in case we need it."

"Great. I'll go help Addie while you see Miss Parsons. She's got our picnic lunch all set in the kitchen. We'll put it in the wagon with a blanket and Addie's paints."

Kat left Jesse in the Red Flyer and ran inside while Francis went upstairs.

Minutes later, Francis entered the sitting room with Addie on his arm. The Eisenbergs, Miss Renee, Eva Parsons, and Kat were there to receive them. Addie nodded to each, raising an eyebrow at Sarah, who was gawking at her. "Paris has been liberated!" Addie celebrated with a smile. The *Post-Dispatch* headlines had announced the news that morning. Taking Kat's hand in hers, Addie said "Good day" to her boarders and turned to go.

Of them, Eva Parsons was the least surprised at what she was seeing. During the past two months she had quietly observed the child's influence. Floorboards seemed to talk back as Kat pranced from room to room and window curtains to giggle as she ran past them; furniture, wall hangings, and flower vases had been rearranged to suit Kat's eye. Even the turquoise kitchen clock had been moved to another wall, away from the windows, because Kat said that the sun shining in your eyes made it impossible to read the time. Slow to adjust to this change, Eva continued to look between the windows for the hour and was amused each time she did so.

Francis helped Addie off the porch. As the three began walking down Steuben Place, Addie on Francis's arm and Kat beside her pulling the Red Flyer with Jesse as passenger, the Eisenbergs, Miss Renee, and Eva Parsons watched from the porch. As soon as the three turned the corner onto Christopher Street and were out of sight, Miss Renee ran off to describe the scene to everyone in town who would listen to her.

The formal entrance to Defoe Park was through an arched, wrought-iron gate overgrown with ivy that obscured all but the letters *ARK*. Addie paused under the arch and breathed in the summer air. Francis and Kat looked at her. She lifted her back, then her neck, and finally her head, like the frond of a fern unfolding. She stretched her arms out wide and grabbed handfuls of air, then chuckled to herself. When she was aware their eyes were on her she said, "Well, what are we waiting for? Show me the buttercups."

"They're over there," pointed Francis. Off in the distance the west meadow was sprinkled with yellow.

Kat bent down and took off her sandals. Addie watched for a moment, then lowered herself onto the red wagon and unlaced her fine black calfskin shoes and removed them. Next she lifted her long skirt above her knees and released her cotton lisle stockings from the pale pink snuggy she wore, and rolled the fine black hose down off her legs and feet. Francis turned his eyes away. After putting her hose and her shoes in the wagon, she stood up and curled her bare toes in the grass and took Francis's arm once again.

When they reached a large maple, Francis took the blanket from the wagon, careful not to touch Addie's hose, and spread it under the tree. He and Addie sat down together while Kat ran off to the open meadow with Jesse and performed a cartwheel and somersault.

Addie patted Francis's leg beside her, then clapped her hands together as Kat managed a straight and sturdy headstand.

"How did she do it?" Francis asked, still finding it hard to believe that Addie was out-of-doors.

"Do what?" Addie asked, distracted.

"This picnic? You?"

Addie didn't answer his question. Instead, lines from a poem by Amy Lowell came to her, and she recited them from memory:

> You are like the stem
> Of a young beech-tree,
> Straight and swaying,
> Breaking out in golden leaves.
> Your walk is like the blowing of a beech-tree
> On a hill.
> Your voice is like leaves
> Softly struck upon by South wind.
> Your shadow is no shadow, but a scattered sunshine;
> And at night you pull the sky down to you
> And hood yourself in stars.
> But I am like a great oak under a cloudy sky,
> Watching a stripling beech grow up at my feet.

Just then Jesse came running toward the maple and began attacking some imaginary form on the blanket. As Addie was petting Jesse and talking to Francis, Kat dropped to her stomach, some distance from them, and peered at the blades of grass. Before her very eyes a caterpillar wriggled and squirmed out of his old skin, and she leaped to her feet and hurried to the maple to tell Francis and Addie what she'd witnessed. As she approached them she heard Addie mention the name "Homer" and asked her, "Is that the one who wrote those long poems?"

"Greek epics," said Francis.

"Yes, darling, that's who Homer, my cat, was named after."

"How come you don't have him anymore?"

"He died years ago, Kat."

"Did you bury him someplace nice?" Kat asked as she plopped down on the blanket.

"Yes, I did. I wrapped him in a towel and took him to Washington Square Park just before dawn, and dug a shallow grave at the base of a chestnut tree between the exposed roots."

"Like a nest in the ground."

"Just like that, Kat."

"Were you real sad?"

"Yes, dear heart, I was. So I stayed and watched the sun come up."

"I'm the same way about the sun."

Francis rose and excused himself, saying, "I think I'll wander over to the flowerbeds."

"Very well, Francis. We'll have our picnic when you return."

"Are you gonna paint now?" Kat asked Addie.

"Perhaps after lunch. I'm still gathering."

A sudden movement caught their attention. A gray squirrel ran down a tree in a circle of beech that stood in the middle of the meadow like children playing ring around the rosie. Once down the tree, the squirrel took a beechnut in his mouth and ran back up. Addie winked at Kat, then leaned back against the trunk of the maple and listened to the leaves rustle overhead. A chipmunk darted out of his burrow several yards off, and Kat pointed to it. With the hip-hip of a woodthrush Kat remembered what Addie had said about taking his song into her heart, and she looked into the old woman's eyes to see if Addie was doing this. Just then a jay screeched, and Kat and Addie laughed out loud.

Spotting Francis across the meadow, Addie asked, "Would you like to hear a cute story?"

Kat sat up, attentive.

"When Francis was five, his mother brought him to my house and left him with me while she went out. Poor devil was so shy he went and hid behind my sofa when his mother left. I let him be, thinking he'd come out when he was ready. Well, he fell asleep in back of the sofa, all curled up like Jesse is right now. After a while I tiptoed around, picked him up, and held him in my lap while I rocked in my rocker. When he stirred awake, I closed my eyes and pretended to be asleep. He crawled down from my lap, got his teddy bear, brought it over to me, and put it in my lap. Moments later I heard him chattering away in the kitchen, and I went to see what he was up to. There he was, sitting at the table talking to an imaginary playmate he called Dooder. When I asked if Dooder was a little boy, he said no—and no again when I asked if Dooder was a girl. Then, very matter-of-factly, Francis explained that Dooder looked like a potato chip. I laughed just as you're laughing now, but Francis was serious—and upset with me for laughing. I apologized, but I'm not certain he's ever really forgiven me."

A much older Francis poked his head around the maple and asked, "What's so darn funny?"

"Good heavens!" Addie cried with a start. "You nearly scared the daylights out of me!"

"Addie was telling me about Dooder," Kat volunteered.

"Oh, she was, was she?" Francis walked out from behind the tree. "Did she tell you he resembled a potato chip?"

"Yep!"

"Don't pay any attention to her, Kat. She's a crazy old lady." Addie winked at Kat, and Francis knelt down on the blanket and set about unpacking the sandwiches, fruit, and cookies, and the port wine he'd brought along for himself and Addie. "I've got a better story for you, Kat."

Addie judged by his manner that he was up to no good. "Let's have our lunch first."

Francis paid no attention to Addie's suggestion and began: "Years ago Addie worked for Cooper Publishing in St. Louis—"

"Hold your horses, Francis. If you're fixing to tell that story you best consider your audience."

"Fair's fair," he said.

"Don't be smug, young man," Addie chastised him.

Sensing no real threat in her voice, Francis said, "If I don't tell it now, I'll tell it later when you're not around."

"Well, if you must . . ."

Kat's interest was piqued, and she was glad Francis had won. Francis passed around the sandwiches and began again. "Mr. Cooper had a son Addie's age who also worked for the firm."

"Not my age! Calvin was more than five years older. It's a

191

good thing you *are* telling this in front of me."

"Calvin Cooper was married, Kat, but apparently he hadn't lost any interest in other women."

"Apparently?" scoffed Addie. "Calvin wasn't that discreet. Everyone knew he was unfaithful and that I was not one of his doxies."

"I didn't say you were, but Calvin certainly was taken with you. Probably because she paid him so little attention," Francis added, winking at Kat, who was devouring his every word.

"Is that the Cooper whose name you took?" Kat asked Addie.

"Cooper is a very common name, Kat. Go on with your story, Francis . . . now that you've opened that can of worms."

"One day Calvin sent a messenger to the art room with a note asking Addie to come to his office immediately and to bring a needle and thread."

"I don't know whether women nowadays carry a needle and thread on their person, but we always did back then."

"Addie went to his office, and when she entered, Calvin told her to close the door and have a seat." Francis opened the bottle of port and poured himself and Addie a glass before going on with the story. "When she was seated in Calvin's office he produced two buttons and explained that they were from the fly of his pants and that he wanted Addie to sew them on for him. Addie agreed to do that for Calvin and asked him to step out of his trousers in the other room and hand them to her. But Calvin said he couldn't step out of his trousers because someone might come in or he might be called out."

"Probably cut the buttons off himself, just so . . . never mind. Go on, Francis."

"Addie knew Calvin would do just about anything to have his way with her, so she finally agreed to sew on his buttons as he wished if he would do her a favor."

"I wanted to illustrate a book on the pony express, and he'd been fighting me on it for weeks. At that time the women artists in the company illustrated only children's books."

Francis took a swallow of wine and continued his story. "Calvin agreed to the deal, and as soon as Addie had his promise in writing, she took out her needle and thread." Francis paused to take a bite of sandwich. "Are all the sandwiches peanut butter?" he asked Kat.

"Yep. What happened next, Flowerman?"

Up till this point Addie had been amused by the storytelling. Now she wondered what had ever possessed her to share the story with Francis, and how much of it he intended to relate to Kat. Would he use good judgment?

"Now, you've got to picture this, Kat," Francis went on.

"Francis! This is a child sitting here!"

"It's all right," Kat assured her. "I'm a grown-up child."

"Nonetheless . . ." Addie said with a stern look.

Francis heeded her warning and continued, "While sewing on the buttons Addie had an idea of how she could get even with Calvin."

"Yes! Yes!" Kat cried. "What did she do?"

"After I sewed on the buttons I stitched the flap of his fly closed, and he hadn't a notion of it."

Tickled silly, Kat fell over on the blanket.

"About an hour later," Francis went on, "Calvin stormed into the art room boiling mad, marched over to Addie's table, and whispered through his teeth, 'Miss Dupre, I can't go to the toilet.' Addie looked up from her work and said, loud enough for everyone in the room to hear, 'I'm sorry, sir, perhaps you should see a doctor.' Then, before going back to her work, she added, 'Sir, maybe you also should learn to sew.' This infuriated Calvin and he told her she was fired, but instead of getting excited, Addie said calmly, 'I'm sorry to hear that, sir. I hope you'll be able to explain how it is I got your trouser buttons,' and she pointed to his two black buttons on the front of her blouse. The other illustrators in the art room were laughing by this time. Calvin, madder than Cain, grabbed Addie's scissors off her desk to cut open his fly, saw her two pearl buttons sewn to his trousers, and stormed out of the room."

"Oh, wow! You sure outsmarted him!" exclaimed Kat.

"Cooked my own goose. I lost the pony express assignment."

"But he promised you in writing," Kat protested.

"That piece of paper was as worthless as a Confederate dollar," Addie laughed, making a move to get up. With the support of the tree trunk she managed on her own, then waved to the two on the blanket and wandered off into the meadow.

Kat rolled onto her stomach, her chin in her hands, and watched Addie. Never before had she seen the woman at a distance. She was stately, walking with her shoulders back and her head held high. Her long skirt billowed as she crossed the meadow.

"I wonder why she waited until now to come out?" Francis pondered aloud.

"I only invited her last week," Kat answered.

Francis looked at Kat, impressed. That *was* the answer, he realized. Until then no one had invited her. The townfolk ridiculed Addie for being a recluse, but had any of them truly welcomed her into their lives?

A half hour later Addie came back into view. She was too far away for Kat or Francis to tell whom she was motioning for, but Kat jumped up and hurried to her.

Addie held out a bunch of wild sweet williams she'd picked. "Let's go for a little walk, just you and me."

Addie's hand felt dry and warm, and Kat wished she could live in that moment forever.

"You liked Francis's story, didn't you?"

"He was real funny telling it, and so were you. Every time he got to a juicy part your eyes got real big."

"I was afraid he'd shock you, but I guess you're shockproof now." Addie gave Kat's hand a squeeze.

After a long moment Kat asked in a tentative voice, "Do you ever get scared?"

"Oh, yes, often."

"What kind of things scare you?"

Addie hesitated before answering, "My mother."

"Is she still living?"

"Inside me."

"Why does she scare your insides?"

"I remember an occasional cross word or disappointed look."

"I thought only kids were scared of their mothers."

"We're always children, even when there's no one alive who remembers us as such, because we remember." By then the two had reached a flowerbed, and Addie noticed dried leaves that had been pinched off and piled to the side to be gathered up later. "Look there, Flowerman has been here."

"Do you know what scares me?" Kat asked, looking away.

Addie turned her eyes to Kat. "What, child?"

Kat's voice trembled as she said, "Andy. I don't think he's coming home . . . ever."

Addie put her arm around Kat, saying, "It's possible he may not." She could feel the child's body shudder. "I've said good-bye to many people in my lifetime. Some were sudden . . . and some were long good-byes, lasting years. Either way, it's very hard."

"I don't know what I'll do if he doesn't."

"When the time comes you will know."

"But it presses down on me so."

Addie bent down to Kat. "Ah, yes, I know that feeling. Life is hard, on all creatures, but it seems to me we suffer the most. Perhaps that's because we forget the real business of life is to enjoy it. The birds know that, and our little gray squirrel . . . When I paint, I am like them."

Addie felt her knees about to cave in on her, so she stood up, biting her lower lip as she did. What to do for this suffering child? she thought. I offer her words, but words are small comfort. Kat put her hand in Addie's, and they started back to their picnic. "I think I've failed you," Addie confessed to Kat.

"Uh uh, you gave me flowers."

Addie let go of Kat's hand once again and put her arm around her, thinking, no one knows the sweet salvation of a child better than an old woman. "Kat, do you know the color of those blossoms?"

What a silly question, thought Kat, as she answered, "Red."

"But not the red of a fire engine or your wagon. They're cerise. A touch of nobility in the flame . . . and that, my passionflower, is why I picked them for you."

195

Kat and Addie were nearing the old maple. When Francis saw them approaching, he pulled the blanket out in the open and set up the easel. While he lazed in the afternoon sun, Addie painted and Kat stroked Jesse.

"What kind of wood is your paintbox made out of?" Kat asked.

"Cherry."

"Do cherries grow on the same tree that that wood came from?"

Francis lifted his head off the blanket and said, "Yes," then lay down again. What an odd thing not to know, he thought. But the mind's like that, he mused. It skips over things, missing this and catching that, often grasping something complex before understanding something elementary. While Francis amused himself with his own thoughts, Addie conversed with Kat.

"There are several kinds of cherry trees, Kat. The one you're most likely to come upon is a wild black cherry. It grows very tall and as wide as you are long."

"Are there any around here?"

"Yes, there probably are, though I don't recall one offhand. Francis, is there a cherry tree in Hawthorn?"

"What?" Francis asked, startled at the sound of his name. Addie repeated herself, and he replied, "There's one behind the Catholic rectory. I'll point it out on our way home."

Kat touched the top of Addie's paintbox and said, "It's real smooth, like the inside of my baseball mitt."

"Mmm, and it's a fine hard wood. Excellent for furniture and cabinets because it doesn't warp or split."

"Why did you say you're like the birds when you paint?"

"The birds celebrate life singing and I paint. It's doing what we mean to do with our full force."

"I like to paint, but I'm not any good at it."

"Why don't you show me?"

"Maybe I'll do a real painting for you sometime. And I know just what I'll do too ... Are your toes cold? They look kinda blue."

"Do you think I should put on my shoes?"

"I'll put them on for you while you paint." As Kat laced up the first shoe she realized she'd forgotten Addie's stockings. "You don't need your stockings, just your shoes," she said. "Do you want me to read to you while you paint?"

"That would be nice, wouldn't it, Francis?"

"What?" Francis asked, startled again.

"Enjoy your reverie, Francis," Addie laughed. "Kat's going to read to us from Amy Lowell."

Kat read several poems. When she grew tired, she closed the book, lay beside Addie, and did something Jesse often did. She reached out her arm until she could feel Addie's skirt, and then, and only then, she closed her eyes.

Addie was painting for recreation. It was impossible for her to paint in earnest when she was with other people. But she was delighted to sit there and mix the colors and dabble on the canvas while Francis and Kat lay restfully at her side. Before long, however, she became chilled and a bit cramped and woke her companions. Francis packed up the wagon, and Kat put the leash on Jesse.

As they walked toward the wrought-iron gate, the August sun was sinking in a sky brushed with clouds. Before leaving the park, Addie turned and looked back, sighing. Francis took the picnic basket from the Red Flyer and handed it to Kat, so that Addie, weary from the outing, could ride home in the wagon. As he pulled the Red Flyer, Addie sat with her two legs dangling over the end and Jesse James asleep on her lap.

The trio turned onto Steuben Place and headed toward the boardinghouse. Francis was the first to spot the dozen or so people standing on the courthouse lawn. "I wonder what that's all about," he said.

Addie turned her head to look just as Daniel Brooks waved and hurried to greet them.

"What's going on?" Kat asked Daniel.

"Everyone's come out to see if Miss Renee was right. And she was!" Daniel exclaimed, seeing the old woman in the wagon.

"Heavens to Betsy!" Addie laughed. "They've come to see if I've truly flown the coop."

As the wagon pulled up in front of the boardinghouse, the curious townfolk stared from across the street. Johnny McGee reached deep into his pocket, pulled out a two-dollar bill, and handed it to Joe Riley. Forgetting herself, Miss Renee slapped Eva Parsons on the back, and Eva nearly spit out her false teeth. Betty Lou and Annie dashed across the street to join Daniel, now walking behind the wagon staring at Addie, who stared back at him, grinning. Sol Eisenberg shot out of the drug store with his apron still on, Sheriff Kramer stood agape on the courthouse lawn, and George Howard, who had been to see a patient on an outlying farm, pulled his maroon Packard to a halt at the corner of Main and Steuben and got out just in time to see his daughter help Addie from the Red Flyer.

Addie stood up, her back to the boardinghouse, and waved to the crowd with both hands, then turned and started gingerly up the walk. She paused halfway and instructed Francis to pull up the boardinghouse sign. "Take that in," she directed, "and change it to read 'Adeline Dupre's Boardinghouse.' And skip the 'For Refined Ladies and Gentlemen.' "

When she reached the porch, Addie turned around, missing Kat. The child was standing on the sidewalk beside her wagon. "Come here, my sweet," she called, and Kat ran to her.

Addie placed Amy Lowell's book of poetry in Kat's hands, saying, "This is for you. Keep it." The two stood facing one another, looking into each other's eyes. Their private day together had turned into a promenade, making their parting sudden and very public. Both hearts ached. Addie was not content to have it so. She held onto Kat's gaze and shut out the world around her. She leaned down and kissed Kat softly on the lips, then waited for Kat to turn and walk on before she turned also and went into the boardinghouse.

⊷§26§⊷ **I**t was good to be home and sit in the chair by the window. Maybe I'll go out in another fifteen years, Addie mused. Ah, what a silly old lady I am!

Addie sighed and played with the peas on her dinner plate, moving them this way and that with her fork, as her mind wandered from the present to the past. She imagined herself a young woman walking along a gravel road outside St. Louis, past an apple orchard and farmhouses, to a small pond hidden in a woods five miles west of the city.

Sometime earlier Addie had ventured into the woods and discovered the pond. She went to the pond often after that and took Thea with her once. Less daring than Addie, Thea had to be coaxed into going on the adventure and upon entering the woods had held firmly onto Addie's arm. The two girls followed the path into the woods, and when they saw a stray cow drinking at the water's edge, Thea's chocolate eyes opened wide in astonishment. She threw her arms around Addie's neck, crying, "You always have the best surprises!"

But Addie always had a terrible time holding onto a surprise for Thea. She wanted to tell Thea everything she knew and felt. That day at the pond the two young women slipped out of their bloomers and placed them neatly on a grassy spot beside the small lake, then eased themselves into the freezing water. Addie wasn't much of a swimmer—she paddled about like a puppy dog—but Thea was like a dark swan in the water. The old woman smiled radiantly as she remembered Thea gliding on top of the water, droplets of water glistening on her nose and cheeks. Addie had paddled into deep water that day to keep up with Thea, but when she suddenly realized she no longer could feel the sandy bottom with her feet, she panicked. Because she didn't want Thea to know she was frightened, she didn't call out to her, but Thea turned and saw the look on her friend's face and swam to her rescue. In the shallow water Addie and Thea embraced. It was their first embrace, and it had scared them both.

How peculiar humans are, the old woman mused. Frightened by our natural instincts.

Addie had recalled that summer day of her youth when she wandered off in Defoe Park, leaving Francis and Kat under the maple. Now, alone in her sitting room, she was visited once again by the sights and smells from her past. Though it was late and she was tired, she wanted to be in her studio with Thea.

As the old woman climbed the stairs she felt a sharp jab in her chest and felt her heart flutter. With her left hand on the rail for support and her right hand on her breast, Addie willed her way to the top floor of the boardinghouse, entered her dark studio, and stood in shadows before the painting of Thea. "Perhaps I did not love wisely, Thea . . . I did love well." Feeling no resentment or regret, Addie walked over to the small, round window where the ceiling slanted and looked out at the night. The lamppost lights on the courthouse walk looked like stars in a midnight sky. Suddenly another sharp pain cut across Addie's chest, and she looked around for a chair. Her straight-backed chair under the skylight seemed a long way off. She struggled toward the center of the room, frightened. Then wondrously she saw Kat's face before her, and the pain eased and she sat down in her chair.

Francis must have returned her paintbox, for there it rested in its place on the chest beside her easel. It is in small gestures one learns she is loved. Addie saw Kat's hand folding her bed sheet over and stroking it. After a moment the old woman lifted the lid of her paintbox; then she took up one of her fine brushes, wet the hairs of it with her tongue, and dabbed it on some green paint. Her right hand trembled as she began to paint, and she held it steady with her left hand as she formed the letters on the inner surface of the paintbox. She put down her brush and sighed, then closed her eyes.

The Howards' telephone rang shortly after ten o'clock. Janet answered it and turned to her husband. "It's Francis Spenger, for you."

George took the phone, and Janet went to the couch and sat

down beside Kat. Francis's tone had alarmed Janet, but she tried not to show her concern as she waited and watched her husband's face become somber.

"Are you certain, Francis? ... Yes, of course, I'll be right over." George set down the phone and turned to his family.

Janet stood up, but her husband raised a hand as a sign to her. She'd seen that look countless times. His eyes said, "Stay, please. I have to go to someone." George took his black bag from the shelf in the front closet, and Janet sat back down and put her arm around her daughter.

Kat also understood the meaning in her father's eyes, and she pulled away from her mother and ran after him. "Papa, wait!" she cried at the front door. "Papa, I'm gonna come too." George didn't look back as he hurried down the walk, not bothering to take the time to start the Packard. Kat turned to her mother inside. "Mama!" Janet opened her arms, and Kat ran to her, crying, "Is it Addie?"

"I don't know, Kat."

"Something bad's happened. Something real bad."

"I'm afraid so, Kat."

"I wanted to go with him, but he wouldn't turn around."

Janet took Kat into the kitchen and sat her down at the table, then took a seat beside her. The kitchen was Janet's refuge. Whenever her children were injured, that was where she took them. Kat understood and knew that her mother would get up from her chair in a moment and warm some milk in the small saucepan on the stove.

The two watched one another and didn't speak as this ritual was performed. When Janet returned to the table with two cups of warm milk, she said, "Darling, all we know is that Papa was called to the boardinghouse by Francis. Someone needs Papa more than you or I do right now. We'll wait together and drink our milk."

Kat rubbed her thumb along a groove in the pine table. The groove marked her place at the table and had always been there. As Kat sipped her milk, tears came to her eyes. Janet laid her hand gently on Kat's to assure her child that she was not alone.

When Kat and her mother finally heard the front door open, they hurried to the living room. Kat's father was standing there with his black doctor's bag in one hand and the cherry-wood paintbox in his other. As soon as Kat saw the paintbox she ran from the room through the kitchen and out the back door. George put down his medical bag, patted Janet's shoulder, and followed his daughter out to the yard.

George found Kat beside the old oak, her forehead against its trunk. He put his hand on her head, and Kat turned into his arms. His daughter's small body quaked against his, and he felt tears come to his eyes. He picked Kat up and carried her to the back steps, where they sat with the light from inside at their backs.

"I've been a doctor for twenty-five years, and I still don't know what to say. I'm no wiser."

Kat finally found the strength to ask, "What happened?"

"She was an old woman. Her heart stopped."

"No."

"Yes, Kat."

"No. I don't want that."

"I don't either, but it has happened."

"It's not fair. She was young today."

"Yes, in spirit she was."

"Why did it have to happen?"

"I don't know why, sweetheart."

"She didn't do anything wrong."

"Right or wrong, everyone dies one day."

"Not me. I'm not going to die. I'm not going to die!"

"She wanted you to have this," said her father, handing her the paintbox.

Kat held the box to her face with both hands and wept.

"She loved you very much, Kat ... Open the box, sweetheart." When she had, her father pointed to the words inside and said, *"Pour Kat, au revoir, Addie."*

"What does it mean?"

"It means the paintbox is for you ... and good-bye. But it's a special kind of good-bye. *Au revoir* means good-bye but not

202

gone. It's a rare thing to love as you and Addie have loved. It will last forever, Kathleen."

Kat held the box against her chest, and George put his arm around his daughter and held her.

That night Kat slept in her parents' bed between her mother and father. It was a comfort for Janet and George as well. They didn't say it, but both were thinking of Andy. Huddled close together under the bedcovers, they talked about a happier day.

"Do you remember your sixth Christmas?" George asked Kat.

"No," she whispered.

"I do," said Janet. "You were so excited that Christmas Eve you couldn't sleep, so you crawled into bed with us."

"Andy heard us talking in here and came in to see what was going on," said George.

"He was a grown boy of seventeen, but he was so envious of the fun we were having he climbed in with us too," Janet laughed softly.

George chuckled, remembering Andy giving in to the child in him, and then said, "It was damned crowded with the four of us in this bed. You finally fell asleep, but the three of us never did. We stayed awake and talked till morning."

"What did you talk about?" asked Kat.

"That was the Christmas Andy wrote out the deed to his fort, giving it to you," her father answered.

"I remember *that*."

"He'd kept it a surprise until that night. When you fell asleep he had to tell us," said Janet.

"I'm glad I was asleep, 'cause if I'd heard it, it would have ruined the surprise. What did I give Andy?"

"Don't you remember? You painted him a picture of yourself."

"I did?"

"Uh huh."

"I didn't know I painted then. Did it look like me?"

"Yes, but you painted your eyes bright yellow."

"Why'd I do that, Mama?"

"You said because cats' eyes were yellow."

203

"That was silly."

"I thought it rather clever of you," said George, and he kissed his daughter's forehead. Kat cuddled close to her father and fell asleep.

The next day Kat sat in her fort staring at Addie's painting, the tin box on one side of her, the cherry-wood paintbox on the other, and Peggy Sue across from her. It was Monday, her day to water the plants. It wasn't possible that Addie wouldn't be there, either upstairs at her window or in the studio painting. Her father had told her Addie was dead and that everyone died one day. But the oak tree didn't die—why did her friend have to? Kat rubbed her hand over the smooth wood of the paintbox; she imagined she was in the park and all she had to do was look up and Addie would be there talking to her about cherry trees.

Kat raised her head to look at the patterns on Addie's face and saw that Addie wasn't there. She was alone. Her jaw started to shake, and she put her hand in her mouth to hold it still.

"Kat?" someone called from below. "Kat, are you up there?" She looked out the door of her fort and saw Francis standing beside the old oak. "Can I talk with you?"

Kat unfurled the rope ladder, and Francis climbed up and into her fort.

"Your mother told me you might be up here."

Kat sat huddled with her arms tucked in, her knees up, and her eyes lowered.

Francis looked around the interior of the fort and said, "So this is Kat's place."

Kat nodded without looking up.

"It's a wonderful place . . . Seems like a very long time since we had our picnic, doesn't it?"

Kat nodded again, still unable to look at him.

"Addie was happier than I've ever seen her."

Kat shook her head back and forth violently.

"I know it seems to have . . . " Francis could not go on. He looked out the window and cried silently.

"She never saw my place," said Kat.

Francis wiped his cheeks dry and whispered, "I'm sorry."

"Where is she, Flowerman?"

"They came and took her last night."

"Who?"

"An ambulance came."

"I know when people die they can't talk, but do you think maybe they can still hear?"

"I don't know, Kat, but I think if you've got something to tell Addie, she will somehow hear you."

"I want to tell her I wish she hadn't gone."

Francis reached out and put his hand on Kat's foot.

"And I want to tell her thank you for the paintbox." Kat unfolded her arms and picked up the box. "And I want to tell her I love her."

"She knew that, Kat."

"It was so nice yesterday. Why did it have to end this way?"

"Nothing beautiful ends without some tears."

Kat looked at the long, thin fingers on Francis's hand. How different they were from the old woman's.

"I'm not much of a baseball player, but I remember you saying once that when you feel bad you play catch and it makes you feel better. That's why I came over. To see if you'd like to play some catch."

Kat wiped her face with her tee shirt.

"But we'll talk if you'd rather."

"I'd like to talk some more and then play." After a long moment Kat asked, "Did you know Thea?"

"Yes, I did."

"Did you know she's in St. Louis?"

"Yes."

"Did Addie ever go visit her?"

"I think so, Kat. She made a couple of trips to St. Louis the first few years I lived here."

"Will someone tell her?"

"I sent her a telegram this morning."

"Did Addie die in bed?"

"No, she was in her studio."

205

"I'm glad."

"Why is that?"

"Because it's her place and because Thea's there."

"Kat, you don't have to work at the boardinghouse this last week."

"It's my job."

"I know, but Eva and I spoke this morning, and she offered to take care of things for you."

"I'll go help her then."

"The new sign is up."

Kat pulled her foot from Francis's hand and looked at him accusingly. "Isn't it going to be Mrs. Cooper's anymore? Can't it be Mrs. Cooper's?"

"Yes, of course. That's not what I meant. Yesterday Addie asked me to change the sign to read 'Adeline Dupre's Boardinghouse.' "

"She did?"

"Yes."

"And that's what the sign says?"

"It does."

"Can we go look at it?"

"Would you like to go now?"

Kat picked up the two baseball mitts and started down the ladder.

Hawthorn's non-denominational cemetery was located between Bryant and Waller streets on the west side of Linden. When the children of Hawthorn passed the cemetery they always held their breath. They believed the superstition that if you didn't, you'd be the next to die.

The night before Addie's funeral Kat had a nightmare and woke before dawn, shaking and sweating. In her nightmare she had been unable to hold her breath at the funeral, and Reverend Wiley had written her name on a page in his black death book. Kat sat up in bed, turned on her light, and held her pillow to her until the scary dream was gone. Then she tiptoed out of the house in her maroon-and-navy-striped pajamas, climbed the oak, and fell asleep with Jesse.

When she woke up a couple of hours later, Jesse was biting the rubber band around her stack of baseball cards. He successfully bit through the rubber, and as it snapped back in his face he let out a howl.

Kat took a piece of string from her tin box, saying, "Jesse, you're such a silly." Jesse blinked his eyes and shook his head. "It's true, Jesse." She tied the string around the cards, then pulled up her pajama pants leg, scratched a mosquito bite until it bled, and lifted her leg and licked her wound. Jesse cocked his head and looked at her. He truly was like no other cat she'd ever known. Sometimes when he looked into her eyes she felt he could read her mind. He was more human than cat. Suddenly it occurred to Kat that if she took Jesse to the funeral with her it wouldn't be the least bit scary.

Before leaving the fort, Kat poked her head through the roof hatch. Hawthorn hadn't had its first frost, but a few of the oak leaves had turned yellow, and the others had faded. In a little more than a week summer vacation would be over, and Kat no longer would work at the boardinghouse. She would return to school and a new teacher. At that moment Kat wished she had a fairy godmother with a magic wand who could make the oak leaves tender green again and give her back her summer and Addie.

The Howards joined the small circle of friends at graveside. The Eisenbergs' potted geraniums rested on the ground in front of Sol and Sarah. Beside the red geraniums were Eva Parsons's African violets, and standing next to Eva was Miss Renee with her lipstick plant. Francis had brought along a garden trowel and his marigolds. He would plant the flowers when everyone left.

After Reverend Wiley gave his blessing, Janet Howard stepped forward and laid the last roses from her garden on top of the grassy mound. Then someone from beyond the circle stepped forward. Francis helped the outsider to the grave, where she placed a small bouquet. Kat looked up at the woman's face and recognized her. The woman's hair was white, but her eyes were the same chocolate brown, and that long, graceful neck could not be mistaken. Kat's heart beat hard against her chest as she stepped forward, opened her book, and read:

IMPRESSIONIST PICTURE OF A GARDEN, *by Amy Lowell*

Give me sunlight, cupped in a paint brush,
And smear the red of peonies
Over my garden.
Splash blue upon it,
The hard blue of Canterbury bells,
Paling through larkspur
Into heliotrope,
To wash away among forget-me-nots.
Dip red again to mix a purple,
And lay on pointed flares of lilacs against bright green.
Streak yellow for nasturtiums and marsh marigolds
And flame it up to orange for my lilies.
Now dot it so — and so — along an edge
Of Iceland poppies.
Swirl it a bit, and faintly,
That is honeysuckle.
Now put a band of brutal, bleeding crimson
And tail it off to pink, to give the roses.
And while you're loaded up with pink,
Just blotch about that bed of phlox.
Fill up with cobalt and dash in a sky
As hot and heavy as you can make it;
Then tree-green pulled up into that
Gives a fine jolt of color.
Strain it out,
And melt your twigs into the cobalt sky.
Toss on some Chinese white to flash the clouds,
And trust the sunlight you've got in your paint.
There is the picture.

Kat took the hand–painted card from the book before she closed it and placed the painting of a dipper bird beside her mother's roses. When she had done this, she walked to Thea and placed the book of Amy Lowell's poetry in her hands, saying, "This is for you. Keep it." Before the tears in the old woman's eyes ran down her cheeks, Kat turned and started away. Janet made a move to follow her daughter, but George took his wife's arm and whispered, "Let her walk on alone."

Kat walked with her shoulders back and her head held high, remembering Addie in the meadow. Her steps became long and graceful, and she seemed to float down Waller Street.

EPILOGUE On Sunday, October 1, 1944, the last baseball game of the season was played. That day the largest American League crowd ever to assemble in Sportsman's Park watched the St. Louis Browns defeat the New York Yankees. The Browns won the American League pennant, and the trolley-car World Series began on October 4th. The Browns won the first and third games but lost the others, and therefore the championship, to the St. Louis Cardinals.

Pete Gray of the Memphis Chicksaws was traded to the St. Louis Browns the following season and became the second man in history to play professional baseball with only one arm.

On September 2, 1945, Far Eastern Time, the formal Japanese surrender took place aboard the U.S.S. *Missouri*, ending the Second World War, and soon after Andrew Howard returned home to Hawthorn.

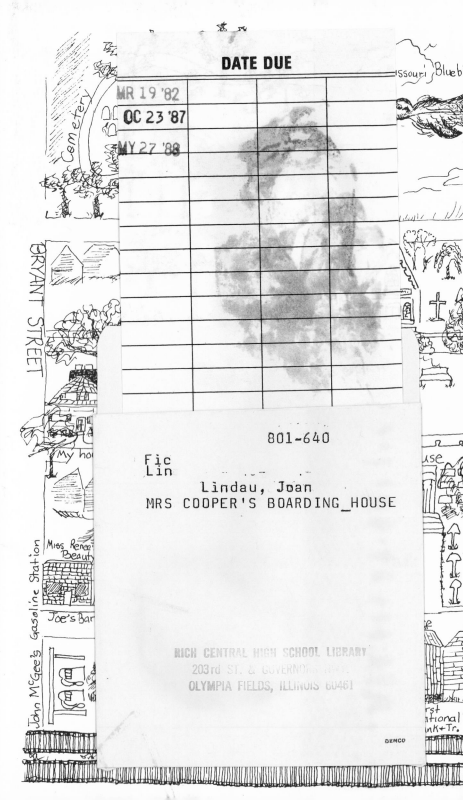

DATE DUE

MR 19 '82			
OC 23 '87			
MY 27 '88			